Praise for the Dark King series by
DONNA GRANT

"Loaded with subtle emotions, sizzling chemistry,
and s— ——————————— —————— choices
[Grant— —————————— ————— choose
their l— ——————— 4 stars)

"Vivi— —————————————————— ——racters
grab the reader's attention and [——————————————————
——————————————— —————— Reviews (Top Pick)

"T— —————————————————————hly
en— —————————————————ery
de— —————————————will
su— —————————————ews

"[— —————————————————vil-
do— ————————————————and
ov— ————————————————ews

"S— —————————

—————ekly

"Ms. Grant mixes adventure, magic and sweet love to
create the perfect romance[s]." —*Single Title Reviews*

Praise for the Dark Sword series

"Grant creat— ——————————————— centuries after
the Celts an— ————————————— —omans, deftly

merging magic and history. The result is a wonderfully dark, delightfully well-written [series]. Readers will eagerly await the next Dark Sword book."

"Another fantastic series that melds the paranormal with the historical life of the Scottish highlander in this arousing and exciting adventure."

"These are some of the hottest brothers around in paranormal fiction."

"Will keep readers spellbound."

THE LEGEND

DONNA GRANT

From St. Martin's Paperbacks

This is a work of fiction. All of the characters, organizations, and events portrayed in this novel are either products of the author's imagination or are used fictitiously.

THE LEGEND

Copyright © 2017 by Donna Grant.

For information address St. Martin's Press, 175 Fifth Avenue, New York, NY 10010.

ISBN: 978-1-250-08341-8

Our books may be purchased in bulk for promotional, educational, or business use. Please contact your local bookseller or the Macmillan Corporate and Premium Sales Department at 1-800-221-7945, ext. 5442, or by e-mail at MacmillanSpecialMarkets@macmillan.com.

Printed in the United States of America

St. Martin's Paperbacks edition / July 2017

St. Martin's Paperbacks are published by St. Martin's Press, 175 Fifth Avenue, New York, NY 10010.

10 9 8 7 6 5 4 3 2 1

To Mark—

You were the best brother. I miss you more
than words can express. You were taken from us way
too soon, but I know you're still looking out for me.
And you always will. I love you.

ACKNOWLEDGMENTS

It takes an amazing team to get a book ready to hand to a reader. My deepest thanks to:

Julia for the Russian translations, the SMP art department for the amazing cover, Titi, Justine, Jordan, and the others in the marketing and publicity departments, Alexandra Sehulster for helping keeping me on track, Monique Patterson for her expert editorial input, and Natanya Wheeler for believing in this series.

CHAPTER ONE

Northern outskirts of Austin

Two Dallas Area Men Charged with Identity Theft

Callie stood on the sidewalk in the warm sun with a grocery bag in each hand, staring at the headline of the newspaper with her heart thumping in dread. She didn't need to read the story to know that it was about her family.

There wasn't a person in the state of Texas who didn't know who the Reeds were. And it sickened her.

No matter how much distance—physically, mentally, and emotionally—she put between her and her family, they still managed to affect her life.

Numb, she turned and continued on her way. She knew she needed to be alert and attempt to spot those who might be watching her, but she couldn't generate the energy.

She caught sight of Mercy, her pride and joy. As she reached the red Dodge Challenger, she clicked the key fob and released the trunk latch. She set the bags inside and closed the trunk, recalling how just a few hours earlier, she'd wished to put a certain someone inside it.

Wyatt Loughman.

The infuriating man knew exactly how to exasperate her, even without words. And he never seemed to get riled up about anything. Which only pissed her off more.

She adjusted her sunglasses as she made her way to the driver's side and unlocked the door. As she opened it, she heard her name. Instinct made her turn her head—only to have a feeling of alarm envelop her.

"Lookin' good, cuz."

With her stomach knotted in anger and revulsion, she looked into the blue eyes of Melvin Reed. Women stared at the handsome face and nice body wearing the latest designer fashion, unaware that the man's soul had been sold to the Devil long ago.

"What are you doing here?" she demanded.

His smile widened as he sauntered up to her, his eyes squinted against the blinding sun. He let his fingers trail along the car, nodding in appreciation at the vehicle. "No hello or nothin'? That's not very nice."

"I'm not nice. What are you doing here?" she repeated.

"If you checked in with the family once in a while, you'd know."

It had been over three years since she'd last spoken with the *family*. And she wasn't in a hurry to change that. "I'm busy."

"Ah, yes," he said and leaned back against Mercy.

Her hackles immediately rose, and she inwardly cringed at the thought that he might be scratching her baby. However, it was the bitterness and hatred she heard in his tone that made her fingers itch to grasp the handle of the knife tucked up her sleeve.

"So, you're still working for the Loughmans." Melvin laughed and hooked a thumb in a belt loop of his jeans. "How is ranching these days?"

She was grateful that her family didn't know her job had gone from ranching to being a part of the Black Ops group—Whitehorse—set up by Orrin Loughman.

Callie tightened her fingers around her keys. "It's good."

"You're a long way from home, cuz."

The threat was there in his eyes—and his voice. A part of her wished he'd try something so she could take him down. But causing a scene in the middle of town wasn't part of the strategy she and Wyatt had.

Though, to be honest, they didn't have much of a plan.

Still, there was a bigger picture. And it didn't involve settling petty differences between her and her family of criminals.

Not now, at least.

That day would come. She could only run so far before she had to face her relatives and put her foot down once and for all.

She smiled, showing Melvin she didn't scare easily. "So are you. *Cuz.*"

Without another word, Callie got into the car and drove away. She looked into the rearview mirror to find Melvin watching her. His arrival felt like an omen that things were about to come crashing down around her.

No matter how hard she tried, she couldn't shake off

the unease at Melvin's appearance. At least the drive to the remote house was uneventful. However, her nerves were strung tight by the time she parked the car and turned off the engine.

She unloaded the groceries and put them away. Then she walked out the back of the house and stood in the September sun on the porch, looking out over the expansive land. It didn't take her long to spot Wyatt doing his check of the perimeter.

His strides were long, confidence pouring off him. The wind ruffled his dark brown hair that fell to his chin. He ran a hand through it, shoving the front strands to the side as he knelt on one knee to inspect something. It gave her a great view of his hard jawline and the shadow of a beard.

When he stood and continued on, her heart skipped a beat as she took in his long legs, narrow hips, and chest that widened into a V.

The clothes couldn't hide the corded muscles beneath, but that's not what made people take notice of him. It was the intense and powerful aura that surrounded him.

Though he could be harsh—and oftentimes cruel— Wyatt Loughman never sugarcoated anything.

As she knew from personal experience.

She crossed her arms over her chest and watched the way he moved with catlike precision and care. She still remembered the first time she'd seen him. It was a day that had changed her life—and he didn't even know it.

As a teenager, she'd sought employment at the Loughman Ranch. It had taken her almost a week to convince Orrin that she could do the work and not let him down.

Sadly, the notoriety of her family had already started to shape her life. Orrin had reluctantly agreed, but she'd seen the look in his eyes. He didn't think she could keep her word.

What they didn't know, was that she'd decided she wasn't going to go into the family business. Her parents were pushing her hard, and she feared that despite her wishes, her kin would win.

The Loughmans were the best family around. Even then, she knew of the brothers, as everyone did, but she'd never spoken to them. And no one had anything bad to say about the family—as individuals or a whole. The fact that they owned a ranch was a plus since she'd always loved horses. All that combined to make them a good steppingstone to cutting ties with her relatives.

The next day, Callie had shown up at the ranch. Orrin put her to work immediately. She'd been ecstatic to be doing something that felt right to her soul, her body, and her morality.

It was as she'd checked the fences that she had her first real look at Wyatt. Nearly fifteen years later, she could still recall every detail of that moment.

How the summer sun had baked her, how the sky had been devoid of clouds, how the sweat had trickled down Wyatt's bare chest as he raised the ax.

She could still hear the thump of the blade as it fell, and the crack of the wood splitting. Her mouth had gone dry as she gazed at the perfection of his rippling sinew.

Years of working on the ranch had honed his muscles, defining each and every one. His dark hair had been short then and soaked from sweat and the water he'd poured over his head.

That was the first time she'd truly noticed—and wanted—a man.

There was nothing soft about Wyatt. His mother's murder had turned him into a loner whose lips rarely lifted in a smile. But that hadn't dissuaded her.

In fact, it had made her want him all the more.

Callie sighed. The years had strengthened Wyatt's muscles even more and smoothed some of the rough edges. But he was still the same cynical man as before.

Yet, there had been a brief period where things were different. A time when hope had shone so brightly that it blinded her.

But when the sun leaves, the darkness consumes everything. So it had been with her. She hadn't allowed herself to wallow in her grief long. Instead, it turned to anger that burned strong enough to chase away the shadows.

It still blazed.

Never in all her life had she imagined she would see Wyatt again. He'd sworn never to return to the ranch. But fate had a way of ignoring such things.

The job Orrin had taken to steal a Russian bioweapon, Ragnarok, had altered several lives. All three Loughman brothers were pulled from missions and sent back to Texas to find their dad.

Callie had had no choice but to work with Wyatt in an attempt to locate and save the man who had become like a father to her. Orrin had given her the strength to turn away from her family once and for all.

She wouldn't let him down now.

If that meant she had to spend time alone with the pigheaded asshat, Wyatt, then she would suck it up. For Orrin.

Here Orrin was, with three strong sons, all of which had gone into different branches of the military to become living legends. Yet they blamed Orrin for their mother's death, refusing to return home.

They had no idea how much Orrin loved or missed them. They didn't know he had friends send him reports and pictures of his sons so he could remain in their lives in some way.

They didn't see his melancholy and unshed tears on Thanksgiving or Christmas when his calls and texts went unanswered.

She would've done anything to have a dad like Orrin, instead of one who tried to persuade her to commit fraud. None of the Loughman boys realized what an amazing man they had as a father.

Orrin's life being put in jeopardy brought them all together again. It was no surprise that Wyatt's thinking hadn't changed about Orrin. However, Owen's and Cullen's had.

It made her long to hit Wyatt over the head and toss him in her trunk.

"Dumbass," she murmured.

Wyatt's head swung to her as if he'd heard her from two hundred yards away. She was caught in his deep gold eyes that seemed to smolder with a fire of anger and skepticism. His skin, darkened by the sun, accentuated those amazing eyes.

The dark shadow of a beard highlighted his hollowed cheeks and firm jawline. She knew how soft and sensual his wide lips could feel against her skin.

A shiver went down her spine as she remembered rapture-filled nights in his arms. Of his lips along her neck while he whispered—in detail—how he planned to bring her pleasure.

She shook off the past as he made his way to the porch. He stopped before her, his eyes framed by thick, black lashes focused on her face. "What happened?"

"Nothing."

"You've never been a good liar." He looked her up and down. "Your shoulders are hunched, which means you're stressed. Tell me what happened."

How she hated that he knew her so well. She couldn't say the same. He'd been gone, and he kept everything hidden and held tightly in check. The walls he'd erected were so tall and thick that no one could get through them.

She shrugged and looked away, only to have her gaze drawn back to his face. If she didn't tell him now, he'd find out anyway. It was better if it came from her. "My cousin is in town."

"Which one?" he asked.

Callie wasn't fooled by his soft tone. "Melvin."

A muscle ticked along his jaw. "Did he say anything to you?"

"He approached me, wanting to know what I was doing in Austin. If he's in town, that means my family is expanding their reach."

"They've been doing that for some time."

For the second time that day, she was in shock. How the hell would Wyatt know what her family was up to? "What?"

"Their business reaches as far south as Galveston and as far west as El Paso."

Was he joking? No, Wyatt didn't kid about anything.

She was shocked and dazed at the news. "How do you know that?"

"I made a point of knowing. Why didn't you?"

"I wanted to forget them." Perhaps that had been the wrong thing to do since there was obviously much her family had done over the past decade.

He was silent for a moment. "You needn't worry about your family. They won't bother you."

"That's not the impression I got from Melvin. Not that you need to concern yourself. I can handle them."

"They won't bother you," he repeated before walking past her and into the house.

Now just what the hell did that mean? And why was he so sure?

CHAPTER TWO

Rage crackled and hissed within Wyatt. The Reeds knew to keep their distance from Callie. He'd made sure of it. What the fuck was Melvin doing harassing her again?

"What do you mean they won't bother me?" Callie asked as she followed him inside the house.

Wyatt clenched his teeth. That comment should've never passed his lips, but the deed was already done. If he didn't give her some type of answer, she'd pester him for eternity. Though she didn't need to know the entire truth.

"They know you don't want anything to do with them. They won't waste their time trying to recruit you," he said.

She paused. "Yeah. You're right."

He grabbed a bottle of water from the fridge and turned to her. It physically hurt to look at her, she was so goddamn beautiful.

Her sun-kissed skin had a gold tint to it, making her long-lashed, light blue eyes stand out in her oval face.

Full, bring-a-man-to-his-knees lips were slightly parted as she stared at him.

A tilt of her head brought her long, chestnut hair falling over one shoulder in thick strands. One lock fell against her cheek, the end brushing against the corner of her mouth.

The white V-neck sweater she wore was thin and molded to her breasts, while dark denim encased the lower half of her body. She barely reached his chest, but he'd learned long ago that what Callie lacked in height she made up for in determination, spirit, and skill.

As he drank, he looked his fill. He allowed himself this small violation to the rules he'd put in place for himself concerning her.

With the water finished, he tossed the empty bottle into the trash. She walked past him to the dining room where her computer was set up.

For a week, they'd kept their distance from each other, rarely speaking. He told himself that this was a mission like any other.

Except it wasn't.

Because she was there.

Willful, impetuous, fierce Callie.

He moved so he could see into the dining room as she began working. Life had been stacked against her since before her birth.

But she looked any obstacles in the face and told them to kiss her ass. Despite her family's illegal empire of fraud, identity theft, extortion, and larceny, as well as their predisposition for being alcoholics, Callie had gone her own way.

He'd told his father it was foolish to hire her because Wyatt hadn't thought she would last longer than a week. A year later, and Callie had not only come every day, but she'd worked longer and harder than most men.

Over those months, Wyatt watched as his father taught her to ride and shoot. No longer did she cower, she walked with a self-confidence she'd lacked before.

As much as she flourished on the ranch, however, not all was good in her life. Wyatt recalled the conversations at dinner where his youngest brother, Cullen, told them how Callie was being bullied at school by members of her large family.

She never spoke of it, never complained. Not once. Even when Orrin asked her how things were. Wyatt wasn't the only one who began to think of Callie as more than just a ranch hand.

Maybe it was because of the interest his father had taken in her. Wyatt didn't know or care. Somehow, Callie had come to be important to all of them. His brothers watched over her at school. And Wyatt kept guard at the ranch. Not that the Reeds would dare venture onto Loughman land.

All seemed to be going well. Until one day, Callie didn't show. She was never late, so her absence alarmed everyone. Wyatt had immediately known something was wrong. He'd saddled a horse and went looking for her.

An hour later, he found her beaten and unconscious at the edge of the property. There were marks on the ground where he could see she'd pulled herself toward the ranch. Seeing her lying so still had brought back memories of finding his mother after she'd been murdered.

And something snapped inside him.

Wyatt brought Callie back to the ranch. While his father, uncle, and brothers doctored her, he went to the Reeds. There, he unleashed his fury on those responsible for her thrashing.

By the time he left, he had a busted knuckle and a bloodied lip, but he felt immensely better seeing all of the men either knocked out or rolling around on the ground, moaning in pain. And with the beating, he'd let every Reed know to leave Callie alone—or he'd return.

She didn't know he'd been the one to find her that day in the woods. Callie didn't like feeling defeated—or being reminded of it.

It was because of his mom and Callie that Wyatt had begun his quest to save others. It eventually brought him to Delta Force. The counter-terrorism unit worked hard to dismantle and bring down extremists.

"You're staring," Callie said without looking up from the keyboard.

"I'm thinking."

She shot him a wry look. "About what?"

"The information Cullen and Mia gave us last night."

Callie sat back in the chair and lowered her hands to her lap. "Russians and Americans working together in a secret organization that wants to take over the world. It's been on my mind, as well. At least Orrin is free."

"We've not heard from him."

She flattened her lips. "Orrin and Yuri are gone. One of Yuri's men told Cullen that they left together. Are you suggesting the man lied?"

Wyatt knew he hadn't because that man was an undercover agent for the CIA who had once been with Delta Force—Maks Petrov.

"No."

Her eyes narrowed as she tucked a strand of hair behind her ear. "I know Delta Force works closely with the CIA."

"Your point?"

"My point is that I think you know more than you're telling me."

"So?"

She rolled her eyes and made a sound in the back of her throat. "You may not care about Orrin, but I do. He's the father I never had. If you know something, then tell me."

There was no reason for him not to tell his brothers or Callie about Maks, other than he was so used to keeping secrets that it became difficult to reveal anything.

To anyone.

"I know you know something," she said as she pushed back the chair and stood. "I heard you on the phone last night. We're supposed to trust each other so we can stay ahead of the Saints. You know, the group after us, the ones who killed your aunt and uncle, those who tried to kill us at the ranch? But you're making it difficult."

He blew out a breath because he knew she was right. "The man Cullen and Mia spoke with in Virginia is Maks Petrov. He was part of my team before he went to work undercover for the CIA. In Russia," he added.

Callie blinked, unfazed by Wyatt's revelation. "Is Maks Russian?"

"His father was Russian."

"Did Maks lie about Orrin?"

"Major General Markovic and Orrin left the warehouse together. Yuri's men, including Maks, helped them escape."

She stood there for a moment before she closed the distance and slapped him. Fury burned in her eyes. "How dare you keep that from us. Or was it just me?"

"All of you."

Her nostrils flared in anger as she continued to glare. "You're a cold bastard, Wyatt Loughman."

She turned on her heel and walked out the front door. He knew exactly what he was, but too many years had passed for him to suddenly change his entire way of life.

He walked out the back door to do another perimeter check and give Callie time to calm down. There had been no sign of anyone nosing around, fortunately. He and Callie traded off going into town, but it was only a matter of time before the Saints found them. Melvin spotting Callie was a bad sign.

Wyatt wondered if she knew that two more of her kin were facing jail time in Dallas for identity theft. Though it was probably better if he didn't bring up her kin since it was such a sore subject, and she was already pissed at him.

He rubbed his cheek where it still stung from her slap. He'd deserved it. The sad part was that he hadn't even realized he should've told everyone about Maks until she'd brought it up.

The life he led made him shut down his emotions, but the truth was, every bit of love, hope, and happiness died the day his mother had—when he'd learned just how horrible human beings truly were.

Cold, he most definitely was. How else could he get through each day? Being with Callie was a particular type of torment. No matter how much fate piled on her, she kept a hold of hope with an iron grip.

She was stronger than he could ever think to be, and she didn't even know it. He'd tried to tell her once, long ago, but like usual, the words had locked in his throat.

Every day he fought against terrorists targeting innocents with suicide bombings. Every radical he brought down was cause for celebration, but he simply moved on to the next. It was a never-ending war.

Now, he was in the middle of another one—a new one that changed all the rules. And this time, his brothers and Callie had been brought into it with him.

Who were these people running this secret organization? It was no mystery that these clandestine organizations wanted power and world domination. The fact that the Saints were willing to have a bioweapon created told him how serious they were.

Though the bio-agent was safely locked away on the base at the ranch with Owen and Natalie, there was still a chance that the Russian scientist could create more.

It was why Wyatt had calls in to his contacts, because the scientist, Dr. Konrad Jankovic, had defected to the U.S. and was even now in D.C. Wyatt needed to get to Jankovic and put an end to the mad scientist before more of the weapon could be made.

At least he didn't have to look for his father any longer. If Orrin had freed himself, then he had his own agenda.

Wyatt blew out a breath. At night, he heard Callie pacing in the lone bedroom she occupied. He saw the searches she did on the computer for anything pertaining to Orrin or a man fitting his description. He knew of the texts exchanged between her and Natalie.

What he'd never tell her was that he agreed to search for Orrin because of her. Too many years of hating Orrin for his mother's murder made it impossible for him to want to help his father in any way.

He felt Callie's presence before he heard her. Standing still, he waited for her to join him as he looked out over the back of the property.

"I'm sorry," she said tightly.

He glanced at her. "You were right. I should've told you."

"You keep too many secrets." Her head turned to him. "You're not alone in this, you know. I'm here with you."

"I usually have my team, so I'm not alone."

She arched a brow. "You've always been alone. You made sure of that."

It bothered him that she was right. No matter how much he tried to hide, she always saw everything—and called him out on it.

But being alone was what kept him going. "A habit that kept me from telling you about Maks."

"A practice you need to break."

"I'll try to remember that in the future."

She looked forward. "You were sent to find Orrin. Now that your father appears to no longer be kidnapped, I'm sure you could make an argument to return to duty."

It was true, and something he'd thought about last night. Then he'd heard her moving about in the next room, and he'd forgotten all about it.

The problem was, staying with Callie meant he was

constantly reminded of what they'd once had—and what he'd left behind. Yet he couldn't seem to walk away from her now.

"Is that what you want?" he asked.

"You don't want to be here. You made that clear at the ranch."

He took a deep breath and released it. "The Russians went after Natalie for what she knew. The Saints ran Cullen and Mia off the road and down a mountain, nearly killing them. They'll come for us next."

"You're staying to fight, then?"

"And to protect you."

Blue eyes met his. "And Orrin?"

His father wasn't a bad man, but Wyatt couldn't forgive him. But this wasn't about his feelings. This was about Callie and what she wanted. "We'll find him."

"The odds are stacked against us."

He shrugged since it was nothing new. "That's just how I like it."

CHAPTER THREE

Finally!

This was the Wyatt she'd been waiting to see since he'd arrived at the ranch a few weeks before. Callie knew from the reports Orrin had shared with her just how lethal a weapon Wyatt was.

Why had Wyatt been holding back with her? She was curious about his actions but relieved that he finally seemed to be set on the same course as her. She'd been about to give up.

"Should we leave?" she asked.

Wyatt's gold gaze was sharp as he scanned their surroundings. "This defense is good. Traps are set for anyone who thinks to sneak up on us. We have the higher ground, as well."

She looked down into the sloping valley below. The arid climate didn't provide the tall trees or thick foliage she was used to, but it didn't seem to faze Wyatt.

"Owen and Natalie are at the ranch protecting Ragnarok," she said. "A weapon we don't understand yet. Cullen and Mia are on the hunt for the scientist. We have no idea where Orrin is or if he needs us."

"My father doesn't need our help. And we're going after Jankovic."

She cut him a look. "Need I remind you of the doctor, Kate Donnelly? The one who Yuri kidnapped, who had to save Orrin."

"I'm well aware of the doctor and how she helped Cullen and Mia."

Callie took in a calming breath. "My point is that everyone seems to be doing something. We split up at the ranch to separate the Russians, but that was before we knew that our own country was involved in this. Let Mia and Cullen hunt the scientist. We should return to the ranch and join forces."

"It won't matter where we are. The sect is coming for us. I'm not going to bring them to the ranch with the possibility of them winning and finding Ragnarok."

She opened her mouth to talk, but he quickly continued.

"I'll also not meet up with either of my brothers to give the Saints a chance to take two of us out at once. The bastards are going to have to fight each of us."

His gold eyes flashed dangerously, and she realized he'd been thinking about this from the very beginning. "So you want us to wait for them? Like sitting ducks."

"We'll draw them out, yes."

"Cullen thought he and Mia had taken out two of the top men in that crazy organization, but that wasn't the case. What makes you think we will?"

"I'm going to make sure of it."

She scratched her eyebrow. "I'm all about confronting these wackos, but we got a taste of what they can do at the ranch. We had Cullen and Owen there for help.

And before you ask, this has nothing to do with me thinking you can't defend this area."

"I think it does."

"I believe you'll do everything you can with what we have. But we have no idea how many they'll send. Even with the high ground, it'll only be a matter of time before we're overrun."

He faced her then. "What do you want to do?"

Callie slid her gaze to the house before turning around and looking at the area. If they left, the Saints—with their many supporters—could keep her and Wyatt on the run or corner them somewhere.

As much as she hated to admit it, Wyatt was right. This was the best place for them.

"I don't like being on the defensive," she said.

One side of his lips lifted slightly. "Defense has a tactical advantage."

"I'll get back to the computer then and see if I can come up with any information on those involved with the Saints."

Wyatt followed her into the house. "Have you heard anything from DC?"

"As a matter of fact, I have," she said as she sat down at the table and opened the emails. "Hewett continues to send encrypted messages, but I'm not opening them."

"Why not? There could be information we need within them." He placed a hand on the table near hers.

Her heart kicked up a notch whenever Wyatt was this close. It reminded her of hot summer nights and pleasure so intense she still dreamed about it, waking with his name on her lips and her body aching for him.

"Callie?"

She inwardly shook herself. Damn him for affecting her so. "Mitch Hewett will know if I open the messages. Right now, he has no idea if I'm dead or alive. That gives us an advantage."

"Not for long."

"Any lead we can get is a good thing. Hewett is still suspected of betraying Orrin."

Before Wyatt could answer, her computer dinged as an email came in. Callie frowned as she looked at the unknown sender. But it was the subject of the email that made her smile.

"What is it?" Wyatt asked.

She sat back. "It's from Orrin. I taught him how to hack into a server and send me an email about a weather forecast for whatever city he was in."

"This is DC weather."

"Yep." She had a difficult time thinking when she felt Wyatt's fingers near her neck as his hand rested on the back of the chair.

He leaned closer to read the screen. "What if it is Hewett?"

"It could be Hewett trying to trick me. But it's not."

"Surely you can figure out a way to open it without the sender knowing in case it is Hewett."

She looked up and met his gaze. There was such certainty there that she wanted to figure out a way to do it. "Yes."

"I'll leave you to it then."

She closed her eyes as he walked away. She hated Wyatt being so close to her, but after he'd moved away, she missed him. Just as she'd missed him when he left for college.

Not that she had any sort of hold on him. Their brief time together ended well before he departed the ranch. He'd shown her just how little he thought of her during those months before he left.

A realist, she'd known there was no use holding onto hope when it came to Wyatt Loughman. Once he made a decision, there was no changing his mind in any capacity.

He was done with her. Had been done with her. Thankfully, she'd managed to put him out of her heart. That lovesick schoolgirl was long gone.

She looked at the computer, took a deep breath, and focused. Then she opened a new screen and began keying in a sequence of commands to help her get in the back door of the server so she could read the encrypted emails without leaving a trail. She knew the email was from Orrin, but at this point, they couldn't be too careful.

In all the years she and Orrin had worked with Hewett, Callie had never felt the need to hack the system. Now, she wished she'd have worked at it earlier.

Every direction she took was cut off quickly. But she didn't give up. She kept at it for another three hours before she realized someone was in *her* computer.

Shock, fear, and anger rose up in her all at once. She was the one who did the hacking—not who got hacked. Her fingers moved quickly to shut out the intruder. While she was writing the last bit of code, a picture popped up.

Just as she was about to move past it, the Americans in uniform caught her eye, causing her fingers to halt. The picture was from a newspaper and showed a desert village in what looked like the Middle East. There was one man in particular who snagged her attention. He was looking at something to the left with only a portion of his face visible. But she'd know him anywhere.

"Wyatt," she murmured.

Another window popped up, showing a clipping from a Middle Eastern newspaper written in Arabic. Callie hesitated. Did she remove the intruder, the picture, and the article? Or did she find out what they wanted?

Her gaze returned to the picture of Wyatt. There was no way she could ignore this—whatever *this* was. Her decision made, she quickly translated the article to read that a terrorist group had attacked Syria in an attempt to target a Delta Force team who had captured their leader.

"Shit," she murmured, her blood turning to ice.

She didn't know who was sending this or why, but she wanted them out of her system. Callie redoubled her efforts to get to the coded message and block the intruder. Once the trespasser was gone and new firewalls were up so no one else could get in, she put everything she had into accessing the back door to the server.

Since it was a government system, it was tightly monitored with all the latest security to keep hackers out. However, she had an advantage, a side door she'd learned about through a friend years ago.

Callie found the way in and immediately pulled up the latest email. Her excitement that confirmed it was indeed from Orrin was swiftly replaced by dread.

They're coming for Wyatt.

Four words. That was all Orrin had sent. Not how he'd found out, or where he was. Just a warning.

"How's it coming?" Wyatt asked from the kitchen doorway.

Callie looked up at him but couldn't get any words past the lump in her throat. Something must have shown on her face because he was at her side immediately.

"Orrin sent this?" he asked. Then kept reading. "Who's coming?"

With a click, she showed him the two pictures. If she thought he was closed off before, it was nothing compared to now. She could literally feel the wall that came down over his emotions as he looked at the computer.

"What happened?" she asked.

For long seconds, he was silent. Then he said, "We went to Syria to take out a radical group. There was a local man who gave us intelligence on the extremists and their location. It was through him that we found the leader."

She saw Wyatt's hands fist at his sides, his body taut with anger. "You got your man."

"That photo of the bombing was taken by the same group of terrorists we thought we'd dismantled. My team was driving through the village on our way to the base to head home. The only one who knew our destination was the man who helped us to find the terrorists."

"I see."

He didn't look away from the laptop. "No, you don't. I lost three men that day. There were twenty killed in the village. My team found our informant hours later. He begged for his life, saying the extremists had threatened his family. So he told them where we'd be. And the terrorists then killed his entire family anyway. Including the dog."

Callie thought she might be sick.

"We've been hunting those same fuckers ever since," Wyatt stated angrily.

"How would they even know where you are?"

His eyes swung to her. "My guess is that the Saints don't include just Americans and Russians. I'm beginning to think it's a whole lot bigger."

"You think they'd work with other terrorists?"

"Who else wants to take out so many?"

She looked back at the bombing. "These are the people coming for us?"

"Yes."

When Wyatt returned his eyes to the computer, she closed the laptop and stood, facing him. "You were doing your job."

"To stop innocents from being killed."

"There will always be innocents who lose their lives. Just as there are those who deserve death and escape it."

"Not these men. Not any longer."

It excited her to see this deadly side of him. The alpha baring his fangs and issuing a growl of fury. Wyatt's gold eyes were alight with determination.

She knew that anyone foolish enough to get in his way would die—painfully. The last thread holding back Wyatt's true nature had been snapped in half.

He didn't have the nickname Denali, which meant The Great One in Sanskrit, because he sat on the sidelines. Wyatt earned his spot on Delta Force and moved into a leadership role because of the vicious, savage way he fought.

He gave no quarter as he sniffed out his opponents. He was merciless to those who bullied the innocent, ruthless in bringing the perpetrators to justice. He was an avenging angel for those who needed him.

With his eyes trained on her, he took a step closer. "I'm going to kill the bastards once and for all. Here. Now."

The Saints were growing in numbers by the second, and she feared there was much more they didn't know. But now they knew who was coming. It didn't matter when because they could prepare.

Orrin had given them that.

This fight went beyond the bioweapon. This was a battle for the freedom of the entire world. And right now, the only one standing between a secret killer organization and the rest of the world was Wyatt.

She smiled at him. "And I'll be standing right beside you."

CHAPTER FOUR

He was as prepared as he was going to get. Wyatt had set traps that would alert him and Callie if anyone approached—while doing damage to the trespassers.

There were pistols, rifles, ammunition, and knives in every room of the small cabin, as well as stashed around the property.

But it wasn't enough.

He hid in the woods, letting the dark surround him as he became one with nature. It was his time to sort through all the information he and Callie had gotten over the last couple of days and combine it with facts from his encounter with the Russians.

The multiple run-ins he'd had with the terrorist group in Syria made him wish that Callie were elsewhere. The terrorists were the type of people who would like nothing more than to get their hands on her.

He didn't let her know about his trepidation. Callie was inside the house, still trying to determine what the hacker had found when they'd entered her computer. Though she didn't say it, he knew she suspected the Saints.

Cullen had warned that their reach was long. Wyatt had been thinking of the clandestine group ever since his father had sent the warning.

Callie confirmed that the picture and newspaper article hadn't come from Orrin based on the ISPs. There was a small possibility that the terrorist group was responsible, but as he'd listened to Callie talk of how quickly and elegantly the hacker had gotten into her computer, the more he suspected the Saints.

If it hadn't been for Natalie grabbing the wrong papers by mistake while she was still working at the Russian Embassy in Dallas, they wouldn't even know about the Saints. Owen and Natalie had survived several clashes with the Saints, but that didn't mean they were safe.

Wyatt ran a hand down his face. It had begun with just the Russians. He thought it was in retaliation for his father's theft of the bioweapon. However, once Cullen was in Delaware with Mia, they'd learned the Saints included Americans and Columbians, as well.

And now, Syrians.

Wyatt thought back to a rumor he'd heard almost ten years earlier about an alliance between people from all over the world. Supposedly, they met to combat global warming. Since he was in the middle of combat, the climate wasn't exactly first on his mind, and he'd quickly forgotten about it.

That rumor got him wondering. Associations came together every day for any number of reasons. Some small, some as large as the United Nations, and some even more sizable than that.

A coalition like the Saints would take years to build

to its current scale, but he was beginning to suspect the group was much bigger than any of them anticipated.

He thought back to the attacks at the ranch, at Natalie's house, and in Dallas. The Russians had taken center stage. Why?

To draw them off the scent of who was really behind it all?

If it hadn't been for Yuri Markovic, they wouldn't even know of America's involvement. It sickened Wyatt to know that his own country—the nation he'd fought for, had been wounded for, and had been prepared to die for—was involved in such a group.

Maks would've revealed the truth when he was able. As it was, their conversation on the phone the previous night had shed more light on things.

Things that made Wyatt extremely uneasy because Maks was unsettled enough to disappear from the CIA for a while. Nothing alarmed Maks, so when he said he thought there were Saints within the CIA . . . Wyatt listened.

Maks verified that the Russian government was comprised almost entirely of Saints and that they had worked their way through all levels of the American government, as well.

It was easy to see why the Saints had such an extensive reach seemingly everywhere. It was another reason why Wyatt wished to remain where they were. At least here, he and Callie had a chance.

Out on the road, they didn't know who was friend or foe, or who they could trust. Not to mention, it would be simple for the Saints to track them.

Not that Wyatt thought they could remain hidden

much longer. No, he fully expected the Saints to make an appearance very soon. The difference was that he was prepared to make a stand at the cabin.

And anyone who came their way was an enemy.

His head swung to the house. There was a single light on in the dining area where Callie still worked. The blinds were closed, preventing him from getting a glimpse of her.

It was nearing two in the morning when he made his way back to the cabin. He silently entered the house, locking the back door behind him. After checking the front of the house, he walked to Callie.

There was a half-empty glass of wine beside her as she searched lines of code that gave him a headache just looking at it. Her brow was furrowed, and lines of strain bracketed her mouth.

He didn't want to startle her, so he walked on one of the floorboards that creaked.

"I heard you come in the back," Callie said without looking at him. She motioned with her head to the gun that rested beside the laptop. "I keep it close."

Wyatt made his way to the table and pulled out a chair to sit. "Have you found anything?"

"Yes, and I'm pissed off." She shoved the laptop away and dropped her head back as she stared at the ceiling. "They're smart. And patient."

He didn't need to ask to know she spoke of the Saints. "What happened?"

"I found where they entered my server over a week ago. They've just been sitting there, waiting. And I didn't know it."

"You can't blame yourself."

She lifted her head to look at him. "But I do. Everyone has their jobs. This is mine, and I failed. Because I didn't check my server before trying to hack Hewett's system, they were able to easily get into my computer and look around at everything."

"What did they find?"

"Well, nothing really," she said with a scrunch of her face.

He stretched his legs out in front of him. "Then what's the problem?"

"It's what they could've found had I not moved everything to a triple-secure server."

"Meaning?" he urged.

She blew out a breath. "I made a map of everywhere we've encountered the Saints. I added in Natalie and Mia, as well. I then layered the map of all the missions Orrin has taken over the last five years to see if there was a pattern."

"I gather there was."

"Yes. But that's just the start of what I've been doing."

He listened as she went through the numerous ways she'd been compiling information on the Saints. Her work would rival that of any intelligence organization. It was no wonder Orrin had recruited her to work for Whitehorse.

"I took the names of the Saints Mia and Cullen killed at the warehouse. I made a tier of names. Right now, the slots are mostly blank until we find out who is in what position, but we had to have a place to start."

"That we did," he said, awestruck at her resourcefulness.

And reminded of the many reasons he'd always found her so damn captivating.

Unlike most of the girls around his hometown, Callie hadn't hidden her intelligence. She worked it, using it to her advantage in school and in life.

Rarely had he witnessed someone with the kind of drive and determination that rode Callie. He saw it because the same emotions goaded him daily. Maybe that's what had drawn him to her.

No, that wasn't it. He knew what it was—her infectious laugh.

She took a sip of her wine. "I should know better. I'll be checking often from now on, but I think the Saints got what they wanted."

"To startle me," he said. "I've been hunting the terrotist group for years. I have no problem facing them."

"Well, I do because it won't be just the terrorists. The Saints will be with them."

Wyatt frowned as a thought took root. It wasn't mere coincidence that Callie's family was in town. Even though the Rccds did conduct their business all over the state of Texas, Austin wasn't a town they ventured to much at all, unlike Dallas.

"What is it?" Callie asked.

He didn't want to tell her of his thoughts since he knew how upset she became at the mention of her kin, so he kept his musings to himself. "Just piecing it all together."

"You and me both."

"Were you ever able to read Hewett's coded emails?" he asked to change the subject.

She rolled her eyes. "I've been a little busy protecting our information and stuff."

"Well, when you get to it . . ." he said as he rose, hiding his smile.

"Are you kidding me? You act as if I've not been doing anything. Oh. The nerve," she mumbled.

He walked to the kitchen. Even after all the years apart, it was still easy for him to incite such a reaction from her. He only did it because he liked to see her spike of anger. It made her blue eyes glitter.

Wyatt grabbed a bag of sunflower seeds and stretched out on the couch. There was a rifle beneath the sofa, and a 9mm strapped to his leg.

Without a word, Callie rose and stormed off to the bathroom. She slammed the door, but it caught on a bathmat and left a crack. There was the squeak of knobs as she turned on the faucets. A second later, the sound of water coming out of the showerhead could be heard.

From his angle on the sofa, he saw through the crack in the door into the bathroom mirror, which gave him a direct view of Callie. His mouth went dry when she began to take off her clothes.

Her back was to the mirror, but that didn't stop his blood from heating and rushing straight to his cock. She turned slightly, and he saw the swell of the outside of one breast.

He knew the weight of them, knew how sensitive her nipples were. He knew the feel of her silky skin. He knew . . . everything about her.

He was jerked out of his memories when she entered the shower and yanked the curtain closed. Wyatt closed his eyes and slowly brought his body back under control.

His time with Callie was over. Even if he wanted to start it back up again, he'd burned that bridge epically. Besides, she no longer looked at him with interest.

In fact, each time her gaze landed on him, it was with annoyance or distaste. Apparently, he'd been right fifteen years earlier when he'd told her he was nothing more than an infatuation.

It was too bad he couldn't say the same for himself. Distance didn't matter because Callie was never far from his thoughts.

He'd tried to lie to himself for a time and say it was because she was like a sister, but that didn't really explain why he kept tabs on her family to make sure they kept away from her.

Three years ago, he'd returned to Texas when he learned they were going to blackmail her into returning to the family. He'd actually been at the Reed house when Callie drove up.

She never knew he was there, and she never would. He'd said his piece to the Reeds, reminding them of his promise from years earlier. The family had promptly left her alone after that. Only when Wyatt was sure that they intended to uphold their end of the bargain did he return to his team.

A sister. He snorted. No, he'd always lusted after Callie.

And he always would.

CHAPTER FIVE

Wyatt waited until he was far from the cabin with the sun just coming over the horizon before he dialed a number and put his cell phone to his ear as it began to ring. When the call connected, there was nothing but silence on the other end of the secure line. He quickly stated his team designation. "Apollo, checking in."

"Hold the line," came the terse, female reply.

He didn't have to wait long before a gruff voice quickly asked, "Wyatt? What the hell happened?"

"I wish I could tell you, Bobby." Wyatt blew out a breath. "Suffice it to say that I'm all right."

Bobby, another Texan, snorted loudly. "I know that voice. I've been friends with you and fighting beside you long enough to know that the shit has hit the fan."

"In a manner of speaking."

"It must be important for you not to share with me."

Wyatt grimaced. He and Bobby had been to Hell and back together. There wasn't much Bobby didn't know. Wyatt considered him a friend—not something he did often—but he wasn't sure who was a Saint and who wasn't.

"Well, fuck me," Bobby grumbled as the silence lengthened. "Are you returning to the unit?"

Wyatt glanced at the house where Callie was already back at work on her computer. "I plan on it."

"That's good enough for me. But you didn't call on the secure line to shoot the shit. What can I do for you?"

It was on the tip of Wyatt's tongue to ask Bobby to locate Orrin. It would ease Callie's mind and allow her to focus on other things, but there was another pressing matter that had him contacting Bobby.

"This call is twofold," Wyatt said.

"I'll do what I can. You know that. I owe you."

That was Bobby's normal response ever since Wyatt had pulled him from a Humvee that had been hit by an IED. That improvised explosive device had killed two other men. "That debt has been paid."

"Never, my friend," Bobby argued.

Wyatt might be stubborn at times, but Bobby took it to the next level as he well knew. "Melvin Reed."

"The Reeds again, huh?" Bobby asked.

"I know he's in Austin. I need to know his exact whereabouts."

"I'm searching his cell phone. Got it, now getting the coordinates and sending to your secure email. That was easy. What's next?"

Wyatt closed his eyes, debating with himself some more about whether to let Bobby and the others know about the terrorists. Their unit had collided with them many times, but they'd yet to eradicate the terrorists from this world.

"Wyatt?" Bobby pressed.

Releasing a long breath, he said, "I can't go into detail on the how or the why, but I was warned that I'm being targeted. By our favorite bad guys."

"Where are you?" Bobby demanded furiously.

"No."

Bobby kept talking. "I know you're in Texas somewhere. I can have our entire unit there in twelve hours."

"No," Wyatt said again.

"Why the fuck not?" Bobby challenged. "It might take a while since you aren't on your usual cell, but I can keep you talking and get a trace on you. I don't want you fighting these sons of bitches alone."

Wyatt squeezed the bridge of his nose with his thumb and forefinger. "Bobby, please."

"There has to be a reas—. Holy shit. You don't trust me."

Wyatt knew his friend would come to that conclusion. They were too good at their jobs not to. "If I could explain it, you'd understand. I can't trust anyone."

"Yet you called in."

"I'm off the grid. I have no other choice."

"Not far enough if Ahmadi and his group can find you," Bobby pointed out.

Wyatt dropped his arm. "I told you about Ahmadi so you and the others are warned in case they come for any of you."

"You don't believe that. You think they're targeting you specifically," Bobby said.

"I do."

"This all points back to you being yanked from our mission. I can't get anyone to tell me anything, and now that I have you on the phone, you won't fill me in either."

"I wish I could. I really do."

Bobby blew out a breath. "And I want to help. I'm not liking this conundrum, Wyatt."

"Me either."

"Ahmadi and his men will come at you hard. They'll take out anyone near you."

"I know."

"I'll be here if you change your mind," Bobby said.

Wyatt knew he was blessed to have such a friend. And he hoped Bobby had nothing to do with the Saints, because he'd really hate to have to kill his friend. "Thanks."

He disconnected the call and logged into his email through his phone to see the coordinates for Melvin Reed. It was time he had a little talk with Callie's cousin.

When Wyatt entered the cabin, his gaze went straight to the table were Callie sat. She twirled a long strand of hair around her finger as she read something on the computer.

"I'm going to drive around the area," he said.

Her head turned to him, her blue eyes pinning him. "Looking for something in particular?"

"I just want a look."

"Okay."

He snagged the keys to her car and headed outside. Once inside the Challenger, he started the engine and drove away. Every so often, he'd look at his phone and the coordinates on the map to see how close he was getting to Reed.

Usually, when he was in this type of situation, his vehicle wouldn't stand out as the red did. Everyone noticed the color, which made it difficult to remain concealed. The only positive was that in a city the size of Austin, it made hiding easier.

When Wyatt finally reached the coordinates—a questionable bar—he pulled off to the side of the road and shut off the engine. Then he sat behind the tinted windows and watched the area, taking note of the comings and goings of those around him.

It didn't take long for his gaze to land on Melvin. The tall blond had perfect features and the blue eyes that were a Reed trait. He stood talking to two women while flashing his wide smile.

Wyatt fisted his hands. The urge to smash them into Melvin's too handsome face was overwhelming. Upon closer inspection, he noticed that Reed remained off to the side of the building where there didn't appear to be any cameras. That made it easier for Wyatt since he didn't want to be seen either.

He exited the car and walked the opposite direction, only to swing back around behind the bar to sneak up on Melvin. Wyatt waited at the side of the building and listened as Reed attempted to get both of the women to go back to his hotel with him.

When the girls finally got into their car and drove away, Melvin turned to walk toward him. Wyatt moved back a few steps and waited. As soon as he was within reach, Wyatt grabbed Melvin, slamming him against the brick.

"Son of a—" Melvin's voice stopped abruptly when he saw Wyatt.

Anger churned in his gut. Wyatt raised a brow. "Nothing to say?"

"What do you want?" he asked with a sneer. "I've not done anything."

"Really? So approaching Callie yesterday was nothing?"

Melvin's Adam's apple bobbed as he swallowed nervously. "I just wanted to talk."

"Bullshit." Wyatt took a menacing step toward him, balling up his fist. "The truth."

Melvin lifted his chin defiantly. "Kiss my ass, soldier boy."

Wyatt smiled at the punk. "I could kill you with one hand and not leave a mark on your body. I found you in a city of two million. Those are just some of the things this 'soldier boy' can do. Do you really want to piss me off any more than I already am?"

"Callie belongs with her family," Melvin said after a brief hesitation.

"She gets to decide what she wants—as I told your father, her father, and all of the other lowlife, alcoholic criminals in your family. She wants nothing to do with any of you. Respect her wishes."

Melvin's blue eyes flashed in fury. "Or what?"

"Do I really need to spell it out for you?"

"Beat me up or threaten me some more. You won't do more than that," he said with a sneer.

Wyatt smiled coldly. "Are you so sure of that?"

Some of his bluster faded. Melvin glanced to the side toward a new, white Cadillac Escalade. "I can't go back without her."

"You're not going anywhere near Callie again. This

is the only warning you're going to get. Next time, you won't even see me coming."

"She's my family!" Reed shouted. "You can't tell me what to do with my own blood."

Melvin grew bolder and pushed at Wyatt's chest, attempting to shove him back. Wyatt didn't budge. He glared at the imbecile. "Callie is my family. We Loughmans protect what's ours to the death."

"This isn't over."

"It is if you want to remain alive."

Wyatt started to walk away. Years of honed instincts and nasty situations around the world had his senses more attuned. He heard the sound of Melvin palming the handgun and drawing it from the waist of his jeans.

Before the gun could be pointed at him, Wyatt turned and grabbed hold of Melvin's wrist, twisting and squeezing until Reed had no choice but to release the weapon or have his bones snapped.

"Okay, okay," Melvin said hurriedly as Wyatt added more pressure.

Reed went down on his knees, his face contorting in pain. Wyatt could feel the bones beneath his hand. It would take just a little more force to shatter them.

He didn't hide his rage. Every time he looked at any of the Reeds, he saw Callie lying unconscious, bloodied and broken in the woods. He recalled how she'd looked so lifeless in his arms. He remembered how small and vulnerable she'd appeared as he held her. How there had been tear streaks in the dirt and blood on her face.

"Please," Melvin whimpered.

If it were up to Wyatt, he'd do more than break Reed's

wrist, but Callie had never wanted to hurt her family. She just wanted them to leave her alone and allow her to make her own decisions.

Reluctantly, Wyatt released Melvin. Then he picked up the gun and tucked it in the back of his jeans, pulling his shirt down to cover it. He didn't look Reed's way again as he strode to the Challenger.

Once back at the cabin, Wyatt walked to the rear of the house to put the gun with some of his other weapons. He came to a halt when he saw Callie standing in the morning sun, hanging up some clothes to dry on the line.

The way the sun shone its golden rays around her gave her an ethereal look. The ends of her long, chestnut locks stirred in the breeze.

He fought the urge to walk up behind her and kiss her neck right below her ear on the spot that made her moan. He longed to wrap that long hair of hers around his hand and hold her head steady as he kissed her with all the pent-up desire he'd held inside for the last fifteen years.

"Hey," she said as she turned around and saw him. "How'd it go?"

Much to his frustration, it took him a second to remember where he'd been. Anger mixed with his desire, making it difficult for him to keep the emotions in check. "Fine."

She laughed and started toward the house. "I was beginning to wonder if you were going answer. You were gone longer than I anticipated."

"I think we should head into town tonight."

Callie came to a sudden halt and looked at him strangely. "Did you hit your head?"

"No." He frowned at her. "Why?"

"We're supposed to stay hidden, remember. Why do you wânt us out there to be found?"

He gave her a flat look. "Give me more credit than that. We're going to be holed up here for a while, so we should get enough groceries to sustain us. While we're out, we can get something to eat."

"Now that sounds more like the Wyatt I know," she said with a shake of her head and continued toward the door. "When you first mentioned it, you made it sound like a date."

Her laughter followed her inside the house. Wyatt remained outside while coming to grips with the fact that he did want to take Callie out on a date.

"I'm in a shit storm of trouble," he mumbled to himself, thankful no one was around to see his predicament—especially his brothers, who would take great enjoyment in his suffering.

CHAPTER SIX

Callie was all too ready to get out of the house that evening. It was rare that she became frustrated while working, but that's exactly what had happened today.

No matter how hard she tried, she had yet to discover where the hack on her laptop had originated.

To make matters worse, she couldn't shake off the lingering indignation with Wyatt that he hadn't been asking her out earlier. The flutter of excitement and delight when she thought they were going out to dinner as a couple had been swiftly smashed to smithereens.

She looked in the bedroom mirror and grimaced. She should've known better. In the brief time she and Wyatt had been together there hadn't been a date. She hadn't been upset about it then. Who would want to be seen out in their hometown with her?

But now? Well, now was different. Now, she wanted to be taken out to dinner, to be treated as if he were more interested in her than anything else in the world.

"Get over yourself," she said to her reflection. "We're running for our lives. There isn't time for dating. Besides," she added. "You don't want anything to do with him. He's cold, callous, and only cares about himself."

She gave a firm nod to herself. But deep in her heart, the pep talk had no effect. She hated herself for how she couldn't seem to get over Wyatt.

Orrin had pretended not to notice when she would hungrily search the reports that came in for anything having to do with Wyatt. There had even been a few years when she'd broken free of Wyatt's hold on her.

Then he'd returned to the ranch—shattering all her walls with a single look.

God, she was pathetic. Callie turned away, unable to face her reflection. She'd fallen fast and hard for Wyatt and loved him fiercely. None of that had done any good. It seemed the harder she'd tried to hold onto him, the more he'd pushed her away.

Callie walked from the bedroom. A quick look inside the cabin confirmed that Wyatt was nowhere to be seen. She searched outside and found him leaning back against her car with one ankle over the other, and his arms crossed over his chest. His eyes were closed, but she knew he wasn't sleeping.

He wore dark jeans and a simple T-shirt, but there was nothing simple about him.

She walked out of the cabin, locking the door behind her. "Are you sure about both of us going?"

"Yep." His eyes opened and landed on her.

She stared into the golden irises and tried to ignore the thumping of her heart. "Then let's go."

He climbed into the driver's side and started the engine. Once she was seated, he backed Mercy up before driving away. Normally, she hated when others drove when she was there, but right then, she couldn't find the strength to care.

"You're quiet," he said.

She shrugged, keeping her gaze out the window. "I'm just thinking."

"About?"

Since when did he care what was on her mind? Callie turned her head to him and frowned. "Let's see. I have so much to choose from. How about locating Orrin. I'd love to talk to him to learn what happened and see if he has information that could help us. Then there are the Saints and everything that involves them. And let's not forget the guys who are coming after you."

"I'll take care of them."

"I have no doubt, but you forget that we're paired up. That means what comes for you, comes for me and vice versa."

"I'm well aware of that."

She held back a snort of skepticism and turned her head back toward her window. The landscape was nothing but a blur as her unfocused gaze turned inward.

Wyatt might be a heartless asshole, but he'd become a legend for ignoring risks to his own life in an effort to save others. She knew that he would look out for her when they were cornered, whether it was by the Saints or other terrorists.

It wasn't until the car came to a halt that she blinked and looked around. They were in front of a restaurant called Sophia's. Since she'd expected some kind of diner where they could be in and out quickly, she was more than confused.

"What's this?" she asked.

Wyatt opened his door as he said, "A restaurant."

Now he wanted to be a smartass. She got out of the car and walked beside him to the entrance. The hostess took them through the establishment with its vibrant teal seats and dark, tufted leather booths. The walls, columns, and archways were all brick, which tied in nicely with the wood floors and wooden ceiling.

She slid into one of the half-moon shaped booths, still unsure what was going on. This restaurant wasn't Wyatt. There were cameras everywhere, which meant the Saints could find them easily. Hell, for all she knew, there were Saints dining right alongside them.

"Relax," Wyatt told her.

She shot him a hard look. "Did you get baked in the sun? What are we doing here?"

"Eating. I can't tell you how long it's been since I sat down at a restaurant."

"We're on display because of your craving?" she asked incredulously.

He looked at her over his menu. "Don't be so dramatic. Besides, tell me you weren't hungry for something you didn't have to fix yourself."

She was about to admit just that when she saw his lips twitch. Then he raised the menu higher. But she was sure he'd been about to smile.

One look at the Italian-American cuisine items on the menu, and her stomach rumbled. Everything looked positively delicious. Her mouth watered for all of it. Then she got a glimpse of the desserts and nearly groaned when she spotted the tiramisu.

"There's no telling when we'll be able to dine like this again," Wyatt said. "How about a bottle of wine?"

"You don't ever need to ask if I want wine. The answer will always be yes," she said, glancing up at him from the menu.

After the waiter left with the wine order, Wyatt said, "I remember when you used to sneak some of Orrin's beer. I'd never have pegged you for a wine girl until you bought a bottle recently."

"I still have the occasional beer, but my preference is wine. White or red. But I truly love champagne."

He raised a dark brow. "Really?"

"Pink champagne is my favorite. I don't know why, but it is." She had no idea why she shared such personal information with him. It wasn't like he cared—or would even remember.

He sat back when the waiter returned with a bottle of pinot noir. Once the glasses were filled, Wyatt turned his glass around and around. "You've changed."

"People tend to do that."

"You've changed a lot."

She met his gold gaze. "It's been several years. When you left, I was still a kid. I'm a woman now."

"You were never a kid, Callie."

He had a point there. The Reeds hadn't let her be a child. They'd forced her to grow up and see the harshness of life at a very early age.

She folded her menu and set it aside. "No. I don't suppose I was."

"Do you enjoy working with Orrin?"

"Very much," she replied. "I have a purpose. Then there's Orrin himself. He took me in and made me feel a part of things. Your aunt and uncle became my family as well."

Wyatt took a drink of the wine. "I know what it's like to walk in and find someone murdered. I'm sorry you had to find Virgil and Charlotte that way."

At first, she didn't know what to say. Wyatt never spoke of his mother—ever. So for him to mention even a kernel of something was a big deal.

"I can't walk into that house now without seeing. . . ." She trailed off, unable to finish.

His hand covered hers. "I know."

She blinked back tears. If anyone could truly know what it had been like to walk into the house and find family murdered, it was Wyatt.

"It's one of the reasons I left," he confessed. "I can't look at the house without seeing my mother's body. So living there those years afterward was pure hell."

"The ranch is my home. I don't live in that house, but I don't know how I'll be able to go back."

Wyatt's lips parted, but before he could speak, the waiter arrived to take their orders. His hand dropped from hers, and she missed the warmth and simple affection it had provided her.

After the waiter departed, she expected Wyatt to continue with their conversation, but the mood had been broken. Callie was saddened by it because she'd felt a true connection to him. Something she'd only glimpsed while they'd been lovers.

"I think we should buy several more prepaid phones while we're out," he said.

She added it to the list she kept on her cell phone. "There's a man who lives near here who makes ammunition. Orrin uses him often. His name is Carl Turner."

"Can you contact him?" Wyatt asked.

Callie smiled as she said, "Already did this afternoon. I gave him a list of our weapons and the ammo that we had. He'll have what we need."

"You trust him?"

"I did. Now I don't trust anyone."

Wyatt leaned his forearms on the table. "Not even me?"

"I don't have a choice but to trust you."

"Does that mean you'd rather not?"

"It means I don't have a choice."

Wyatt shook his head. "So you don't."

"I know you don't want to be here with me any more than I want to be with you. You could've gone to Dover in Cullen's place to look around the Air Force base," she stated.

"I could've, yes," Wyatt said.

Now that got her curious. "Why didn't you?"

"I know how important you are to Orrin."

She rolled her eyes at his statement. "That's the best you could come up with?"

"Either of my brothers could've guarded you, but I can do it better."

There was one thing Wyatt had never lacked, and that was confidence. He had it in spades. The worst part about it was that he was right. Cullen and Owen were experts at what they did.

But Wyatt was a master.

"So you decided to pair up with me for Orrin?" she asked.

Wyatt lifted one shoulder in a shrug. "That's part of it."

"And the other part?"

"Just know that I get the job done."

She pushed aside her wine glass to cross her arm over the other on the table. "Oh, no. You're the one who made the statement about it being *part* of the reason. You say something like that, then you have to be prepared to answer the resulting question."

"Does it really matter?"

"Yes."

His eyes narrowed slightly. "Why?"

"Because I know how you feel about me."

"Do you?" he asked softly.

She should've known better than to keep pushing when he used that voice. She should've remembered how he used it to draw people in and lull them right before he came in for the kill. "You made your feelings perfectly clear long ago."

"Is that right."

"It sure the hell is."

He took a drink of wine and slowly lowered the glass to the table. "Interesting."

"What is? My memory?"

"Yes."

"I have the memory of an elephant. So just tell me the other reason for teaming up with me."

He let the silence lengthen until it became almost unbearable. Then he said, "I wanted to know the woman you've become."

CHAPTER SEVEN

For a second, Callie didn't move, unsure if she'd heard Wyatt correctly or not. Why would he care about the woman she'd become? He'd once told her that she meant nothing to him.

"You find that difficult to believe?" Wyatt asked.

She nodded. "You could say that."

"Why?"

"Why?" she repeated in disbelief. "You're seriously asking me that?"

His gold eyes were steady as he watched her. "I am."

"No."

His brow creased in a frown. "No, what?"

"No, I'm not going to do this. I'm not going to bring up the past and relive it."

"I'm not asking you to."

"But you are," she insisted.

His frown deepened. "How?"

"You can't be that obtuse. You want to know why I find it difficult to believe that you're interested in the person I've become? The answers lie in a past that I've no wish to revisit."

A muscle in his jaw clenched. "It seems the past is very much a part of the present."

"I wouldn't say that at all."

"You have your opinions of me for things I did over a decade ago."

She laughed, shaking her head at him. "The fact is, you haven't changed. You're still the same Wyatt who can cut a person to shreds with his eyes and his words."

"I—"

"I've just about gotten in the back door of Hewett's servers," she said, changing the subject. "I should be through tomorrow. Then, I can decrypt the messages and see what he wants."

"He wants to know where you're at."

She was surprised at how easily Wyatt shifted to the new conversation without so much as a look. "He'll remain in the suspect column until we find out otherwise."

"Everyone stays in that column for now."

"Including your friend Maks?"

Wyatt's eyes jerked to her. "Maks didn't just come to the aid of Cullen and Mia, he helped Markovic and Orrin escape."

"That doesn't mean he's not a Saint."

"If he were, he wouldn't have disappeared so that even the CIA can't find him."

She scrunched up her face. "That still doesn't clear Maks."

"Don't trust him then, but I do."

During their meal, the conversation turned to where Orrin and Yuri Markovic might have headed. Through dessert, they went over places they could go if they were able to escape an attack on the cabin.

By the time Wyatt asked for the check, Callie was happily stuffed. She walked contentedly from the restaurant to her car with Wyatt just a few steps behind her.

It wasn't until she opened the passenger door that she saw the folded paper fall out. She got into the vehicle and discreetly retrieved it. There was no need to wonder who'd put it there. She knew—her family.

She kept the note hidden in her palm as she gave directions to Wyatt on how to get to Carl's house. It was to the southeast of Austin, far enough away from the city to offer seclusion, but close enough to bring in clients.

It took them thirty minutes to reach Carl's property. The place looked deserted, but once they drove over the cattle guard then past a fence, the buildings came into view. There was an older house, which had been kept in good repair, and two large, metal buildings off to the right.

"Park over there," Callie told Wyatt, pointing to the buildings.

They exited the car and came to stand before it. Callie used that time to carefully put the note in her back pocket. As they began to approach the door, they heard the racking of a pump shotgun. Immediately, they came to a halt.

"Carl, it's Callie. You're expecting us," she called.

A moment later, a man with an old baseball cap on his head with wisps of white hair poking out emerged. He had a beard that fell to his chest, and blue eyes that hadn't faded with age. He wore a white shirt and denim overalls.

There was a smile on his face as he lowered the shotgun. "Callie girl. It's good to see you. It's been much too long."

"Hi, Carl," she said and walked into his outstretched arms.

When she stepped back, Carl's gaze moved to Wyatt. He studied Wyatt for a long while before hooking his thumbs into the pockets of his overalls. He then walked around Wyatt slowly.

"I'll be damned," Carl said when he stood before Wyatt. "The shit must have really hit the fan for you to be here."

Wyatt held Carl's stare. "You know me?"

"Of course, I do. I've been working with Orrin since before you were born, son. I even made the trip to Hillsboro to celebrate the birth of his first child: you." He turned away, shaking his head while mumbling, "Do I know him?"

Callie shrugged when Wyatt looked her way. She hadn't a clue that Orrin and Carl's friendship went back so many years, but it explained why Carl readily dropped whatever he was doing to help Orrin out.

They followed the old man inside the first metal building. The front of it looked like any other workshop might with various engine parts lying about and tools hanging on the walls.

It wasn't until they reached the back that you saw the workstations used to build weapons, and others for producing the ammunition.

Callie watched Wyatt's face. It beamed as if he'd come down on Christmas morning to find everything he'd asked Santa for under the tree. Carl stood by Callie as Wyatt walked between each of the tables, touching and examining everything. Though Callie was impatient, Carl merely smiled.

Finally, Wyatt turned to Carl. "When this is over, I'd love to come back and talk to you about specifications on a rifle."

"You're welcome here anytime," Carl said. His smile dropped as he pulled out his cell phone and looked at the list Callie had sent him of their weapon and ammunition supply. "It looks like y'all are preparing for war."

Callie hesitated in answering. It wasn't that she didn't trust Carl. The fact was that she didn't know who the Saints had recruited. They were taking a huge chance coming to him.

Wyatt, however, didn't seem to have that problem. He replied right away. "We are going to war."

"This involves Orrin, doesn't it?" Carl asked.

Callie glanced at Wyatt as she nodded. "It does."

"It's why he hasn't responded to my calls."

"Yes."

Carl ran a hand down his beard, his gaze thoughtful as he looked at the floor and rocked back on his heels. "That's not good news. Is he alive?"

"As far as we know." Wyatt folded his arms over his chest. "Orrin trusts you, and so does Callie. However, we've been betrayed."

"We?" Carl asked.

Callie put her hands in the back pockets of her jeans. "Orrin, all three of his sons, me, Mia Carter, and Natalie Dixon."

Carl walked to one of the worktables and sat in a chair. "Betrayal can cut deep. I know. I'm not sure there's anything I can tell the two of you that will relieve your misgivings."

"Try," Wyatt urged.

A smile pulled at Carl's lips, tilting his mustache up on the sides. "I've been building weapons and producing my own ammunition for four decades. I do occasionally sell to an individual hunter or the like, but most of my work is exclusive to people like Orrin."

Callie winced. "That's actually not helping matters."

"The people I do work for have been the same for over twenty years," Carl said.

Wyatt dropped his arms and moved closer to Carl. "What do you know of the Saints?"

"I don't watch football, son," Carl said with a chuckle. When neither she nor Wyatt commented, Carl sat up straighter. He looked from one to the other before focusing on her. "So. That type of group, huh?"

"If you aren't working with them and they find out you've helped us, they might come for you," she said.

The corners of Carl's eyes crinkled as he smiled. "Let them come. My land might not look like much, but I did that on purpose. This is a veritable fort. I have provisions to last me five years, not to mention my armory."

"They're not a group you want to disregard," Wyatt warned.

Carl nodded. "We all have to die someday, but I'll heed your words, son. Now, let's go over this list."

The longer they were away from the cabin, the more unnerved Callie became. She didn't want the Saints to catch them on the road as they had Cullen and Mia. And she and Wyatt still had to get food for the next few weeks.

At this rate, it would be in the early hours of the morning before they made it back.

"While y'all do this, I'm going to run to the store to pick up the items we need," she said.

Both men looked at her, and in unison said, "No."

She blinked at them. How had those two bonded so quickly when Callie had known Carl for years?

"I'd rather we do that together," Wyatt said.

She shook her head. "Why waste time? This way, when we're done here, we can head straight back to the cabin."

"Callie girl, why not go below and look through my provisions. Take whatever you two need," Carl urged.

She could tell by the look in Wyatt's eyes that he wasn't going to hand over the keys to Mercy, which meant Callie wasn't going anywhere.

Just another reason she liked to drive her own damn car.

Holding back the urge to flip him off, she smiled at Carl and made her way to the stairs that led below to his bunker and the stores of food. Once she was down there, she took out the note and unfolded the paper. Scrawled upon it were just six words: *You can't run from us forever.*

She folded the paper back up and returned it to her pocket. When was her family going to take the hint? How many times did she have to tell them she wouldn't join in their criminal enterprises?

How many more instances would she have to firmly and emphatically tell them she was living her own life? By now, they should've gotten the not so subtle hint.

What was it about her that caused them to continue trying to bring her back into the fold? And why was she in this cycle of them pushing and pushing until she took a stand and then they backed off, only to repeat it all again in a few years?

It had all begun when she'd gone to work at the Loughmans'. At first, her family had thought it funny and humored her by allowing her to go. Of course, they took every penny she made, but she hadn't worked for the money.

After over nine months at the ranch, suddenly, her father ordered her to quit. When she'd refused, he hit her. It wasn't long before her mother and the rest of the family joined in.

Then they'd loaded her up in the back of one of the trucks and dumped her in the woods a mile from Loughman land. She'd passed out from the pain, but when she'd woken, she had crawled and dragged herself toward the ranch.

When she came to, Orrin and Virgil were standing over her, telling her that everything would be all right. They'd even called the sheriff. She didn't bother filing a report against her kin. The sheriff couldn't arrest the entire Reed family, and when she returned home— because she had to go home—there would just be another beating.

No amount of talking could change her mind, and finally, Orrin had given up. He'd then lifted her in his arms and carried her to the stairs.

On his way up, Wyatt had stormed into the house. When he'd spotted her, he'd stilled, their gazes meeting. She'd been mortified that he had seen her in such a condition. The one thing Callie hated was for anyone to think her weak. Her size often gave people that impression, and she'd spent years dedicating her life to learning how to defend herself.

Never again would she be beaten down like that—physically, mentally, or emotionally.

It was time her family learned that.

CHAPTER EIGHT

"You could make a stand here," Carl said.

Wyatt stopping making the bullets and looked over at him. "Thanks for the offer, but I don't think that's wise."

"Why? Because you're worried about me getting hurt?" Carl made a sound in the back of his throat. "Son, I was in Vietnam. I served three tours and have multiple scars to prove how easy it is for a bullet or shrapnel to find you. Think about Callie."

It was all Wyatt did think about. Even when she wasn't near, his thoughts constantly drifted to her.

"We could make a helluva stand here," Carl said.

Wyatt thought about the small cabin. It was even more remote than Carl's house, which would keep any innocents from being hit. Even with all the traps he'd set, it was nothing compared to what Carl had.

Just as Wyatt was about to agree to his offer, Callie came up the stairs with several bags of food in her hands. Their eyes met. He set aside his work and turned the stool to face her.

"What is it?" he asked.

She shrugged indifferently. "Nothing. I've been getting food. I also grabbed a few of the burner phones, Carl."

Wyatt started to argue, but stopped at the last second. If he told her that he could see the anger in her eyes, she'd inform him that he didn't know her. There was no way he could tell her that he knew her better than he knew himself, that she'd been with him every step of the way through all their years apart.

"You look pissed," Carl said after he glanced her way.

Callie flashed him a fake smile. "Not at all."

There was only one thing that could rile her in such a way—her family. Wyatt thought back over the evening. The Reeds hadn't been anywhere near her physically, but they could've gotten to her in other ways.

Obviously, his little talk with Melvin hadn't done any good. Wyatt was going to have to follow through with his threat. Breaking the asswipe's wrist was just the thing.

Carl finished making the last bullet in the box and faced Callie. "I told Wyatt y'all should stay here. You'd have an unlimited supply of weapons, ammo, and food. Not to mention the fortification."

"Wyatt has done a great job securing the place we've chosen. We know it. It's better if we return," she said.

Carl shook his head, smoothing a hand down his beard. "Think about this, Callie."

"I am. I have." Her gaze swung to Wyatt. "We need to return home."

Home. He knew she meant it as the place they'd been staying, but for some reason, hearing her say it in the same sentence as mention of him sent a bolt of longing so strong, so pure running through him, that if he hadn't been sitting, his knees would've buckled.

She raised a brow. "Agreed?"

He merely nodded, unable to find words since he was still dealing with the unwanted feelings.

After Callie walked to the car with the bags, Wyatt turned back to the table, only to find Carl staring at him intensely. "What is it?" Wyatt asked.

Carl blew out a loud breath. "If I have to say it, then you're dumber than I thought."

"I don't have a clue what you're talking about."

"The hell you don't, son." Carl glanced out the door to Callie. "You've got it so bad for her, you can't see straight. What I don't understand is why you don't just tell her."

The reasons ran through Wyatt's head, but there were too many to name. "It's . . . complicated."

"Bullshit. Love is always complicated. What you need to ask yourself is if you can live without her. If you can't, then you've gotta do something."

"I screwed it up years ago. There's no getting past what I did."

Carl returned to his work. "Sounds like you've got a problem then."

For the next hour, they worked as Carl shared stories about Orrin, with Callie chiming in every so often. Wyatt hadn't wanted to hear any of it at first, but it was hard to ignore the deep respect and friendship Carl had for Orrin.

So, Wyatt grudgingly listened. By the time the work ended, he'd learned much about his father that he hadn't known. It made Wyatt wish he didn't hold such anger for his father because they had much in common.

With a farewell wave to Carl—and a promise to return soon—Wyatt pointed Mercy back in the direction of the cabin. He glanced over at Callie, who had rolled down her window and was still waving at Carl.

Only when he was out of sight did she roll up the window. Wyatt had gotten to see another side of her, as well. She'd shown that she had earned Carl's respect from her work with Orrin.

"I know you didn't want to hear those stories about your father, but I couldn't exactly tell Carl to stop," she said.

Wyatt pulled out onto the road. "If Carl knows who I am, then he knows the rift between Orrin and me. He talked about my father on purpose."

"They were good stories."

He saw her smile out of the corner of his eye. Many of Carl's retellings had involved Callie. It was a jab at Wyatt. To show that Callie loved Orrin, and that his father was a good man.

"I'm glad you found a place at the ranch," Wyatt said.

She leaned her head back. "Me, too. I honestly didn't think anything could touch the ranch again. But then, I never thought a group like the Saints could exist, much less target us."

"We have a chance to fix this."

Her head swung to him. "Fix it? What do you mean?"

"If anyone but Orrin had accepted the assignment, we wouldn't know about the Saints or Ragnarok."

"We still don't know what the bioweapon does."

"It doesn't matter," he insisted. "My point is that Orrin was smart enough to know something was wrong after they left Russia. Otherwise, he'd never have sent the weapon to you."

She shoved her hair away from her face. "You make it sound like you're glad it was Orrin."

"I am." He hadn't realized it until now with all the information they had, but he recognized that between him, his brothers, and his father, they could strike a lethal blow to the Saints.

Callie laughed softly. "That's something I never thought I'd hear you say. Wait." The smile faded, replaced by a glare. "Do you mean you're glad it was Orrin because he was kidnapped and beaten? Because if you did, that's jus—"

"No," he said over her. "That's not what I meant. I might hold anger toward my father, but even I know how good he is at his job. I've had years to hear it from my superiors."

"Oh. Well. That's good to know."

"How insistent was Hewett that Orrin take the mission to Russia?"

She scratched her chin as she thought. "Mitch just sent the one encrypted email, though he did call me the day before Orrin agreed to do it to see which direction Orrin was swaying."

"Did you tell him?" Wyatt questioned.

"No. I work for Orrin, not Hewett."

Wyatt expected nothing less from her. "You said that you suspected Hewett wanted Orrin specifically for the assignment."

"It was just the way Mitch spoke. It was nothing he said specifically. Just a gut feeling I had," she said with a lift of her shoulders.

"In our line of work, trusting your gut could save your life."

"Then I should've said something to Orrin about it."

Wyatt shook his head and glanced at her. "It wouldn't have done anything but push my father to take the mission to see what was going on."

"Does it bother you?"

It was his turn to give her a frown. "What?"

"That I'm so close to Orrin?"

Wyatt slowed the car in front of a stop sign before pulling away. "Why should that be a problem?"

"He's your father."

"It's a fact I can't change. Another fact is that he's responsible for my mother's death."

"You don't know that for sure."

"I sure as shit don't have any other person to pin it on."

Callie turned her head to look out the side window. "There is so much I could tell you about Orrin to change your mind."

"I suspect this is when you start?"

"No," she declared without looking his way. "You wouldn't really hear me anyway. You've made up your mind, and once you do that, there's no changing it."

He knew she alluded to when he broke it off between them. It was true, once he made a decision, he didn't change his mind. What she didn't know was that it took him a long time to come to such verdicts because he looked at every angle.

Which was why he was so certain when he finally did make his choice.

She suddenly looked his way. "No. I am going to tell

you something. I don't care if you don't believe it. You should know."

"Then tell me."

"Orrin never stopped looking into Melanie's murder."

Wyatt cut her a dubious look. "And in all these years, he found nothing?"

"Ugh," she ground out angrily. "You make me so furious."

"Because the truth hurts?"

"Because you're an ass. He got close several times with leads he uncovered, but each time, someone or something put a halt to it. Everyone who once helped him no longer would have anything to do with Melanie's murder. No one."

Wyatt stared at the dark road as the headlights lit the way. Her words troubled him more than he wanted to admit.

"You know what else?" she asked. "He could never find out who hindered his investigations. There was never a name he could go to, nobody to confront."

"That sounds suspicious."

"You think?" she asked sarcastically. "What else is suspicious, is that we discovered that he had gotten close because he would be given orders that put him in the direct line of fire."

Now that didn't sit well with Wyatt at all. "Is that why he retired from the Navy?"

"It's one of the main reasons, yes. It gave him time to dig into things more, but even more doors were closed against him. He got nowhere. But the point is that he kept trying."

They were approaching the cabin, so Wyatt slowed

the car. When he put the vehicle in park, Callie reached over and turned off the engine, taking the keys.

He looked at her, seeing the fire in her blue eyes, the same heat that told him she was ready to take on the world. She wasn't finished, so he remained to hear what else she had to say.

"You've never been in love. You don't know how Orrin felt to have the woman who bore his children, the woman he'd made a life with, the woman who was the other half of his soul taken from him." She paused, her eyes welling with tears. "Do you know that he never went on a single date after your mother? He's never even looked at another woman. Because he holds her in his heart still. If you think he doesn't care about Melanie's murder or you, then you're an idiot."

She got out of the car and stormed into the house. Wyatt watched her go, her words ringing in his head. The distance he'd put between him and Orrin meant that he knew nothing of his father.

It came as a shock to hear that Orrin hadn't found another woman. And Callie would know. She spent the most time with him.

Wyatt closed his eyes, thinking of his mother. She didn't deserve to die so horribly. It was even worse that no one had been brought to justice for the deed.

Somehow, it all pointed back to Orrin—of that he was certain. It didn't matter how much his father looked into the killing or how he pined for Melanie. The murder was still unsolved.

Until that changed, Wyatt would continue to blame Orrin.

CHAPTER NINE

For the next two days, Callie saw very little of Wyatt. He kept to the outdoors, constantly walking the perimeter. He didn't come in for meals, either. Which suited her just fine.

Ever since their conversation returning from Carl's, she'd been livid. She didn't understand how Wyatt could still hold such a grudge against Orrin. Didn't Wyatt realize how his father suffered?

Maybe he did and just didn't care.

She sat back in her chair at the thought and pushed away the laptop. It would be just like Wyatt. The only thing he did care about was himself.

Why had she ever allowed herself to fall in love with such a cold man? She knew she had no control over her heart, but it didn't make things any easier. If only she could be sure she was, in fact, finished with him.

Every time she thought she might be over Wyatt, she'd catch herself watching him—wanting him. And she'd remember how tender, how loving he'd been in those precious few weeks. During that brief time, she'd seen another side of Wyatt Loughman. The side that showed he could love deeply—if he wanted.

And that's what wounded her the most. He chose not to love her. He'd decided she wasn't worth it and closed himself off.

What had she done—or not done? What was it about her that pushed him away? Even now, looking back, she felt the same heart-wrenching pain.

He'd been everything to her. She'd given him her body, her heart . . . her soul. And he'd teased her with a glimpse of what could be, only to snatch it away from her at the last second.

The cruelty was staggering. She hadn't expected him to turn it on her, but he'd given her an even bigger dose of his ruthlessness. Though she didn't remember all the words, it was the tone she'd never forget.

The impatience and annoyance. The viciousness and finality.

It all said one thing: he was finished with her.

He'd had his fun, and he was moving on.

It had been almost unbearable for her to continue working at the ranch for the next few months before he left for college. She would watch him from the woods. He hadn't even looked for her. Never in her life had she cried so hard as the day he drove away. Because she knew she'd never seen him again.

If Orrin, Virgil, Charlotte, Cullen, or Owen knew what had happened, none of them ever spoke of it. She'd made sure no one saw her tears. Wyatt Loughman had broken her with only a few words. It had taken years for her to pick up the pieces and move ahead.

And she was determined to keep moving. Whatever feelings she still carried for him had to be ignored at all costs. He'd never be able to give her anything but misery.

Knowing that did nothing to diminish the longing, however. There hadn't been a single man she dated who had kissed her as passionately as Wyatt.

Her eyes closed as unwanted memories assaulted her. A sultry July fourth night when, beneath a sky lit up by fireworks, he'd made love to her. It had been magical. That night, more than their bodies had been joined.

She'd seen it in his eyes, felt it in his touch. Tasted it in his kiss.

Callie gave her head a vicious shake to dislodge the memory. She used to sit and wonder for hours what went wrong. Her life had come to a standstill during that time, and she wouldn't go through that again.

Her gaze lifted to the window. The sky was streaked in bold, vibrant reds and oranges as the sun sank into the horizon. It was a glorious sight that she wasn't able to enjoy fully because she was too wrapped up in everything.

There had been nothing from Cullen or Mia on their search for Konrad Jankovic. Callie initially thought Orrin might go after the scientis, as well, but no matter how hard she looked for a sign of Orrin in DC, there was nothing.

Where was he?

Her phone bounced on the table as it vibrated. She recognized the number immediately. Briefly, she thought about ignoring the call, but her family needed to be dealt with.

"How did you get this number?" she demanded when she answered.

Melvin laughed. "We've got good connections, cuz. You should know that there's nowhere you can go, no place you can hide that we won't find you."

"Is that what your little note was about?"

"That was my idea."

She'd always had a particular distaste for Melvin. Perhaps it was because he used his looks and charm to get whatever he wanted, and he didn't care who he took down along the way. "Should I clap for you?"

"What are you doing with Wyatt?"

She'd wondered if they were watching her. Now, she had her confirmation. "He's a Loughman. I work for the Loughmans."

"Not in Austin."

"You don't know what the ranch is doing, so don't pretend otherwise," she retorted.

Melvin laughed again. "You'll never be one of them. You belong with us."

"I'm only going to say this once more, so listen closely. I don't want to see any of you. I don't want to talk to any of you. Don't call me, don't track me down, and don't stop me on the street. I'm finished with all of you."

"We'll be the judge of that," he said angrily.

Callie sighed. "You're just not getting it. No matter what you do, I'm not returning. I won't be party to crime, nor will I be involved with people who actively hurt others for their own gain."

"You're a Reed. We have the same blood. That makes you one of us whether you admit it or not. You'll never be able to run from the truth of that."

"I won't continue to have this same conversation every few years."

Melvin mumbled something she couldn't make out. Then he said, "Tell Wyatt I'm ready for him to carry out his threat."

The line disconnected. Callie lowered the phone, looking at it as if it could give her answers. What the hell had Melvin meant? Wyatt never talked to her family. He hated them. Everyone hated the Reeds.

The more Callie thought about Melvin's statement, the more she had to know the truth. She closed her laptop and walked outside with her phone still in her grasp. Her gaze searched the area for Wyatt, but she didn't find him.

One of the first things they'd done when they got to the cabin was walk the property. Callie picked her way through the underbrush, careful of the traps he'd set. She spotted a rattlesnake and gave it a wide berth.

The first place she decided to check was the stream that ran through the property. She crested the hill and looked down to the water. There was no sign of Wyatt, but she spotted his clothes on a low-hanging branch.

Callie made her way to the creek in time to see Wyatt break the surface. He had his back to her, the rivulets running over his sculpted back to his narrowed hips and into the water. His muscles bulged in his arm as he wiped a hand down his face. Then he turned and froze when his gaze landed on her.

She tried not to look at his dark hair slicked back from his face. She really tried to stop from looking at his wide shoulders and thick chest or his stomach and abs where every muscle was defined as if sculpted out of granite.

Her heart accelerated, her blood heated. Desire thrummed through her, making her ache to feel his touch. But she stood firm in her resolve to ignore her feelings.

"Did something happen?" Wyatt asked.

"Did you speak to Melvin?"

There was a stretch of silence before Wyatt answered. "Yes."

She waited for more, but he didn't elaborate. "Why?"

"I wanted him to leave you alone."

"So you searched him out?" she asked.

Wyatt shrugged.

Callie was taken aback. "How did you even find him?"

"I have contacts."

"Contacts that you'll use to locate my stupid family but not your own father."

He shrugged. "I don't know if I can trust those contacts to find Orrin."

Damn him for making sense. Still, she was enraged that he would interfere with her family. Why would he do something like that? "Melvin said he's ready for you to carry out your threat. What did you say to him?"

"Nothing," Wyatt said as he looked away and walked out of the water.

Callie told herself to turn her back to him or look anywhere elsc but at the magnificent male specimen before her, but she just couldn't manage it.

She drank in the sight of him, noting the many scars that seemed to touch nearly every part of him. Why did he have to be so damn . . . lickable?

He'd sported muscles at a young age, but the years

had hardened his body, tightening it into a lethal weapon that matched his mind.

And it turned her on.

Shameless in his nudity, he stood on the bank and began to dress. "Why did you call Melvin?"

It took a second for the words to penetrate the fog of lust that filled her head. Callie shot him a glare. "I didn't. Melvin called me."

"On the new phones we got last week?"

Callie nodded, the unease she'd felt during the call assaulting her again. "He said they have good connections."

"I don't like the sound of that." He slipped the shirt over his head, hiding his muscles. "What else did he say?"

"That there's nowhere I can go, no place I can hide that they won't find me."

Wyatt's face was set in hard lines when he stalked to her, causing her to step back into a tree. "Does he know where we are?"

"He knows I'm with you. He saw us at dinner the other night. He left a note in the door of the car."

Fury shot from Wyatt's eyes. "Why didn't you tell me about the note?"

"It's my family. My mess."

"It stopped being your mess when they beat the shit out of you."

She looked away, hating the reminder of that awful day. "You don't need to interfere. I can handle them."

"Right," he said with a snort. "What did the note say?"

"You can't run from us forever."

Wyatt turned away with a curse and walked to his boots. He hastily yanked them on. "You should've told me."

"No, we have enough to worry about. My family will have to wait."

He picked up the rifle standing against a tree. "I don't think that's possible."

"Why not? They do this every few years. I'll get rude with them, and they'll back off."

Wyatt gave her a contemptuous look. "You really think that's what happens?"

"Yes." What else could there be?

He stalked past her, saying, "I can't believe you haven't pieced it together."

"Pieced what?" she asked, hurrying to catch up with him.

"Those 'good contacts' the Reeds have could very well be the Saints."

Callie's feet stopped working. She came to a halt as the truth settled around her. Of course, her kin would work with the Saints. The secret organization could've easily discovered the Reeds and reached out to them.

The Saints had already hacked her computer. The only way Melvin could've gotten her new number was by cloning her phone when he'd approached her that day.

Which meant now that he had the number, it could be traced.

Callie threw the cell phone on the ground before stomping on it.

CHAPTER TEN

Washington, DC

Mitch Hewett walked to the coffee shop, his gaze darting about as he looked for Orrin Loughman. It was only a matter of time before he turned a corner and came face-to-face with Orrin. The scenario he'd painstakingly arranged had turned to shit.

All because the Saints had trusted Yuri Markovic.

He'd warned them that it was a mistake, and the proof now lay before all of them.

Opening the door to the coffee house, Mitch strode inside. He paused, looking around until he saw who he was looking for sitting at a back corner table.

The man looked ordinary and inadequate, the kind of person no one would remember walking past, sitting next to, or even talking to.

Which was exactly what Andrew Smith wanted.

With his coffee in hand, Mitch made his way to the table. He eyed Smith. It wasn't his real name, but that didn't matter. No, what was important was the reason for the meeting.

Mitch sat at the table and looked at Andrew's sandy hair and into his nondescript brown eyes. Mitch wasn't exactly sure what Andrew did for the Saints—nor did he wish to find out. In matters such as these, it was better to be oblivious of such things.

Andrew took a deep breath and leaned his arms onto the small, round table. His black trench coat was open, revealing a dark gray sweater beneath. "You're late."

"I had a lead on Callie. I was hoping to have some information for you."

Andrew made a face and looked out the window at the passing people on the sidewalk. "We have Miss Reed taken care of."

"I thought she was my problem?"

"You failed to get to her before the brothers split up and went different directions." Andrew turned his head to face him. "Things have gotten out of hand."

Mitch wasn't going to take the blame for everything. "I'm not the only one who screwed up. We wouldn't even have this mess if Orrin had been dealt with. Instead, Yuri took out Orrin's team and kidnapped him."

"You think you're telling me something I don't already know?"

It was the soft tone and the sharpening of Andrew's gaze that alerted Mitch he might have gone too far. But he wasn't part of the Saints because he gave up easily.

"I'm reminding you," Mitch stated. "Callie is mine to deal with."

Andrew lifted the mug to his lips and took a drink of his coffee before slowly lowering it back to the table. "What's so important about Callie Reed?"

"I think she could be an asset to our organization."

That caused Andrew to lift a brow. "You can't be serious."

"I am."

"We've already agreed to hand her over to her family."

Mitch gritted his teeth. He'd done his own investigating into the Reeds when Orrin initially pulled Callie away from the CIA and into his Black Ops team, Whitehorse. The Reeds were nasty individuals, whose ambitions were as grand—if only the family would stop getting busted and sent to jail.

"Agreements can be altered," Mitch said.

Andrew sat in silence for a moment. "I'll run it by the others."

It wasn't a promise, but it was the only thing Mitch could expect. Right now, that was enough for him. "My team is still looking for Orrin. Owen remains at the ranch in Texas, and we believe Wyatt is still in Texas, as well. However, we've lost Cullen. Have you had any sightings of Orrin?"

"No."

The bite of anger in that one word spoke volumes. "Yuri either?"

"Both have vanished, but it's just a matter of time before those two pop up. We're going to ensure that happens very soon."

Intrigued, Mitch set aside his coffee. "How?"

"We all know how much Orrin loves his sons, even if the boys don't return the sentiment. We've put things into motion that will ensure that Loughman shows up to help his eldest son."

Mitch sat back and twisted his lips. "Don't bet on it. Orrin knows how good his sons are. He'll expect them to take care of themselves."

"Not with what we have coming for Wyatt."

"What's that?"

Andrew smiled coldly. "An old enemy from Wyatt's past that he won't be able to handle on his own."

"What about Ragnarok? One of them has it."

"It no longer matters. We have Jankovic." Andrew then pushed back his chair and stood. He looked down at Mitch and said, "You keep recruiting."

"And Callie?"

"You'll have an answer soon."

Mitch waited until Andrew walked out of the shop and blended into the throng of people before he rose. He was well aware that there were Saints watching him.

The organization was far larger than most who were part of it even knew. The Loughmans were fighting a war they'd never be able to win. Mitch was glad that someone was going to bring Orrin down a peg or two.

Now that he knew the Saints had a plan for Orrin, Mitch wasn't worried about the eldest Loughman hunting him down. Orrin would have too much on his plate—like protecting his sons—to come after him.

Even if Orrin decided to come to DC, the moment the cameras about the city saw his face, the Saints would be alerted. Orrin wouldn't make it two steps before he was taken down.

The headlines would read that intelligence had discovered a plot to kill the President. Below it would be a picture of Orrin facedown on the ground, handcuffed.

And that would be the last anyone would ever see of him.

It had happened more times than Mitch could remember. The Saints were masters of making people disappear.

* * *

"So. That's Mitch Hewett," Mia Carter said.

Cullen lowered the binoculars from his face. He gazed out the window of the vacant floor of a building, following Mitch with his eyes. "That's him. You got the pictures of Hewett and the man he met with, right?"

"Oh, yes," Mia said as she set down the camera. "I'm going to send them to Callie to see if she can find out who the man is."

Cullen turned to the side and looked at his woman. "We got lucky that we were able to catch Hewett with someone. That meeting could've taken place anywhere."

"Yet it was so near his office."

"We're thinking that man with Mitch is a Saint. For all we know, it could be his best friend from college."

Mia shook her head. "I don't think so. Not the way Hewett acted walking into the coffee shop or while they talked. He looked relieved returning to work."

"I wish we knew what their conversation was about."

"We're already taking a huge risk remaining here," Mia pointed out.

Cullen knew all too well. The longer they remained in DC, the more chances arose for the Saints to find them. He felt trapped, which made him yearn to leave the city behind. But their search for Orrin, the Russian scientist, and anything on the Saints kept them in DC.

Mia put her hand on his chest over his heart. "We're going to take the Saints down."

"Eight people are going to bring down an organization like the Saints? We have no idea who is running it or how far-reaching it is. For all we know, the Saints could have infiltrated every government in the world."

She raised a dark brow as her lips curved into a smile. "Then we go into it believing this group of maniacs are that large."

"I love that you think we can do this, but I'm a realist."

"And I'm not?" She gave him a little shove so that he fell back onto the chair. Mia straddled his legs and rested her arms on top of his shoulders.

He groaned as he gripped her hips. When he rose up to claim her mouth in a kiss, she stopped him with a finger to his lips.

"We're not alone," she whispered. "It's not just eight against a million or a billion. There's Kate. She's taken a leave of absence from the hospital to help."

"So, nine," he corrected.

Mia gave him an irritated look. "Have you forgotten about General Davis? He sacrificed himself so that I could get off the base."

"He's dead, love. He can't help us."

"My point is that there will be those out there who can and will help."

Cullen had to admit she was correct in her thinking. "On the flip side of that coin are those who will pretend to help only to betray us."

"Yes. And as you so frequently point out to me, we'll have to follow our instincts on each instance. If one of us feels that it's wrong, then we listen to the other."

"I think the whole idea is wrong." He grunted when she pinched the lobe of his ear.

"That's because you worry I'll get hurt."

"I can't lose you," he admitted. Cullen cupped her face and looked into her black eyes. "All that matters is you."

Her gaze softened as she leaned down and pressed her lips to his. "I don't want to lose you either, but this is bigger than either of us. This affects the entire world."

It was the same argument they had every day. He didn't want Mia anywhere near the fighting. After their car had gone over the mountain, he realized he never wanted to feel that powerless again. He loved Mia more than anything.

Yet, his woman was a force to be reckoned with. She was a skilled pilot who loved to push the boundaries and was more than equipped to handle herself whether she was flying a plane or on the ground in the midst of battle.

But as competent as Mia was, there was always a chance that she would be injured or killed. Every time he thought about her being taken from him, he felt as if his heart were being ripped in two.

Was this pain what his father had lived with all these years? Cullen couldn't imagine what it would be like to discover that someone had murdered Mia. He wouldn't rest until he found her killer.

Then again, Orrin hadn't stopped looking either.

"What is it?" Mia asked.

"I love you."

She cupped his face. "I love you, too."

"I want to have a long life with you. I want to grow old with you. Maybe have a few kids."

A smile curved her lips as she laughed. "Kids, huh?"

"Could be. I'm not ruling it out."

"Then we have something to look forward to," she said huskily.

He splayed his hand on her back and pushed her forward so their lips were nearly touching. "Yes, we do."

Dark eyes searched his face. "Hope is what gets some people through the worst times. This is the worst I've ever been through."

"Your association with me has put your family in danger, as well."

"My father is rich and powerful. He's already begun making preparations and putting precautions in place. I'm not worried about him. I want to find Orrin, but my worry isn't with him either."

Cullen frowned. "Who are you worried about?"

"Callie and Wyatt."

Since Cullen and Wyatt had never been that close, he didn't talk to his eldest brother much. Owen was their go-between, and he hadn't said anything about plans changing.

But Cullen knew firsthand how the Saints could alter things in a millisecond.

CHAPTER ELEVEN

Wyatt stalked into the house, furious that a Reed dared to call his bluff. That's how he knew the Saints were involved. In all of his dealings with Callie's family, none of them had ever attempted to go against him.

Now, all of a sudden, Melvin changed tactics?

This was the Saints. And he'd bet every weapon he owned that Ahmadi and his men coming after him was the Saints' doing, as well.

Wyatt paced the dining area before he stopped and leaned down, putting his hands on the table. He hung his head as the truth revealed itself.

He heard Callie behind him. She was out of breath from running. He squeezed his eyes shut at the desperation that pounded through him to take her into his arms and simply hold her.

How sure he'd been that staying with her would keep her safe. Never had he thought his enemies a half a world away would find him. If he had, he'd have stayed as far from her as he could get. But there was no choice for them now.

If only they'd remained at Carl's.

"Whatever it is you've put together, just tell me," Callie said.

Wyatt opened his eyes and straightened, facing her. "We're going to be hit from two sides."

"The terrorists and . . ." she paused, frowning. Then her eyes went wide as realization dawned. "My family."

"The Saints have set it up. We could handle one attack, but a duel assault?"

Callie slowly walked farther into the room. "It's a setup."

"To kill us."

"Maybe." Her blue eyes met his. "I think they'd be happy to take one of the Loughman sons out of the mix, but I think the real trap is being set for Orrin."

Wyatt dropped his head back to look at the ceiling. Fuck. Callie was right. Orrin already knew about Ahmadi planning something. If his father was aware of that, then the odds were that Orrin knew of the Reeds, too.

That would bring him straight to Wyatt and Callie to try and help—which was exactly what the Saints wanted.

Wyatt lifted his head and looked at Callie. "Can you get a message to Orrin?"

"I don't know," she said with a shake of her head.

"Orrin found you."

"Yes, because we set up a way for him to contact me if he was ever in trouble."

Wyatt flattened his lips. "And neither of you thought that the situation might be reversed and you'd need his help?"

"There wasn't a need. I was supposed to be safely inside the base at the ranch."

"Did he happen to leave you an idea of how to get in contact with him after this latest communication?"

She opened her mouth to answer, then paused. Her lips closed as she frowned and walked to her laptop. She sat and opened the computer. A moment later, her fingers were flying over the keyboard.

Wyatt watched her for a moment before he went to the large window that overlooked the front yard. The cabin was situated at the top of a hill, giving them the advantage for an attack. Austin's arid climate kept the trees from getting too tall. That gave them the ability to see virtually unhindered all around the property.

Who would come for them first? The Reeds or Ahmadi? Or would they attack together?

Ahmadi wanted him dead, which meant their attack would be to decimate everyone and everything around. That was in direct contrast to the Reeds, who wanted Callie at all costs.

Knowing Callie's family as he did, they wouldn't have aligned themselves with the Saints unless they knew for certain that, in the end, Callie would be theirs. It made sense for the Reeds to attack first, but that didn't mean that would be what happened. Ahmadi might wait for Callie to leave before they came after him.

Wyatt turned and looked at her. If they remained together, he could fight beside her against her family and possibly win once and for all against them.

But against Ahmadi—he knew he needed to send her away. If she remained with him, she'd end up dead.

That thought had him facing the window. He couldn't imagine Callie taken from this world. She would be out of reach of her family's claws once and for all, but she would no longer be a part of his life.

Orrin would never forgive him.

He'd never forgive himself.

The sound of her typing was soothing in a way. At first, he'd hated it since it disturbed the quiet, but it didn't take long for it to become a comfort. It filled the silence since she had nothing to say to him, and he didn't know what to say to her.

When she'd come to the stream, he first thought it was to be with him. He should've known better. The past couldn't be undone, nor did he want it to be. What he'd said to Callie years ago still applied.

It didn't matter that he'd lied about having no feelings for her. It didn't matter that he'd lied about just wanting to have some fun during the summer.

With every word that fell from his lips, he'd seen them wound her more deeply than a blade ever could.

He almost hadn't been able to get it all out. Being with her those few months had been as close to Heaven as he was likely to get. She'd freely given him her love, her smile shining brighter than the sun.

But he'd known what his future held. Bringing someone like her into his world of blood and death was a sin. And he hadn't wanted her ending up murdered like his mother.

Not once had he seen Callie cry after he broke it off. She didn't try to talk him out of it or beg him not to end things. She didn't demand a better explanation or call him names as he deserved. Not his Callie.

She'd stood straight and silent, taking it all in. But he

saw her change nonetheless. Right before his eyes, he saw her heart protect itself as much as it could. He saw it because he'd erected those same walls after he found his mother's body. No one had ever even dented those barriers until Callie.

Her tenacity and persistence working at the ranch, as well as her smile and bright outlook on life despite her family affected him. Without even trying, she'd busted through his walls as if they were made of smoke.

He was the one who'd approached her on the premise of teaching her how to throw knives. She was a quick learner, eager to soak up any kind of knowledge be it about the ranch, school, weaponry, or life.

Of all the girls who had tried in vain to catch his attention, there hadn't been anyone like Callie.

Nor had there been anyone like her after he left Texas.

He blew out a breath. If he'd known Orrin would pull Callie into his Black Ops business, he'd have confronted his father years ago. Instead, Wyatt assumed that Callie only helped manage the ranch with his uncle.

All those years, Orrin had put her life in danger. All those years while Wyatt had stupidly assumed the most peril to Callie's life was dealing with the livestock at the ranch.

His ignorance was his fault alone. He'd kept close tabs on her the first few years he was away, but it became too hard when she began dating. For his own peace of mind, he'd stopped being so involved. It helped him find sleep once more, but he never stopped loving her. Though he'd never told her the words, he'd fallen in love with her the first week they began talking.

Before claiming her body, even before their fist kiss, he'd been madly in love with her.

He hadn't cut her out of his life for himself. He'd done it for her. He'd freed her from any ties to him or his family. And he had hoped she would take it.

When he was forced to return to Texas, he'd been thrilled to see her. Until he learned she worked for his father. It made him hate Orrin all the more.

"I think I might have found something," Callie said from behind him.

Wyatt didn't bother to respond. She was too deep in her work to hear him anyway. Instead, he walked the house, checking the weapons and ammunition as well as the locks on the windows and doors.

The two days he'd spent away from the cabin had been both a blessing and a curse. Not once could he stop thinking about her, and it had nothing to do with the danger surrounding them. Their last conversation had been tough to hear. Worse, it had come from her.

He heard and saw just how little she thought of him. At least he didn't need to worry about there being anything between them again. Even if he wanted it, she'd probably just as soon gut him as allow him to touch her.

The hours passed in an excruciating crawl. When his stomach growled, he made them dinner. She ate the hamburger while still working and barely looked up from the screen to acknowledge him.

Wyatt didn't bother her. If she were able to discover a way to get in touch with Orrin, then he would let his father know not to come to Austin. And that Wyatt was sending Callie to him.

While stretched out on the sofa thinking of ways to

get Callie to leave, he heard her typing halt. He sat up and looked her way to find her bent over the table, her head on the laptop with her eyes closed.

He rose and went to her. Carefully, he lifted her in his arms. She sighed as her head rolled to lie on his shoulder. The only other time he'd ever carried her like this was when he'd found her in the woods.

Though he knew he should walk to her bedroom and put her on the bed to sleep, he enjoyed having her in his arms again.

He didn't know how long he stood there holding her before he finally made his way to the bedroom. The lights were out, leaving only the beam from the living room coming through the door to guide him.

Reluctantly, he bent and laid her on the mattress. When he stood and turned to walk away, her fingers grabbed his hand. Wyatt halted and turned back to her, but her hand went slack, releasing him.

He walked out of the room, pulling the door shut behind him. He went to the computer to see if he could tell what she'd been doing, but it was all gibberish to him. He had no idea what any of the code was or how to use it.

He closed the laptop and shut off the lights. Then he went back to the sofa. There would be little sleep for him, but it wouldn't be the first time. He rarely slept before a battle.

His mind was full of plans and ideas. The fact that he knew both enemies intimately helped to determine how they might act or react. Without a doubt, the most lethal of the two foes was Ahmadi.

The Reeds weren't to be cast aside, however. But they

were used to fighting with their charm and smooth talk. This would be an entirely different kind of battle, but they would be prepared.

For Ahmadi, this was a way of life. Most of his men had been born into war. They lived it, breathed it. They wouldn't attack quickly. Based on his past encounters with Ahmadi and his men, they would inspect the area, deciphering where the best place to attack would be.

Wyatt already knew the place they would choose. It was one of the reasons he'd set up even more traps during the past two days. Some were visible—a deception to make his enemies believe they could outsmart him.

He threw an arm over his eyes, his thoughts shifting to Callie. There was no way he would allow Ahmadi to get near her. If they suspected she meant anything to him, they would torture her in front of him.

The irony of the situation didn't go unnoticed. Wyatt had done everything right years ago so Callie would never be in this situation.

And yet, here she was.

When Wyatt finally did see Orrin, he would have a hard time not killing his father.

CHAPTER TWELVE

Outside of DC

Orrin Loughman sat up straighter in the seat of the Range Rover when he caught sight of Konrad Jankovic through the lenses of the binoculars. "I see him."

Beside him, Yuri Markovic grunted. Then said in a Russian accent, "About time. What is he doing?"

"He's on a cell phone, arguing with someone by the expression on his face and the way he's motioning with his hands. Here, take a look," Orrin said, handing the binoculars over.

Yuri peered through the lenses. "He is definitely angry."

Orrin spotted a large, black SUV slowing before turning into the driveway of the house they were watching. The vehicle stopped alongside of a column, and a window rolled down as someone punched a button next to a speaker in the brick.

Orrin nudged Yuri in the shoulder. "Someone has arrived."

Yuri moved the binoculars over to focus on the SUV as the gate opened and it drove to the front door. "A man in a black trench coat just got out."

"Do you recognize him?"

"*Da*. He has been here several times before. And . . . there is something familiar about him."

Orrin pulled out a notebook and pencil, jotting the date and time as well as the vehicle description. "What does he look like?"

"Dark eyes, sandy hair, medium height," Yuri rattled off.

Orrin nodded. "Oh, him. He comes regularly. And you're right. He does look familiar. Get me the license plate number."

Orrin quickly wrote it down as Yuri called out the mix of numbers and letters. It wasn't a government plate, but that didn't mean anything. Ever since they'd been watching the house, there had been only one government car that stopped.

"Now the visitor and Jankovic are speaking," Yuri said.

Orrin looked at the house, grimacing. "We can remain here for the next several months, but the scientist isn't coming out."

"You are probably right," Yuri said. "It does not look as if Jankovic wants to leave, but I suspect they are keeping him there."

"Because they know we want him."

"*Da*."

There was no need for either of them to go into detail regarding what they wanted to do to Dr. Konrad Jankovic. The scientist had no morals and worked for whatever government—or organization—paid him the most.

The fact that he had willingly created a bioweapon

that would prevent women from getting pregnant sickened Orrin. Ragnarok could be released into the air without anyone the wiser. But how long would it take before people began to realize something was very wrong?

"We could go in and get him," Yuri offered.

It was something Orrin thought about every day. "There are too many guards and only two of us."

Yuri lowered the binoculars and turned his head to him. "You do not think we could get through the doors?"

"I know we could. We have the experience and years on the men patrolling. It's the getting out part that would be a problem."

"I think you are right, *stariy droog.*"

Old friend. That's exactly what they were. From years being forced to work together by their governments to an unlikely friendship to brief enemies only to find themselves friends again.

It was strange how life could turn the tables so unexpectedly. Once before it had happened when his Melanie had been so cruelly taken from him and his boys.

Orrin had almost given up on ever finding her killer—until something Yuri said changed his thinking. It had never entered his mind that someone had murdered his wife in order to set him on a course of their choosing. But there was a possibility that the Saints had done just that.

All those years he thought he'd chosen his own path. When in fact, there were others doing it for him, and they did it in a way that he never knew.

Had they also done it to his sons? None of his boys had ever given their hearts to anyone, so the Saints couldn't use that against them. But that didn't mean the organization hadn't been pulling strings the whole time.

"You are thinking of your sons," Yuri said.

Orrin blew out a breath and nodded. "If you're right about the Saints killing Melanie—"

"I am," Yuri interrupted him.

"You're guessing."

"It is an educated guess."

Orrin narrowed his gaze on Yuri when his old friend scratched his jaw. "You know something."

"I do not," Yuri replied with a frown.

"You scratched your jaw when you spoke. You always do that when you're lying. What do you know?"

Yuri sighed loudly. "I only saw Melanie's name in a file. It was crossed out with red ink."

"Where was this file?"

"At the Pentagon."

Orrin let that information settle over him. "I gather it was in an office of a known Saint?"

"It was not an office. It was a conference room with thirty other individuals. Most were from the US, but there were others, like me, from different countries."

"What countries?" Orrin asked.

"China, Australia, Argentina, Mexico, Japan, France, Italy, and the UK to name a few."

Dear God. "And the file?"

"I was walking to my seat and saw a man reading a list of names. Melanie's was towards the top."

"That would explain why the leads I had kept drying

up." Orrin felt sick to his stomach at the betrayal. But he was also so livid he could think of nothing but getting back at the people who had taken Melanie from him.

Yuri's blue eyes held a note of sadness as he looked at Orrin. "I am sorry. I should have told you sooner. I thought you might have given up, and when I learned you had not, I did not want to bring you more grief."

"These people have to be stopped. I doubt I'm the only one they've meddled with. What I do know is that I won't allow them to do the same to my sons."

"I was not in the Saints but a year. I learned very little about them. I have no idea how big the organization is."

Orrin raised a brow. "The listing of those countries at that meeting you attended says they're global. Do they extend to every country? It wouldn't surprise me."

"That does not do us much good if we do not know who is running it," Yuri pointed out.

"You saw no one?"

Yuri ran a hand through his dark hair heavily sprinkled with gray. "I was recruited by a comrade. That same friend was my go-between with the Saints for three months. After that, another man came to see me. I received messages from the Saints through him."

"What about meetings?"

"All with people like me. Never any of the upper management. No names, no faces."

Orrin didn't like the sound of that. "We could be standing right next to them and not know it."

"This war we are starting could end very quickly. For us."

"I'm prepared for that."

"I do not fear death. I fear failing."

It was the same for Orrin. "All three of my sons were home, and I wasn't there with them. I've waited years for that."

"That is my fault. I kidnapped you."

"You were trying to save us all. Besides, I'm not sure my children would've been happy to see me."

"They were looking for you. That should tell you they care."

Orrin wasn't so sure, especially about Wyatt. His eldest's heart was still filled with so much pain. Orrin briefly thought Callie might heal him, but Wyatt had shut her out.

"I hope Wyatt takes my warning about Ahmadi seriously," Orrin said.

"He will. If what you have told me of Callie is true, she will make him."

Every time Orrin thought of how easily they could've bypassed such information, his blood turned to ice. It was by chance that Yuri found the message in his email when he checked the previous night.

Or was it by chance?

Orrin questioned everything now.

"We could contact Callie again and find out where they are. I know you want to help your son," Yuri said.

More than anything. Orrin ran a hand through his hair. "We should stay with Jankovic."

"For all we know, he has a lab within the house and is making more of the weapon."

"That thought has crossed my mind as well."

"If we cannot get him out, then we get inside."

Orrin eyed the house. "We'll have to be quick."

"Once we find him, we kill him."

"Agreed. The guards chan—"

The sound of his burner phone ringing halted his words. Orrin looked at the unknown number, frowning. He glanced at Yuri, then answered the call.

"Orrin?"

At the sound of Callie's voice, he closed his eyes and smiled. "It's good to hear from you, Callie."

"It's really you."

He blinked as he heard the tears in her words. "It is. How did you get the number?"

"Really?" she asked with a laugh. "It took some doing, but I was able to retrace the number you used to send the warning to Wyatt."

"So Wyatt got it?"

"Yes. He's getting ready for them as we speak."

Orrin released a breath. "We don't know how many of Ahmadi's men are coming for him, but you can't go up against them alone."

"We have to. The others want us to run. That's how they'll corner us."

He knew she was intentionally not saying *the Saints* in case someone was listening. And he realized then what the Saints wanted by allowing him to learn about Ahmadi. "They're trying to get me there."

"Don't," Callie said. "We'll be fine."

"Do you have a good location?"

"Wyatt picked it out, so yes."

"Good. Have you spoken to Cullen or Owen?"

Callie said, "I have. Everyone is good. I've been so worried about you. It's good to know that you're okay."

"Any other news?"

"Some, but it isn't important."

He knew that tone. Whatever it was most definitely was important. She just didn't want to share it. "Tell me."

"It can wait."

"Callie."

She blew out a harsh breath. "My family tracked us down."

"Tracked?" Orrin repeated. He knew the Reeds intimately, and though they were good at what they did, tracking someone down wasn't part of their skillset.

"Unfortunately. And yes, by the others."

Orrin fisted his free hand. The Saints were sending two different groups after Wyatt and Callie. They'd never survive. And they wanted him to know that. "You need to gather your belongings and get on the road now."

"I trust Wyatt. He knows what he's doing. I've got to go. I'll call later," she said hurriedly before hanging up.

Orrin lowered the phone as fury consumed him. "The Saints didn't just send Ahmadi after them. They sent Callie's family, too."

"I gather they are not good people?" Yuri asked.

"Some of the worst."

Yuri grunted and briefly raised the binoculars to his eyes again. "I think we should take care of Jankovic tonight."

"Yes."

His head swung to look at Orrin. "Then we get on the road."

"I don't know where Wyatt and Callie are." And he hadn't had time to warn them just what Ragnarok did.

"Then you call and ask them."

Yuri was right. Whether Wyatt wanted to admit it or not, he was going to need help.

CHAPTER THIRTEEN

Callie put down the burner phone she'd just opened when she saw Wyatt walk by the window outside the house. When she'd woken that morning, she had been alone.

But she also knew she hadn't gotten into bed on her own.

She was glad she was by herself, because knowing that she had been in Wyatt's arms did something strange to her. There was a part of her that was angry she'd slept through it, but also glad because she knew she wouldn't have been able to keep her hands to herself.

Even though it had been well over a decade since they had been intimate, it felt weird to be that close to him— whether she was awake or not. There was a barrier between them, one that she relied on to keep from repeating a youthful mistake.

She hid her smile at having spoken to Orrin. It was great hearing his voice. She knew he'd been held and beaten, but he was alive. Hale and hearty. She wiped at the few tears that had escaped and looked up.

Only to find Wyatt standing not five feet from her.

She jerked, startled at not having heard him enter the house.

"What are you doing?" she demanded. "Trying to give me a heart attack?"

"Why are you crying?" he asked instead.

She started to lie. Then she decided not to. She hadn't done anything wrong. "I was talking to Orrin."

There wasn't a single reaction from Wyatt. Not anger that she'd talked to his father without him there. Not a shred of relief that Orrin was indeed alive.

"Don't you have anything to say?" she asked.

He shrugged, twisting his lips as he did. "Not really. I'd wanted to talk to him. And I'm waiting for you to tell me what was said."

"We weren't on the line long. He sounded good, but tired. And worried. He wanted to make sure that we got his warning, and that you didn't dismiss it."

"Why would I?" Wyatt asked.

She barely refrained from rolling her eyes. "Perhaps because it came from him, and you don't want to have anything to do with him."

"What else was said?"

Callie decided not to point out that Wyatt was avoiding any type of response in regards to his father. It just showed how little emotion was there.

"He thought we should make a run for it," she said.

Wyatt nodded slowly. "So you told him about your family."

It wasn't a question. "I did."

"Do you tell him everything?"

There was something in his tone, something that immediately rubbed her raw. And she knew what he really wanted to know. She hadn't needed to tell Orrin anything. He had pieced it together himself like anyone with eyes would.

Callie held Wyatt's stare. "Orrin is part of our team. That means that yes, I told him what I would've—and will—tell Owen and Natalie, as well as Cullen and Mia."

"Stand up."

That took her aback. "Excuse me?"

"Stand up. I want to test your close quarters combat skills."

She guessed they were finished talking about Orrin. "Do you want to call him back?"

"Not now."

It was hard to keep up with Wyatt's moods and thinking sometimes. They could flip as fast as lightning. Callie decided not to remind him that she had gotten the better of him at the ranch so that he landed flat on his back. She'd just show him again.

"Afraid?" he asked when she remained seated.

"Puh-leeze. I was thinking of moving the table out of the way."

"Then let's move it."

She didn't know why, but she was suddenly wary of Wyatt. He wasn't acting as standoffish as normal. If she didn't know better, she'd say he was beginning to open up to her as he had when they were younger.

Ha! Like that would happen again.

She got to her feet and moved the seat she'd been sitting on while Wyatt grabbed the back of a chair in each hand, setting them out of the way. Callie then took the last one and her laptop to safety. When she turned around, Wyatt had taken care of the table.

He stood on the oval, braided rug and stared at her as if silently daring her. When it came to him, she was always ready and willing to accept his challenges.

Before she'd barely taken a step onto the rug, he rushed her, grabbing her about her middle. Callie twisted, but she couldn't break his hold or get into position to hurt him. Then he threw her over his shoulder.

Her humiliation was complete.

"I expected better," he said and set her down.

Yeah, well, so did she. She wasn't going to give him some lame excuse about not being ready, because there weren't do-overs in battle.

"What are you waiting for?" she asked when he merely stood there.

There was a ghost of a smile before he took a step toward her. She was ready for him this time. With a sweep of her leg, she had him shifting his weight. Then she sent a punch into his gut while pushing against his chest with her other hand.

Callie smiled down at him from his position on the floor looking up at her. "I expected better," she tossed his words back at him.

For the next hour, they traded turns bringing the other to the ground. She hated to admit that Wyatt more than tested her skills. He showed her moves she'd never seen before, causing her to reevaluate some of her strategies. Even with the bruises she knew she'd have the next day, she was glad Wyatt had made her do this.

She laughed when she realized the current hold she had on him wouldn't give her the advantage—but then neither could his. His answering grin made her stomach flutter.

God, he was stunning when he smiled. She found herself lost in an ocean of gold as she stared at him. It was then she grasped that their bodies were pressed together. One of his arms was locked around her, the other holding one of her wrists.

His smile melted away slowly. Their ragged breaths filled the silence of the room. The hold couldn't be more intimate. She was all too aware of her breasts crushed against his chest. Her nipples hardened, and an ache began low in her belly.

One of them would have to be the first to relent, to let go and step away. To admit defeat.

She couldn't seem to make herself release him. He overwhelmed her. His scent, his power, his spectacular body.

She'd seen him naked just yesterday. He'd always been gorgeous, but the years had refined his muscular body until he was a work of art.

Her mouth watered just thinking of running her hands over his flesh, of taking his arousal and stroking the hardness. Then feeling it slide inside her. She bit back the gasp that image induced.

He could never know that he still had power over her. If he did, he'd control her with just a look. That same desire-filled look that used to bring her to her knees.

That's when he was just becoming a man. He'd had years to practice and hone his skills. Her legs went weak just thinking of what he might do to her now.

Despite her best intentions, she must have let something show in her eyes, because his darkened. And God help her, but she knew that look. She felt his cock hardening between them, causing her blood to heat even more.

She wanted him, hungered for him.

But to go down that road again would be folly. Why then wasn't she stepping away?

And why wasn't he?

That thought made her heart skip a beat. Her lids closed as his head lowered. Just as his lips were about to touch hers, the laptop beeped, signaling that one of the traps had been tripped.

Without a word, they stepped apart in unison. Callie grabbed her laptop and sat on the sofa to pull up the layout of the house as Wyatt came to stand beside her. The alarm set up on the perimeter was one she'd brought with her from the ranch.

"I'll be back," Wyatt said as he strode from the house.

She let loose a sigh once he'd gone. Though she'd wanted his kiss, she was glad they'd been interrupted. Wasn't she?

Callie pressed her hands against her swollen breasts. Her body thrummed with need. But she could be strong. She could withstand Wyatt's allure.

She closed her eyes, hating that she wasn't as confident of that statement as she had been even thirty minutes earlier. Now that she'd had his arms around her again, that she'd felt his arousal, her willpower was weakening.

In an effort to tamp down the rising tide of desire, Callie remained on the couch. She thought of kittens and puppies, of cleaning her guns, of scrubbing toilets— but nothing could dislodge Wyatt from her mind.

Her eyes snapped open when he called her name. She sat up and found him walking inside with an armload of wood. The nights were getting rather chilly, but she couldn't tell at the moment with her body heated to such a degree.

Wyatt knelt near the hearth and stacked the wood inside. "It was just a deer."

"It's too bad I didn't have any video cameras left for us to bring."

He gave a shake of his head. "Owen and Natalie need them more on the ranch. It's a much larger area to fortify than ours."

Ours.

That one word had the power to give a pretense to things. She and Wyatt were working together, but that's where it ended. Whatever fantasy she'd allowed herself to believe a short time ago was gone.

The reality, the truth was that Wyatt was a loner. He didn't need or want anyone or anything. He counted only on himself for everything he needed. There would never be an *our* with him.

No matter how much she'd once longed for it, no matter how much she had cried for it, there was no changing him.

Natalie might have gotten her happy ending with Owen. Mia might have even found love with Cullen. But there would be no such outcome for her.

Callie couldn't even feel sadness for that fact anymore. At one time, it had caused her to cry herself to sleep. But acceptance had changed her. She might not like the way Wyatt was, but there was nothing she could do.

There was no mention of their near kiss as he walked out of the cabin and didn't return for four hours. There were no words spoken when they ate dinner. Not even when he started the fire and she made coffee.

What was there to say, really? It wasn't as if she would bring up their near kiss. She wanted to forget it as she attempted to put up a wall again—a wall that Wyatt had somehow torn down without her even knowing.

Too bad she couldn't do the same to his. How she'd love to smash all of them. To make him empty his soul of all the anger, hate, hopes, and dreams that he'd tucked away there. If only she had that kind of power.

She stared into the flames and admonished herself for her thoughts. What did it matter how she felt about Wyatt or how he felt about her? An attack from her family as well Ahmadi—and possibly the Saints—would come at them any day.

The odds of either of them coming out of it alive were slim. To the Saints, Wyatt was better off dead. At one time, her family would've done anything to bring her back into the fold, but now, she wasn't so sure. They could be coming to kill her for all she knew.

This could be her last night on Earth. And what was she doing? Silently griping about what she couldn't change. Why? When she should be grasping at what little enjoyment or happiness she might be able to find.

She glanced at Wyatt, who stood in the kitchen. What would it matter if she gave in to her heart's desire? There would be no promises, no declarations. Only sated need.

When she looked at him again, he was staring at her with desire burning in his eyes.

CHAPTER FOURTEEN

He wanted her.

He craved her.

No longer could Wyatt pretend otherwise. The truth had become painfully evident when they had been locked together, their bodies rubbing against each other just hours earlier.

Had the perimeter alarm not gone off, he would've kissed her. It was the thought of tasting Callie's lips again that caused him to look at her now.

She was staring into the fire. As he gazed at her profile, he wondered what she was thinking. Did she long for his touch once more? Did she remember the pleasure they had found in each other's arms?

Or had he burned that bridge once and for all?

He held out hope. It was slim, but her reaction to him couldn't be denied. Not the way her breathing had changed or how her lips had parted. Most definitely not the way her blue eyes had filled with need.

His balls tightened thinking about it. And when her lids had slid closed, his only thought had been to claim her lips, to let her know how he'd hungered for her kiss all the years they'd been apart.

But the damn alarm had interrupted everything.

Now, he might never get that chance again. Callie was a master at remaining just out of his reach. Perhaps if he were more of a charmer, like Cullen, or even as open as Owen, there might be a chance for him.

But he was neither of those things. He was hard, cold, and closed off to the world.

Callie had been the only one to get close to him, the only one to ever touch his heart and make him long for a life that could never be his.

This was where Owen would urge him to let Callie know that secret, but Wyatt didn't dare. It would leave him too exposed. Admitting it to himself was one thing, but no one—absolutely *no one*—could ever know.

His thoughts came to a screeching halt when Callie's head turned, and their eyes clashed. The palpable desire he saw made his body pulse with a yearning he hadn't dared to give in to. But there was no turning away from it now.

From the very beginning, Callie had a hold over him. She swayed him with a smile or a look. He didn't know if she grasped the power she had back then—the power she still had.

Because if she did, with just a few words, she could make him invincible—or break him.

She rose from the couch and stood to face him. There was no other choice for him but to go to her, to go to the only woman he'd ever wanted.

When he reached her, she turned him, shoving him back onto the sofa. He looked up at her and was consumed with lust. Callie stood between his legs not as the young girl he remembered, but as a woman who knew what she wanted—and got it.

Her head tilted to the side, blue eyes shamelessly looking over him. He swallowed a groan and grabbed her wrists. A seductive, teasing smile pulled at the corners of her lips before she placed one knee on the outside of his hip.

His mouth went dry as she straddled him, her breasts even with his face. Before him was a temptress, who would accept nothing less than all of him.

She glided her hands up his arms and over his shoulders before sinking into his hair. Then she arched her back and rolled her head to the side before letting it fall backward.

The moan he'd been holding back rushed past his lips. He gripped her on either side of her ribcage and leaned forward. His lips touched the space just below her neck in the middle of her chest.

"Wyatt."

His name whispered in that husky voice of hers stirred something deep and primal within him. He wrapped an arm around her while he yanked at the collar of her sweatshirt to expose a slim shoulder.

He nipped and kissed the skin there before moving across to her collarbone. All the while, the long, silky strands of her hair teased his arms and hands with whispered touches.

Her head shifted to the side to give him better access to her neck. Slowly, he worked his way up the column of her throat to her ear and licked the spot that always drove her wild.

Just as he'd expected, her response was immediate. Her nails sank into his scalp, and her hips rocked against his cock. He gently sucked on the delicate skin until her breathing was as erratic as his heart.

Only then did he return his lips to her throat and kiss his way up to her chin. But he didn't take her lips. Her head lifted, and their eyes clashed.

For long seconds, they stared at each other, the longing, the hunger growing with each breath. The only sound was the popping of the fire. Without realizing it, they moved toward each other.

Her hands came around to caress his jaw as her gaze lowered to his mouth. Her thumb swept across his lower lip. He hesitated in kissing her because once he did, there would be no turning back. He only had so much self-control, and she was quickly sapping him of what was left.

She lifted her eyes to him. Then she leaned forward and placed her mouth over his.

For a heartbeat, Wyatt didn't move. He was afraid that it would shatter the moment. But when her tongue skimmed along the seam of his lips, he couldn't hold back.

Gripped with desire so overwhelming, so consuming he had no choice but to succumb, he held the back of her head, his fingers tangled in her chestnut locks, and he kissed her—letting her feel and taste the years of longing, of his aching to have her again.

He had to know the texture of her skin, her warmth. Her softness. No longer could he wait. He took her arms and moved them above her head. Then his hands slipped beneath the hem of her sweatshirt and impatiently pushed the cloth upward.

As soon as the shirt was gone, they were kissing hungrily again. With just a twist of his fingers, he unhooked her bra. The garment was tossed aside. He wrapped an arm around her before shifting them so that he lay atop her.

Her warm flesh against his palm as he caressed upward from her waist was exactly what he'd longed for. But that wasn't all. Not by a long shot.

He broke the kiss and rose up enough to look down at her. The sight of her hair spread around her with her lips swollen from his kisses caused his cock to jump. His gaze moved lower to her breasts.

His mouth went dry when he saw her dusky nipples already hard. Callie always had the most amazing breasts. There was a rough intake of breath from her when he cupped one perfect globe and massaged it.

Her eyes rolled back in her head, her lips parted on a silent moan. He rolled one tip between his fingers while leaning down to tease the other with his tongue. Her answering cry was just what he wanted to hear.

Just as he was about to get settled to feast on her breasts, Callie surprised him again by once more taking control and pushing against his shoulder to roll him. He tumbled off the sofa onto the floor with her still in his arms.

She leaned over him, her hair falling in a curtain around him. He was so turned on by her aggression that he was more than willing to see what she would do.

Her lips brushed against his, but when he tried to kiss

her, she pulled away. Then she sat up, giving him a view of her bare chest in the light of the fire.

"Take off your shirt," she commanded.

He eagerly complied. This new side of her was something he could definitely get used to. Callie had always known what she wanted and had never been afraid to ask for it. But this was a whole new level.

With her hands spread wide, she leisurely caressed his chest, gliding over his muscles and lingering at his wounds. His gaze never left her face as her eyes followed her hands. He couldn't tell what she was thinking, and he hated that.

Suddenly, she rolled back onto her feet and stood. Wyatt rose up on his forearms, afraid that she'd changed her mind. He should've known better.

Callie removed her shoes, then shimmied out of her jeans before slipping her underwear off. His gaze swept her naked form from her breasts to the indent of her waist to her flared hips then lower to her muscular legs.

He held out a hand. As soon as she placed hers in his, he pulled her down beside him. Then he rolled to his side and let his hand move over her body.

"Have I changed much?" she asked.

He touched the swell of her hip. "You've filled out more in all the best places. Have I?"

"I don't know," she replied saucily. "You still have your clothes on."

The smile formed before he realized it. Not one to disappoint, he stood and removed the rest of his clothes. When he finished, he let her look her fill.

"Well?" he prompted after several quiet minutes.

She got to her knees and began to touch the scars on

his legs before moving to the ones she'd already investigated on his upper body and arms. Then she climbed to her feet and walked around to his back.

His wounds were proof that he had survived. He barely noticed them anymore, but he began to wonder if she found them offensive. Did she think them unsightly?

When they were younger, she had often commented on the beauty of his body. He'd laughed about it then, but that memory returned, putting doubts in his head now.

Her hand trailed behind her over his butt as she walked to stand before him. "Yes, you've changed. You're stronger than before, more filled out." She reached up and ran her middle finger along the outside of his eye. "You have lines from squinting in the sun."

"Is that all?" He didn't know why he asked. He should've just left well enough alone.

A slim brow lifted. "You're a warrior, Wyatt. Your body proudly carries the marks of battle—and victory."

With one hand, he yanked her against him and claimed her mouth in a savage, fiery kiss. She had always brought out the best in him. With her, he could be the kind of man she looked at with pride and delight.

She ended the kiss and sat on the floor before leaning back, propped up on her arms.

"Are you going to join me or stand there staring?" she taunted.

"I'm enjoying the view."

With a carnal smile, she spread her legs, giving him a view of her sex and the triangle of trimmed hair. "Still want to wait?" she teased.

The last of his self-control vanished. He knelt between her legs and held himself over her with his hands.

"Please," she begged, the smile gone. "I need to feel your weight atop me."

He lowered himself, settling between her legs.

Her eyes closed as she sighed contentedly. "I missed this."

"I missed you."

The words were out before he could stop them. But if he thought they would have any effect on her, he was wrong. She acted as though she hadn't heard him while running her hands over his back.

He was glad she hadn't heard. That way, he didn't have to explain or lie. And he wouldn't repeat such a mistake. It didn't benefit either of them.

He hissed in a breath when she ground her hips against him. He knew what she wanted, because he wanted it, too. But it wasn't time yet.

He wanted to hear her scream in pleasure first.

CHAPTER FIFTEEN

Callie was on fire with an ache that only Wyatt could ease.

"*I missed you.*"

His words rang in her head like the tolling of a bell. They were so unexpected, so astonishing that they blindsided her. There were no words because she didn't want to think about what his whispered confession meant.

She only wanted to *feel*.

To take the promise of pleasure he offered.

All thought ceased when he kissed down her stomach to the junction of her thighs. She held her breath, waiting. He lightly nipped the tender flesh of her inner thigh, causing her to gasp and then moan.

His large hands spread her legs, holding them open. She looked at him to find his gold eyes on her. A shiver of awareness, of pure, unadulterated longing went through her like lightning. Every nerve ending sizzled, her muscles tightening. Her breath stopped.

His mouth hovered over her, his warm breath fanning

over her womanhood. With agonizing slowness, he lowered his head and ran his tongue over her.

Her heart skipped a beat when his eyes closed, and he moaned at the taste of her. At this rate, she would go up in flames.

But she should've known that this was only the beginning with him.

He used his thumbs to spread her woman's lips then he licked, laved, and teased her swollen clit. Her head dropped back as pleasure slid through her, wrapping her in its clutches until she was a slave to its bewitching and irresistible lure.

With one look or touch, she turned into a wanton. Once she was in his arms, it was useless to fight the inevitable. Her body knew the ecstasy that awaited—and yearned for it.

He was the master of decadence and hedonism, as if he'd been schooled by the gods on how to bring her to unimaginable heights.

And she, the willing sacrifice, submitted completely.

The flames of desire soared, engulfing her. It coiled low in her belly until she was a quivering mass of nerves. She couldn't form words to beg Wyatt to end her torture. All she could manage was to sling her head from side to side as he brought her ever closer to that pinnacle.

And just when she was about to go over the edge, he stopped.

A cry of despair welled up within her, filling the room. He held her immobile with just his hands and a look. She met his gaze, trying to form the words while begging him with her eyes.

She whimpered when his mouth once more returned

to its exquisite torture. The slow circles of his tongue around her clit were driving her mad. Unable to stop herself, she tried to put her hand on her sex to give herself the direct contact she craved.

"No."

That one simple word halted her.

Her sex convulsed, waiting for what he would do next. He wasn't touching her, and it was driving her mad. Then something touched her face. She jerked her head away.

"Easy," he whispered.

She held steady as he covered her eyes and tied the material. Then her hands were gathered above her head and tied. Excitement strummed through her.

When he finished, he slid a hand around her breasts, never touching her aching nipples. That same palm moved lower. She raised her hips, eager for his to touch. He gently pushed her hips down and ran his fingers along the edges of her sex. It was maddening how his touch could affect her in such a way—but she welcomed it.

Her attempt to touch herself only prolonged her torment as he moved his hand away and settled between her legs once again. He then bared her clit, swirling his tongue around it before sucking it between his lips.

Callie gasped then cried out at the intense pleasure. She was pushed to the edge of release quickly, where he held her. If only he would give her the shove she needed, but he had other ideas. He kept her on the brink time and again, allowing her to build to right before climax, then pulling away.

She sighed when his tongue licked her sex before

moving to her entrance. Her body tensed expectantly when she felt his tongue sink into her ever so slightly, but then it was gone, leaving her desperate for more.

It was becoming too much. She had to have release. She pulled at the restraints at her wrists, but they held tightly, keeping her in place.

Her futile attempts were halted when his tongue returned to her entrance, slowly sliding in and out of her several times. The slight penetration only added to the sweet anguish.

When he moved away from her, she strained to hear. The blindfold enhanced her other senses, exciting her. Her ragged breathing masked his movements. He was close. She could sense that.

His hand cupped her sex. She bit her lip, waiting expectantly. One of his fingers slipped inside her with agonizing slowness. A second was added before the fingers curled up inside. She moaned and tried to shift her hips to take the fingers deeper.

Thankfully, he complied. He moved his digits in and out, unhurriedly. She arched her back when he pushed them deep and held still.

If only he would touch her clit or breasts or move faster, she could climax. She wanted to touch him, to feel his heat and muscle against her. To kiss him and taste him. To wrap her fingers around his thick arousal and stroke him.

As if he knew her mind was drifting, he moved his fingers inside her.

"What do you want?" he asked.

She licked her dry lips. "You know."

"Tell me. I have to hear it," he urged.

Her stomach quivered at the low, sexy tone. "I want you."

"What do you want me to do?"

Oh, God. He was going to make her say it. All of it.

"I want you inside me," she said before swallowing. With that first sentence out, she grew bolder. Somehow, the blindfold made it easier to say the things she saw in her mind—she wasn't sure she could otherwise. "I want to feel you deep within."

He withdrew his fingers from her slowly. "What else?"

"I want our bodies sliding against each other."

"Hmm," he said with a moan rumbling his chest. "And?"

Her breath hitched when the pad of a finger swirled around her clit. "I . . . I want to lose control. With you," she added before he could ask.

God, how she'd missed this—missed him. He'd always had such expert command over her body, pushing her to the limit and allowing her to explore her most intimate fantasies.

With him, she felt beautiful, wanted.

With him, she gave in to the base desires she otherwise ignored.

With him, she was simply . . . herself.

Wyatt was the only man who didn't make her think she needed to hide her flaws, needs, or cravings. He'd always accepted everything that she was without question or judgment.

A tear slipped out of her eye and fell down her temple. Fortunately, the blindfold hid it. Wyatt couldn't see how the longing he'd released distressed her.

It wasn't him. She refused to allow him to be the cause.

It was everything else—Orrin's kidnapping, Virgil's and Charlotte's murder, the attacks, her family coming for her again, and the Saints.

It wasn't Wyatt.

It couldn't be him.

"Where are you, baby girl?"

It hurt to hear his endearment for her on his lips after all these years. "With you."

"No, you weren't. Which means I'm not doing my duties correctly."

Few people knew how tender and downright sexy Wyatt could be. Even at a young age, she'd known Wyatt would protect her. He hadn't changed.

"Tell me what you were thinking," he demanded as he thrust a finger deep inside her.

She arched her back. "I'm thinking of you."

"Now you are."

"Don't let the world intrude. Not tonight."

There was a beat of silence before he whispered, "I won't."

With that promise, it was easy for her mind to let go of everything. He pulled his finger from her and ran his hands from her hips up to her breasts, squeezing her nipples before caressing down her sides.

And just like that, her body was his again.

"You're going to scream for me," he announced as he moved over her.

Excitement filled her. "Yes," she answered breathlessly.

She forgot to breathe when the head of his cock butted

against her entrance. Her sex clenched, impatient to have him inside.

Her head rolled to the side when she felt his lips at her ear. Then he whispered in that deep, seductive voice of his, "I ache to be inside you."

"Yes," she replied eagerly.

"I want you."

She rubbed her cheek against his since she couldn't touch him. "Take me. I'm yours."

Always have been.

That last bit she kept to herself.

His arousal pressed against her delicate lips before he pushed inside. She yanked against her bonds to touch him as her body stretched while he slowly entered her until he was seated fully.

The sound of his heavy breaths told her he was as affected as she by their joining. They remained locked together for another second before he began moving his hips.

Suddenly, her blindfold was yanked off. She opened her eyes to find him staring down at her with his gold eyes lit by an internal flame of desire.

The bonds holding her were loosened. She pulled her hands free and wrapped her arms around his neck. With her palms running along his back, she felt the muscles move with him.

Everything about Wyatt made her ache with desire. There was no use denying that, not when she was in his arms.

His tempo increased, pushing her to the edge once more. Their bodies slid against one another, slick with sweat. She was wound so tightly that, at any moment, she would peak. His thrusts went deeper as his hold tightened around her.

"Together," he said.

She met his gaze, unsure if she could hold off her orgasm until he was ready. He'd kept her at the brink for so long that she craved the release. Then it was upon her, the first waves of pleasure battering against her.

"Now, baby girl."

That was all she needed to hear. The climax was powerful, wracking her body with shudders of white-hot ecstasy. Her eyes closed as she was held in the clutches of the violent orgasm.

All the while, she felt Wyatt above her, pounding her body to prolong her pleasure until he stiffened with his own release.

It felt like an eternity before she came back to herself. When she opened her eyes, it was to find him smiling down at her.

"What?" she asked.

"I told you I'd make you scream."

She couldn't remember doing that, but then again, he'd always made her scream. "Was it loud?"

"I think they heard you in the next county."

It was impossible not to smile. The ease between them was familiar, right. She didn't want it to end.

He gave her a soft kiss before pulling out of her and rolling to the side. When he raised a brow in question, she snuggled next to him.

The morning light would change everything, but she had asked for tonight—and he was giving it to her.

CHAPTER SIXTEEN

There wasn't much in Wyatt's life that he regretted. Once a decision was made, he stuck by it. But he mourned the life he could've had with Callie.

If his mother hadn't been murdered.

If his father had found the killer.

If he hadn't joined the military.

If his heart hadn't turned to stone.

But he'd loved Callie too deeply. Some days, it was easier to push his feelings aside. Other days, it threatened to smother him—like now.

As he held her in his arms, he couldn't believe he'd gone so many years without her. If only he could freeze time and keep them as they were, but he didn't have any superpowers. He was but a man who had made enemies, and now, those enemies were coming for him.

Wyatt stared at the ceiling while listening to her breathing even out as she drifted into sleep. Being with her, making love to her, had shown him how lonely he was.

It hadn't been evident until he returned to Texas. And

the more time he spent with Callie, the clearer it became.

He wasn't whole unless he was with her.

For almost two decades, he had walked through the days only half alive. He'd known it when he left Texas, but that ache had dulled, blunted. Blurred.

Now, it was in crystal clear focus once more.

Maybe that's why he'd been so damn good at his job, because he hadn't cared if he lived or died. He readily walked into the toughest of situations, and somehow, always walked—or limped—out.

Many times, he'd been wounded and even spent some time Stateside in a VA hospital to recuperate, but then he returned to his unit, ready to do it all over again.

He took missions that would have otherwise gone to men with families, because no one cared if he died. Those other men had people counting on them. He had . . . nobody.

Now, the only precious thing in his life was in danger. It hadn't sat well with him when it had just been the Saints, but having Ahmadi and the Reeds closing in put everything into perspective.

He turned on his side to face Callie. It was unfathomable that she was in his arms again. He grazed the back of his knuckles along her cheek and down her jaw.

"Hey, baby girl," he whispered.

She groaned in annoyance and nuzzled her face against his arm. He smiled, regret twisting his gut. How he wished he could leave her sleeping, perhaps wake her in the early morning hours as the sunlight came through the window and then make love to her again. But it wasn't meant to be.

As the evening had worn on, a particular feeling had begun nudging him. He knew it well. Danger was fast approaching—and he had to do something.

"Callie."

She let out a huff and opened her eyes to glare at him. "What?"

"We need to leave."

Her gaze cleared of sleep with a blink. "Why?"

"A gut feeling."

Since they agreed to trust each other's instincts, he wasn't surprised when she asked, "When?"

"Now."

Without another word, she sat up and grabbed her clothes to dress. Wyatt did the same, and then put out the fire. In the next half hour, they packed all the food, clothes, weapons, and ammunition they could carry.

He put a hand over hers when Callie grabbed her keys. "Mercy stays here."

Callie started to open her mouth to argue then nodded. "Are we stealing a car?"

"We'll be on foot."

She didn't bat an eye as she zipped her computer into her backpack and handed him one of the two new burner phones. "I programmed each of the numbers into the other. I also added in Orrin's number. Just in case."

Wyatt looked at the cabin now bathed in darkness. "I promised you the night."

"I'd rather have my life."

Always practical, he thought with an inward smile. "Ready?"

"Yep."

He walked to the back door and slowly opened it,

peering out. Then he slipped through the opening. Callie was quick to follow. Once the door closed silently behind her, he led her around the traps he'd set, picking up weapons as he went.

She stayed close behind him with a pistol in one hand. So far, he hadn't seen any evidence of others approaching the cabin, but that didn't mean anything. His intuition had told him to leave that night, and he wasn't going to question that—especially if it saved Callie's life.

The cabin being as secluded as it was, they walked for a couple of miles without encountering any other houses. It wouldn't be long before they hit a city. Luckily, there were still areas around Austin used exclusively for ranching.

Wyatt didn't like trespassing on someone else's land, but the situation certainly called for it. And he would make sure to stay away from any houses to keep from being spotted.

They'd been walking for almost an hour before Callie asked, "Where are we going?"

"I have no idea."

"Wow. You didn't even try to lie."

He slowed so that she came even with him. "There's no point."

"Do you have a general direction you've pointed us in?"

He shook his head at her, disappointed. "Don't you remember the lessons I gave you about using the stars as a guide."

"Obviously, not," she replied testily. "I knew I should've just pulled out the phone."

"We're headed north."

She jerked her head to him. "Why?"

"I had four directions to choose from. I chose north."

"For a reason," she pointed out.

He pressed his lips together before sighing. "I'm taking us back to the ranch."

"Good," she stated.

He'd expected an argument, but he should've known better. "We need to alert Owen and Natalie that we're headed back."

"I'll do that in the morning. What about Orrin and Cullen?"

"What do you think about giving Cullen and Mia the information on Jankovic and letting them track down the scientist since we seem to have our hands full."

She adjusted her backpack. "I've been sending everyone updates on what I find, so I think Cullen is already doing just that."

"I was hoping you'd say that."

"Were you?" she asked with a sidelong look.

Neither had spoken about what had occurred between them, and he had a feeling that she never would. It might be for the best. Besides, his focus was on staying ahead of the Saints, Ahmadi, and the Reeds currently.

For the next three hours, they made their way north, drifting eastwardly as they did and stopping to rest occasionally. When the sky turned a light gray, he spotted Callie yawning.

He was used to going without sleep and hiking through deserts for days at a time, but she wasn't. Though she was tough, she was untrained.

"How do you feel about stealing a car?" he asked.

She shot him a smile. "I think it's a fabulous idea."

The next town is five klicks away. We should get there before dawn. Just enough time for us to find a vehicle and get on the road."

"If you were alone, would you walk all the way to the ranch?"

"Yes."

She made a face. "I thought so. You only want to steal a car because of me."

"Not just because of you. I'd like to get to the ranch in time to prepare for the attacks."

"How long do you think it'll take for everyone to figure out we're no longer at the cabin?"

He shrugged, his thoughts on that very thing. "I'm hoping a few days, but we can't count on that."

"With the way these assholes seem to have eyes and ears everywhere, no we can't. Which means, we shouldn't be seen anywhere."

"We'll fare better away from the city."

She grunted in response. They fell silent as they made their way to the small town. Just as Wyatt expected, there was little movement before dawn. The few awake were opening shops or were ranchers getting an early start.

He took her to a drug store that was connected to a diner. There were a couple of trucks in front of the building, but it was the old VW Bug parked off to the side of the structure that Wyatt was interested in.

"Stay here," he whispered as he set down his bag and weapons.

He hunched over and hurried to the car. Luck was on his side when he tried the handle and the door opened. He climbed inside and pulled the door partly closed. Then he reached below the steering column and yanked out the wires.

All he had to do was get the engine started, and then they could be on the road and to the ranch in just a few hours. That would give them plenty of time to get things ready.

He glanced up to check on Callie and stilled when he saw her talking to someone. The man had his back to Wyatt. It wasn't until she sidestepped, causing the man to turn with her that he saw the gun pointed at her.

It wasn't fury that filled him, but cold, deadly intent. He quietly pushed open the car door and slipped out, squatting beside the vehicle while pushing the door closed.

The man was talking to Callie, but Wyatt couldn't make out what was said. As soon as Wyatt moved away from the car, he'd be seen.

He looked around, trying to determine if the man was alone. It was still too dark to see if there were others inside parked vehicles or not.

His gaze landed on his bag with his weapons. The only thing he had on him was a knife. He pulled it from its sheath at the back of his waist and prepared to stand when he heard something behind him.

Wyatt turned and saw the attacker in time to raise his arm and knock the gun away. He stood and thrust his knife upwards, aiming for the man's gut, but the assailant moved to the side and slammed Wyatt's hand against the car.

He elbowed his attacker in the side of the face twice before slamming his foot into the side of the man's knee. There was a grunt, but this foe didn't go down easily.

The man had skills that were equal to his, and Wyatt had trained in nearly every kind of combat there was. Wyatt slashed with his knife again and again, and each time, the man blocked and evaded him.

A kick came out of nowhere, knocking his knife from his hand. Wyatt didn't slow his attack. The blows happened quickly from each of them. Wyatt spent half the time using evasive tactics to limit the number of hits from his attacker.

One vicious blow to his cheek had Wyatt tasting blood. He leaned out of the way at the last second, causing the man to smash his fist into the driver's side window of the car.

Using whatever they could find to fight, the battle turned brutal as both men realized only one of them would walk away. Wyatt was going to make sure that was him. He wanted to look over at Callie, but to do so might very well be what cost him his life. He had to believe she could take care of herself.

Wyatt managed to get behind his assailant and wrap an arm around his neck. The man elbowed him repeatedly, but Wyatt didn't loosen his hold.

"Who sent you?" Wyatt demanded.

The man laughed in response. When Wyatt was about to question him further, he happened to look up and found Callie gone. Without hesitating, he broke the man's neck. As the attacker fell to the ground, Wyatt grabbed his knife and ran to the bags Callie had left behind.

He scooped up both by the handles and set out looking for her.

CHAPTER SEVENTEEN

Callie had never run so fast in her life. Her lungs burned, and there was blood dripping down her neck into her sweatshirt. She weaved and zigzagged around anything that could give her cover.

There were thirteen rounds left in her Glock 19. Thirteen bullets that had to find their targets. She had no idea how many Saints were after her, but she couldn't waste a single round.

She turned left, intending to get as far from the town as she could. Her best chance was to lose them in the woods. The arid landscape of Austin and the surrounding area gave way to more lush grounds with taller trees.

Branches snagged on her clothes, hair, and face. She didn't pause until she found a set of trees that she could duck behind. Callie closed her eyes for a second and took several deep breaths before peeking around the trunks to see how close the men were.

The wound on her neck stung, but she was lucky that she had shifted at the last second. Otherwise, she'd be dead. She wondered about Wyatt. When she'd been able to glance his way, he was locked in a very physical battle with someone.

She'd debated doubling back to find him, then decided against it. Away from the city, the men after her would have to fan out to look for her. It would give her time to take them out one at a time.

The crack of a limb sounded loudly nearby, silencing the birds. The area grew as quiet as a graveyard. They were close. She looked out in front of her, trying to see as far ahead as she could in order to choose the best route.

She didn't know this region and didn't want to end up cornered somewhere. But it wasn't like she had a lot of time to plan an escape.

With a deep breath, she pushed away from the safety of the trees and crept forward. She stayed low, letting the underbrush assist in hiding her. Fortunately, her clothes were dark, which also helped conceal her.

Thanks to her time working at the Loughman Ranch, Callie had learned how to move quietly through the thickets. That skill came in handy now as she methodically and steadily put more distance between her and the men following.

She needed to find an area large enough to move around in, but which also provided great cover in order for her to start taking the men out. Unlike her attacker—who had a silencer on his gun—as soon as she fired the first shot, her location would be known.

Her throat was already parched. It was a good thing it wasn't summer, or she would be in for a very rough day. Not that the autumn climate would give her much relief. Texas weather could change on a dime any time of the year.

She kept moving from tree to tree, only running when the distance between them kept her visible for too long. The trick was to blend in with the foliage. She could only pray that there wasn't a tracker with the men after her. Otherwise, things would get much more complicated.

Wyatt stashed the bags behind a large bush. He knelt beside them, getting out weapons as he glanced up every few seconds. He didn't know what he would be walking into. He had to be prepared, but he couldn't lug the bags with him if he wanted to creep up on the man after Callie.

Once Wyatt was set with the weapons, he zipped up his bag and stood. The traffic in the sleepy town was getting busier, and that meant more people would see him. It was a chance he'd have to take to figure out which direction Callie had gone.

The concrete gave away nothing. It wasn't until he spotted a drop of blood that he knew he was headed the right way. He refused to think that the blood was Callie's, because the idea of her on the run and wounded sent him into an animalistic rage.

He followed the drops of blood in a path that wound around vehicles, garbage cans, businesses, and other things. It wasn't until the trail suddenly veered to the left away from the town and into the treeline that he smiled.

Five feet into the vegetation, he saw a body slumped against a tree with the victim's chest soaked in blood. Wyatt recognized the clothes as the man who had confronted Callie.

He squatted beside the dead man, looking him over.

A white male in his thirties with no identifiable marks present. Wyatt knew the Reeds, and this man wasn't a Reed, so he crossed them off the list. It also wasn't any of Ahmadi's men. That left the Saints.

Had it been misfortune that put them on a path that intersected with the Saints? Wyatt sure hoped so because the only other option was that the Saints had been following them all along.

As many times as Wyatt had gone off the grid, he knew what to do. Regardless of the reach of the Saints, he and Callie had been more than careful.

He surveyed the ground, spotting the prints of several large boots. The way they trampled over everything erased any evidence of Callie. But he knew she was out there. Just as he was certain she'd been the one to kill the man.

Wyatt straightened and looked around, his gaze moving slowly through the foliage. If he were in charge of this group of Saints, he'd leave a man behind to make sure no one followed.

It didn't take Wyatt long to spot the guard. He kept well hidden, but not good enough. On silent feet, Wyatt crept toward the unsuspecting man.

There was a mechanical click, and his target whispered something. Wyatt paused, listening. When nothing more was said, he moved closer and spotted the headset the Saint wore.

With no time to spare, Wyatt came up behind him, removing the knife from its scabbard at the back of his waist and slit his throat. As the Saint bled out, Wyatt took his headset and rifle before following the trail of boot prints.

*   *   *

Callie was tired and thirsty. The amount of blood she'd lost was only making her weaker. She stopped to rest once more. When she looked back through the trees, she counted seven men.

"Shit," she mumbled, hating that she had a stitch in her side.

She continued onward until the trees gave way to a clearing and a fence. Beyond the fence were miles of pasture. A large herd of cattle grazed nearby.

Callie avoided the ranch and turned to the right, hoping to skirt the property while remaining shielded by the trees. She pressed a hand against the wound on her neck to try and stop the flow of blood.

Every step became a struggle. She hadn't thought she'd lost enough blood to put her in such a predicament. The stitch in her side didn't relent. Adrenaline kept her going, but even that would wear off eventually.

During her training for the CIA and for Orrin, she'd been put in similar situations—though she hadn't been wounded in either scenario.

Though it wasn't often, Callie did get out in the field with Orrin on missions. She'd killed to save another life, so she didn't feel bad about shooting the man trying to take hers. But she'd never been out on her own before.

That didn't mean she wasn't prepared. Orrin had been rigorous in the constant trials he put her through. Some were mental, some physical, some emotional—but all were training he knew she'd someday need.

That day had come.

The training worked to help her mind sort through minute details, but it was Wyatt who kept her going.

She paused, leaning against a tree. By the ascent of the sun, it was already mid-morning. She couldn't believe she'd been out there alone for that long. The shade of the trees kept the sun off her, but the day was turning out to be warmer than usual.

It wouldn't be long before she'd need to take off her sweatshirt or overheat. Without any water, she had to remain as cool as she could.

She was thankful for her two weapons, but she wished she had her backpack. Not only did it have water, but it also had the burner phone. She could call . . .

Her thoughts trailed off. Who would she call? The closest ones were Owen and Natalie, but they needed to remain at the ranch. Besides, she didn't want anyone else to have to fight the assholes after her.

She wiped her forehead on her sleeve and looked behind her. There was no sign of anyone, but she didn't let her guard down. Nor would she until her pursuers were all dead.

Callie started moving again. She'd gone about half a mile when she saw another clearing and the same fence as earlier.

Wyatt touched the blood on the bark of the tree. The twisting of his gut told him it was Callie's. He'd hoped the blood he found in town was someone else's, but it looked as if he were wrong.

It was easy enough to find her trail because Orrin had trained her and given her the same skills as his sons. Knowing which direction Callie would head helped Wyatt stay on her trail.

The Saints spread out looking for her, giving their locations via their communication that Wyatt heard through the headset. At least one of them was a tracker, because every time they veered off course, they would inevitably retrace their steps and find Callie's trail.

Wyatt moved quickly over the land. He didn't stop until he saw the ranch. There, he stared at the cattle for a long time before he looked in the direction Callie had gone. She would keep away from people, which meant she would remain in the woods as long as she could. He realized she skirted the ranch in hopes of keeping hidden.

He turned and followed Callie's trail. From what he could tell, there were at least seven men after her. And he was determined to find them before they found her.

Worry set in when he discovered how often Callie was stopping to rest. He spotted more blood, a thick drop here and there.

He looked up, squinting through the trees. She continued to remain on her feet, which was a good sign, but it wouldn't be too much longer before the Saints caught up with her. As long as she stayed conscious, she had a chance.

"I'm coming, baby girl," he said.

He'd gone another two miles when he looked from the woods and saw the ranch again. There were cattle in the distance, but closer to the fence were five horses. He was about to walk away when he spotted something running in the pasture.

As soon as he realized it was Callie, he rushed from the trees and across the clearing. He slowed when he neared the fence so as not to spook the horses. When he climbed over, all but one of the horses trotted off.

"Come on, boy," he coaxed, holding out his hand.

The gelding snorted and walked toward him slowly. Each second felt like an eternity, but Wyatt remained patient until the horse reached him.

He stroked the velvety nose of the palomino, talking low and smooth all the while. Then he caressed the horse's neck and side, walking around the animal to let the horse get to know him.

Once he returned to the gelding's head, he looked the horse in the eye and said, "I need a ride. Will you take me?"

The horse gave a swish of his tail and moved closer to him. Wyatt grabbed a handful of mane and leapt atop the horse's back. There were some things that a person could never forget, and riding a horse was one of them.

Wyatt gave the horse a nudge, and the palomino leapt into a run, racing across the pasture. Though it had been years since he had ridden a horse, much less bareback, it was engrained in him. He leaned low over the horse's neck, his gaze on the men that had jumped the fence and were running after Callie.

He pressed his knee against the horse, sending the gelding veering toward the men. When the animal spotted the group, its ears pricked forward and he picked up speed.

There was a smile on Wyatt's face when the palomino ran over two of the men.

CHAPTER EIGHTEEN

Callie could hear the Saints gaining quickly. She was fast losing energy, but she wouldn't go down without a fight. She spotted a fallen tree ahead of her and ran toward it.

The sweatshirt chafed against her sweaty skin, causing her to feel the heat baking around her. She pumped her arms and legs, gritting her teeth as the stitch in her side throbbed. As soon as she reached the tree, she vaulted over the massive trunk and landed heavily on the other side.

She turned to lift her Glock when a face appeared over the trunk, knife raised. Callie fell back, startled, as she fired off two shots, dead center of the man's chest. He slumped lifelessly across the trunk.

There wasn't time to get up as another reached the tree. This time, however, she was looking down the barrel of a gun. She didn't hesitate to shift her Glock and pull the trigger a heartbeat before her attacker.

Her face turned away as she squeezed her eyes closed when his bullet landed in the dirt inches from her head. When she looked back, the only thing visible from her position was the man's foot since he'd fallen back over the other side.

Callie heard a commotion and turned onto her hands and knees. Someone grabbed a handful of her hair from behind and yanked her upper body up, as she remained kneeling. She winced, clutching the hand that held her.

"Finally found you, bitch," the man said angrily. "My reward is going to be immense."

He squeezed the wrist of her hand holding the gun, so she had no choice but to drop it or have her bone break. Her other hand reached around to her knife while he talked. She slipped the blade from its sheath and held it against her arm.

"You actually thought you could outrun us," he said and turned her toward him.

She looked into his close-set, dark eyes. "You're going to lose."

"You've already lost," he said with a smirk.

Callie held his gaze as he tightened his fist in her hair. The pain shot from her scalp all the way down her spine, but she didn't move. Her eyes watered, and inside she was screaming. Outwardly, she allowed him to believe he was dominating her, showing her who the victor would be.

Then she smiled and smoothly slid her knife between his ribs and right into his heart. When his fingers loosened in her hair and his eyes widened as he fell to his knees, she leaned close to his face and said, "Who lost, bitch?"

It was the sound of approaching hoof beats that caused her to look up. She ducked as a horse jumped over her and the tree. When she looked up again, it was to see

Wyatt dismounting from the horse and striding to her with long, purposeful steps.

She was so relieved to see him that she reached for him as he dropped to his knees beside her. As soon as his arms wrapped around her, she closed her eyes and held onto him tightly.

"You're hurt," he stated in a gruff voice.

"It's just a graze on my neck."

He pulled back to look at her, his eyes shifted to her neck. "I'm talking about the wound on your side."

Side? What was he talking about? She would know if she had an injury on her side. To prove her point, she looked down to show him, only to stare silently at the blood that stained her right side.

"Let me see it," Wyatt said.

She didn't stop him when he gently pushed her onto her back. "The Saints?"

"All dead," he stated.

Her gaze lifted to the sky and the clouds drifting swiftly past. With the threat now over, her eyes grew heavy, and she let them close, wanting to rest for just a moment.

Wyatt's hands were tender as he lifted her sweatshirt. It made a sucking noise as he pulled it away from her wound. She could feel him wiping something against her, but she was too tired to open her eyes and see what it was.

She began to drift off. She was so fatigued from walking all night, then running from the Saints. If only she could sleep.

"Wake up, baby girl."

Was it a dream? Or had he really spoken to her? She couldn't tell, and it took too much energy to find out.

"Callie."

This time, she knew it was Wyatt by the insistence in his tone. Gone was the affection in his voice. She grunted and tried to push his hands away.

"Open your eyes. Dammit, Callie, stop fighting me and open those beautiful eyes."

It took her a few tries, but she managed to wake up enough to look up at him. His dark hair was disheveled and damp with sweat, and he had a day's growth of whiskers that darkened his jawline, making him oh so sexy. His shirt was missing and showing off that mouth-watering body.

But it was his gold eyes searching her face that made her smile.

"Hi," she said.

He gave her a crooked grin, the kind that always made her heart skip a beat. "I need to tend to your wounds, which means we need supplies. And that means we need to move."

She closed her eyes against the scratchiness and groaned. "Now? I just laid down."

"You've been asleep for twenty minutes."

Her gaze snapped opened. "What?"

"I checked your wound, tied my shirt around it to reduce the bleeding, and I got rid of all the bodies."

While she'd slept. She felt like an utter fool. "You should've woken me so I could help."

"Not with your injuries. We've had a long night and morning, and I don't know what the rest of the day holds. I might need you later."

"Okay," she agreed reluctantly.

Not like she had any choice. She rolled to her side and slowly sat up. Now that she knew of her injury, the pain lashed through her body as if it were struck by spikes.

She clenched her jaw and welcomed Wyatt's help in getting to her feet. Her lids kept slipping closed, and she had to force them back open. Sleep called to her like a lover with promises of a pain-free slumber.

Somehow, she found herself standing next to a horse. She wanted to pet the palomino, but the effort was too much. The animal turned its head to her, its soulful brown eyes seeming to understand the agony she was in.

"Ready?" Wyatt asked.

Her eyelids shut again of their own accord. Ready? Did he want her to ride? Surely not.

She hissed in pain when he gently lifted her in his arms and set her atop the gelding's back. On instinct, Callie grabbed a handful of the horse's mane to steady herself. Then Wyatt mounted behind her.

He wrapped his right arm around her, holding her against his chest as their legs conformed to each other. The pressure of his arm actually helped against the pain. And now that she didn't have to stand, sleep pulled her under quickly.

The moment Callie's head rolled back to his shoulder, Wyatt knew she was asleep once more. Fear wrapped him in its iron grip, tightening around his chest so that he couldn't breathe.

The amount of blood she had lost was staggering. Her entire right side was coated in it. He had no idea how she'd managed to run, fight or even stay on her feet against the Saints in her condition.

He clicked to the horse to start walking. Wyatt wrapped his hand around Callie's that held the gelding's flaxen mane. He had to get supplies to treat her, but that meant bringing her around people—people that could be a part of the Saints.

At least the bastards who had been chasing her were dead. She'd fought like an avenging angel, and it caused his blood to heat thinking about it. She truly was an amazing woman.

He steered the horse toward a barn he saw in the distance. The closer they came, the more buildings Wyatt saw. Then he saw movement. A tractor was being driven, moving hay into a barn while two other men loaded a stallion into a trailer.

Wyatt hated being so exposed, but there was nothing he could do about it. The few trees that dotted the pasture would do him little good in getting to any of the structures to find a first-aid kit.

At the last minute, he steered the horse toward one of the trees closest to the barn and dismounted before he could be seen. Wyatt gently lifted Callie down and set her up against the tree as he looked under the belly of the gelding to see where the three men were.

A fourth man, an older gentleman with a wide stomach and a big mustache, emerged from a barn after the horse had been loaded. There were words exchanged before one of the workers climbed into the truck and drove away with the animal.

The older man and the second one talked for a moment before both walked off in different directions.

Wyatt's gaze shifted to the tractor. There was still a lot of hay to unload, so at least that one would be occupied for a bit.

Wyatt stood and patted the palomino's rump as he walked behind him. "Stay with her, boy. I'll be right back."

The horse snorted and continued munching on the grass. Wyatt glanced at Callie before making a quick run to the barn. When he reached it, he plastered himself against it and peeked around the corner of the entrance.

He could hear horses within, but it was too dark for him to see anyone. He took a deep breath and slipped inside, keeping close to the wall. His eyes adjusted to the dimness of the inside of the building quickly.

Beside him, a horse walked to the gate of its enclosure and stretched out its neck to sniff him. Wyatt held out his hand, allowing the animal to smell him. He walked closer, petting the beast.

When he was at the gate, he looked inside the stall and spotted the wide belly. He smiled at the pregnant mare and patted her neck.

Then his focus shifted back to the barn. It was made very similarly to the one at his ranch, so he had an idea where the tack room would be—which was where a first-aid kit would most likely be kept.

He moved slowly down the center aisle, always remaining near the stalls. When he came to the middle of the long barn with a wide aisle making a T, he glanced both directions to make sure no one was coming, then hurriedly crossed to the tack room.

The door to the space was ajar and the light on. Once inside, he looked at the rows of saddles, halters, brushes, and the like until he found the white box with the red cross on it set on some shelves. Wyatt grabbed the box and turned to retrace his steps when he came to a halt.

There was a faded denim shirt tossed over one of the saddles, and a brown paper bag with someone's lunch sitting nearby. He tried on the shirt, happy to see that it fit, and grabbed the bag before hurriedly retracing his steps.

He wasn't surprised to find the palomino where he'd left him. Wyatt opened the bag and saw an apple and a sandwich inside. He gave the apple to the horse and walked to Callie.

She didn't appear to have moved. He took out his knife and slit her sweatshirt up the side to better see the wound. If the bullet had shifted a hair to the left, it would've hit her kidney. It had done enough damage, though.

He was thankful he wouldn't have to dig the slug out of her as it had passed through. The location meant that it had most likely not hit any vital organs. She would need a hospital, but right now, his concern was to stop any more blood loss.

Wyatt opened the box and set about cleaning her injuries and stitching both the entrance and exit wounds. For the first time administering such work, his hands shook.

Because it was Callie.

He glanced up at her. Her breathing was even, but she appeared pale. He wanted her to open her eyes and berate him, call him choice names for all of his mistakes. She was too quiet, too still.

"Don't leave me, baby girl," he whispered.

He lifted his bloody hands to move her hair away from her neck to see to that wound when he paused. Blood had never bothered him, but this wasn't just any blood. This was Callie's blood.

It was all over him and her, even in her hair. He swallowed past the lump of emotion in his throat. The more he looked at the stains coating his hands, the more furious he got.

Ten men after them. If the Saints wanted a fight, he would give them one they wouldn't soon forget. He would show them retaliation.

He would show them vengeance.

And when he was done, there wouldn't be anyone left standing. No matter how long it took, no matter how many he had to kill, he vowed then and there to take down every last Saint.

CHAPTER NINETEEN

Outskirts of DC

Cullen pulled the SUV over next to the curb in the affluent neighborhood outside of DC and turned off the engine.

"Jankovic is in there," Mia said, nodding toward the large house through the drizzling rain.

Cullen leaned his elbow on the center console and nodded. "Maybe."

Following Hewett out of DC had led them to a car shop. After an hour, Mitch returned to DC, but two other men drove in the opposite direction. Cullen and Mia had decided to take a chance and follow the others to see where it led them.

Mia turned her head and gave him a flat look. "Callie said Jankovic was in DC."

"We're not in DC anymore, sweetheart," he pointed out.

"As near as. Callie knows her stuff."

He ran a hand over his mouth and chin. "I think whoever is in that house has something to do with the Saints."

"It's the scientist," she insisted.

"Why are you so sure?"

She turned her head to him, but her eyes focused on something else. When she didn't answer, Cullen looked at her to find her mouth hanging open and her eyes widening by the second. He followed her gaze to another car across the street and up a ways.

But it wasn't until he looked inside the vehicle that he saw what had taken her by surprise—his father.

"Is it really him?" Mia whispered hopefully.

Cullen nodded slowly at seeing his father in the passenger seat. The driver was none other than Yuri Markovic. None of them moved.

"I have to see him," Mia said. "I have to talk to him."

"Not here." Cullen started the engine and pulled out onto the road, driving slowly past Orrin and Yuri. He met his father's gaze and nodded.

Mia turned around in the seat to watch them, while Cullen looked into the rearview mirror. It wasn't long before the black Range Rover pulled out and did a U-turn on the road to follow.

"Where do we take them and not be seen by the Saints?" Mia asked.

It was a damn good question, one he'd been asking himself. "Somewhere abandoned."

"I saw a closed strip mall a few miles back."

"I remember that," Cullen said, shooting her a smile.

He made his way there, taking precautions to ensure that they weren't being followed. When they reached the abandoned plaza, Cullen drove around to the back, away from prying eyes.

When Mia started to open the door and get out, he grabbed her arm and shook his head. A moment later, the Range Rover appeared and stopped before them about twenty yards away.

Cullen's heart raced when the passenger door opened and Orrin stepped out, unconcerned with the sprinkle of rain. This time, there was no stopping Mia as she threw open her door and jumped out, racing toward Orrin.

Cullen watched as she launched herself at his father. Orrin's smile filled his entire face as he caught Mia in his arms, hugging her. For several minutes, Cullen watched the easy way his father and Mia interacted. Their affection and respect for one another obvious.

Yuri then exited the SUV and spoke to Mia. Cullen knew he needed to get out, and he wanted to talk to his father. The problem was that he didn't know what to say. Too many years had passed without any sort of communication for there not to be awkwardness.

Orrin's gaze moved to him. Cullen opened the vehicle door and slowly stood. He didn't take his eyes from his father as he shut the door. Then he took his first step. The closer he got to Orrin, the more he spotted the faint bruises and cuts from his captivity and torture.

Cullen cut his gaze to Yuri. The Russian was to blame for kidnapping his father and putting him through that hell, but Yuri was also responsible for Orrin's escape.

When Cullen looked back at his father, the impact of the entire situation hit him. For a short time, he feared he had lost his only living parent. That was when he'd realized how much he loved Orrin—and how much he wanted his father in his life.

There were no words needed as Orrin opened his arms and Cullen walked into them. Cullen squeezed his eyes closed when tears threatened. He hadn't wanted to admit that he feared this day might never come.

Orrin pulled back, gripping Cullen's upper arms as he smiled, his gold eyes crinkling. "Damn, it's good to see you, son."

"Hi, Dad," he replied, chuckling.

Mia sniffed loudly before she said, "Now this is a reunion."

"What the hell are you two doing here?" Yuri demanded.

Orrin gave Cullen a pat before he dropped his arms, his gaze turning serious. "I'd like to know that answer myself."

"Callie," Mia said.

Orrin grinned at the mention of her. "Ah."

"And we've been watching Hewett," Cullen explained.

Yuri crossed his arms over his chest and widened his stance as he frowned. "What did you find?"

"Mitch leaves the office frequently to meet up with people," Mia said.

Cullen added, "They could be Saints, they could be personnel in his division. We don't know."

"You won't until it's too late," Orrin said.

Yuri grunted. "Your father did not know that the team he brought to Russia was all Saints."

"What?" Mia asked in shock.

Yuri shrugged indifferently. "It is why I killed them and took Orrin."

Cullen digested that information as his gaze met his father's. "Hewett met with a man in a black trench coat yesterday."

"Plain-looking?" Orrin asked. "Someone you'd forget meeting?"

Mia nodded enthusiastically. "I've got pictures." She ran to their vehicle and grabbed the camera. When she returned, she handed it to Yuri and Orrin.

"That is the same man that visits the house often," Yuri said.

"Why are you watching the house?" Cullen asked.

Orrin returned the camera to Mia. "The scientist who developed the bioweapon I stole from Russia is there."

"Konrad Jankovic," Cullen said with a nod of his head.

Mia winked at him. "I told you."

"How do you know of him?" Yuri asked.

Cullen told them about how Owen, Natalie, Wyatt, and Callie had attended a benefit in Dallas and got the Russian ambassador, Egor Dvorak, alone. Dvorak gave up Jankovic as well as Orrin being in Virginia.

"How is Natalie?" Orrin asked.

Cullen smiled, thinking of his middle brother. "Quite happy now that Owen has won her heart again."

"Now that is good news." Orrin looked down at the cracked pavement, smiling.

Yuri dropped his arms as he looked upward, blinking against the continuous trickle of rain. "We should not remain out in the open."

"He's right," Mia said. "But now that we've found each other, we should work together."

Orrin pivoted and made his way to the back door of one of the shops. He withdrew a long knife from his boot and pried open the door. Then he motioned everyone inside.

Cullen shook off the rain from his head as he closed the door behind everyone. "What's our next move? I gather you two were going after Jankovic."

"*Da*," Yuri stated.

Orrin hesitated, he and Yuri exchanging looks.

It was Mia who said, "I know that look, Orrin. What aren't you telling us?"

"Just spit it out," Yuri told Orrin.

Cullen waited impatiently before his father blew out a breath and said, "When Callie first came to work for me, she set up a system for me to be able to contact her if I was ever in trouble."

"You should've done that as soon as you and Yuri escaped," Mia chided him.

Orrin nodded. "I know, but I also knew the Saints were watching all of you. Yuri and I wanted to keep our whereabouts and intentions to ourselves."

"Understandable," Cullen said.

"I intended to keep to that until a few days ago," Orrin continued. "That's when we came across some information regarding Wyatt."

Cullen's attention sharpened. "What information?"

"While working for Delta Force, he and his team had several run-ins with a rather nasty terrorist force led by a man named Ahmadi. Each got several good hits on the other. One such time nearly took Wyatt's life. He ended up spending several months in a VA hospital in DC with a leg wound."

Cullen ran a hand through his hair. Everyone who

joined the military knew they would one day find themselves in the middle of the crosshairs, but to find out his eldest brother had come close to being killed unsettled him.

"I'm glad these terrorists haven't made their way here," Mia said.

Orrin's face filled with anger. "The Saints brought them in and put them on Wyatt's trail."

Cullen was torn between taking out Jankovic and going to help Wyatt. He'd fought radicals many times, so he knew they wouldn't stop until Wyatt was dead. "You alerted Callie and Wyatt," he guessed.

"I did," Orrin replied. "I sent a message. Callie used her skills and managed to find the number to my burner phone."

Mia's expression lightened a fraction. "You spoke with her, then?"

"For a few minutes. That's when she told me her family was after her."

Cullen spun around and raked a hand through his hair as he paced. The Saints were smart. They were boxing Callie and Wyatt in, which would send the rest of them to help.

"I know how you feel," Orrin said. "It's still tearing me up."

Cullen turned to his father. "Do you know where Callie and Wyatt are?"

"Somewhere in Texas," Orrin said with a helpless shrug.

Yuri's lips flattened in distaste. "I will tell you what I told Orrin. You cannot go. It is what the Saints want of you."

"Of course, it is," Mia said with a derisive snort. "But we can't let Callie and Wyatt be killed."

Orrin merely smiled. "They won't. Wyatt is too good for that. Callie told me they were staying put."

"Which means Wyatt is setting traps," Cullen said.

Mia looked expectantly between the two of them. "What does that mean?"

"It means that no one is sneaking up on Wyatt," Cullen said.

Orrin chuckled wryly. "Wyatt has a knack for such things."

"But against three groups?" Mia pointed out.

Cullen moved his gaze to Orrin. Despite his father's brave face, he was worried, just as Cullen was. Wyatt might be nearly as legendary as Orrin within the military, but everyone had a weakness.

And Cullen knew what Wyatt's was—Callie.

If Wyatt couldn't admit that, then it might very well get them both killed before anyone could help.

"What do you know of Wyatt and Callie having a relationship before he left for college?" Cullen asked.

Orrin vacillated for a long moment. Then he said, "Neither have ever admitted anything to me, but I saw them once. It was dusk, and they were coming back from a ride. They were walking hand-in-hand, leading the horses to the barn when he stopped and kissed her."

"It's what I suspected. It also makes matters much worse."

Orrin blew out a breath as he nodded. "Because Wyatt still cares for her."

"How do you know that?" Mia asked.

His father lifted a dark brow. "Because Wyatt has kept her family away from her all these years."

"Somehow that doesn't surprise me. So what do we do now?" Cullen asked.

Orrin looked at each of them. "We kill the scientist. Tonight."

CHAPTER TWENTY

Wyatt waited almost two hours for Callie to regain consciousness, but she didn't stir. If they remained so close to the barns and activity, it was only a matter of time before they were spotted.

There was a chance the people who owned the ranch didn't work for the Saints, but there was also a good chance they did.

It wasn't something he was willing to risk.

He was trying to figure out how to get away from the ranch when a truck pulled up. An older woman got out, greeting the others. By the way she ordered them around, it was clear she owned the ranch.

But what interested Wyatt was the back of her truck. The tailgate was down, and there was a tarp spread out in the back. It would be perfect cover for them.

He wasted no time gathering Callie into his arms and waiting for the individuals to turn their attention away. It came when they walked into the barn.

Wyatt stood and rubbed his shoulder against the palomino's neck. "Thank you."

Then he hurried to the truck and climbed in the back. He shoved aside the tarp and carefully set Callie down before lying beside her. No sooner had he covered them than he heard voices.

"Want me to get the tarp?" a man said.

"Naw," came the woman's reply, growing closer as she spoke. "I've got an appointment in town that I'm already late for. We'll get it when I get back."

The sound of the tailgate closing drowned out her next comment. Wyatt listened as she walked around the truck and got inside before starting the engine. The vehicle pulled away, and he released a breath.

It was stifling under the tarp, but it kept Callie out of the sun. When the truck hit a hole, she moaned but didn't wake. The longer she remained unconscious, the more worried he became.

As the vehicle picked up speed, he lifted the tarp near his head and looked around the bed. He smiled when he spotted the cooler. Reaching over, he lifted the lid and slipped an arm inside. His fingers brushed ice, then frigid water before finally hitting on a bottle.

He wrapped his fingers around it and lifted. His mouth salivated when he saw it was water. Quickly, he opened it and drained the entire bottle before grabbing another.

This one was for Callie. He put his hand beneath her head and lifted as he placed the bottle against her mouth. Water trickled against her lips before running out of the sides. He then parted her lips with his thumb so that the water could fall into her mouth.

When she swallowed, he wanted to shout with joy. Slowly, he fed her a little of the water at a time until she turned her head away. He was pleased with getting her to drink. Now, if only she would wake.

As the truck bounced along the road, he checked Callie's wounds, careful not to move beneath the tarp too much. So far, his quick stitching job had done the trick.

He laid back and made sure the tarp covered them. His hand brushed hers. Then her fingers curled against his. He closed his eyes, his chest constricting.

Wyatt used the time to relax. He didn't sleep, but he dozed enough to rest his mind and body. With his hand against Callie's and his finger on her pulse, he was able to feel her steady heartbeat.

His eyes snapped open the moment the truck began to slow. When it turned, he pushed aside the tarp to see outside. The trees had given way to open spaces with the occasional building.

Damn. They were headed back to town.

Wyatt turned his head to look at Callie to find her eyes open and looking at him. "Hey," he said.

She smiled sleepily, her eyes drifting shut before opening again as if it took great effort. "Hey."

"Thirsty?"

When she nodded, he brought the water to her lips and helped hold her head up again until she drank her fill. She let out a sigh as her eyes closed again.

It took longer before she managed to lift her lids once more. He smoothed a lock of hair from her lashes. "How do you feel?"

"Horrible," she croaked.

That made him smile. "We're in the back of a truck right now. I'll get us home."

Her lips turned up at the corners at the mention of

home. He didn't stop her when she fell back asleep. It was enough that she had woken long enough to talk to him.

His thoughts shifted to his next move when the truck came to a stop and the engine cut off. The door opened and shut quickly, but he waited several minutes before he sat up enough to peek over the side of the bed.

They were at the edge of town with just enough people that someone could spot them. Wyatt looked for vehicles to steal when he spotted a vacant lot next to them with an older model truck with a *For Sale* sign in the window.

Wyatt slipped over the side of the truck and hurried to the pickup. He tested the handle and found the driver's door locked, but the passenger side wasn't.

He quickly opened the door and hot-wired the vehicle. Then he ran back to Callie. He looked around to make sure no one was watching before he lowered the tailgate and threw the tarp off her. Once she was in his arms, he promptly got her inside the waiting truck.

In minutes, Wyatt had pulled out of the parking lot. As he drove away, a woman walked out of the building to the vehicle that he and Callie had stowed away in.

He couldn't have timed it better.

A quick pass through town brought him to where he'd stashed their bags of food and equipment. He took a few minutes to grab the supplies before pointing the truck north, straight to the Loughman Ranch.

Twenty miles later, he had to stop for gas. He grabbed a baseball cap from his bag that he'd thrown on the floorboard and tugged it low over his face.

He kept his back to the store cameras and his head

down as he filled up the gas tank. Unfortunately, he was paying with cash, so he had to go inside. There was a teenage couple in front of him, so he threw down the two twenties at the register to cover the cost and walked out without saying a word.

Then he was back on the road. He took the cap off since the windows were tinted and glanced at Callie. She was curled in a ball on her left side with her head by his legs.

He combed his fingers through her hair several times before resting his hand on her shoulder. As the miles passed, he thought of the Saints.

They had no idea where he and Callie were at the moment. It took some of the pressure off him, but it wouldn't last long. The Saints no doubt had the ranch under surveillance, but with a property the size of the Loughman's, not all of it could be watched at all times. No doubt they had drones to aid them.

That meant he couldn't just pull up in the driveway if he wanted to keep as much heat off Owen and Natalie as possible. The only way to do that would be to come in from the back of the property. It would mean a long walk to the house, but it would keep the Saints' eyes off them.

Wyatt heard something vibrating in the bags. He pulled over to the side of the road and took out Callie's cell. Though he didn't recognize the number, he answered it.

"Wyatt?" asked a female voice.

He thought he recognized who it was. "Who is this?"

There was some noise as if she handed the phone to someone else. "Wyatt?" Owen asked. "Is that you?"

"Yeah, brother, it's me," he said with a smile.

Owen laughed. "Where are you? We've been calling the two numbers Callie gave us all day."

Wyatt pulled back into traffic. He gripped the steering wheel tightly as he glanced at Callie. "Our plans changed."

"Are both of you all right?" Owen asked after a pause.

"Callie's been shot twice. I've stopped the bleeding, but she's been out most of the day."

"Shit. What happened?"

Wyatt sped down I35 toward Hillsboro. "Orrin sent us a warning that an old enemy of mine was coming after us."

"Who?"

"Ahmadi."

Owen grunted. "He's a nasty one."

"I was willing to stand my ground since we had a good place, but then the Reeds showed up."

"Callie's family? How? Why?"

"The Saints."

"Son of a bitch," Owen ground out.

Wyatt changed lanes to go around a slower car. "That was pretty much my feeling, too. Despite taking days to set up traps for anyone who wanted to attack us, my instincts told me that we had to leave."

"That's when they found you?"

"We left at night and got away without anyone seeing us. We stopped at a town to steal a car, and that's when a group of Saints stumbled upon us. There were only two at first. One came at Callie while another attacked me. By the time I'd taken care of my guy, Callie was gone."

"They took her?"

"She ran. After being shot twice. I found her attacker a short distance away. She put three slugs in him, but by that time, the other eight were after her. I killed the one left behind as guard and followed."

Owen blew out a breath. "You obviously caught up with them."

"I didn't understand why Callie had slowed. They caught up with her, and while she fought and killed three of them, I got my hands on the other four. That's when I saw how badly she was wounded." He paused, choking up thinking about it. "Owen, I don't know how she got as far as she did having lost so much blood."

"She needs to rest. So do you."

"I know. That's why I'm bringing her home."

"Good," Owen stated.

Wyatt looked at the clock on the dashboard. "We'll reach the ranch in about an hour and a half. I'll go to the back of the property."

"I can bring some horses out to you."

"No," he hurried to say. "Don't stray from your routine. I don't want to alert anyone who might be watching. Besides, I'll wait until it gets dark before I bring Callie to the base."

"We'll be waiting."

Wyatt hadn't realized what talking to his brother would do to ease his anxiety. He didn't like having to count on anyone. With his team, they were as cohesive as a single person. Everyone had a job, and everyone did it.

But this was different. This was about being a team, but it was also about family. And right now, he needed his family. It was hard for him to admit, but there it was.

"Wyatt?" Owen called.

He cleared his throat. "I'm here."

"It's going to be fine. Callie is going to be fine."

"Yeah."

"I'll call Cullen and alert him. He and Mia should return to Texas as well."

Wyatt gripped the phone so tightly the plastic crackled in protest. "No."

"But—"

"No. Leave Cullen there. I'm risking you and Natalie enough by returning home. Cullen is doing what he can in Virginia. Besides, the battle will probably be over before he can get to the ranch."

There was a long stretch of silence before Owen said, "A few weeks ago, I'd have said you were just a mean bastard, that you hated your family. But now I see you for who you really are."

"I don't know what the hell you're talking about."

"Sure you do. You worry about all of us. All the time. You know returning to the base means another attack, but you'll do it because you know we can defend the ranch and because you want a safe place for Callie. Yet, you'll go to extremes to keep Cullen away—to protect him."

Wyatt wanted to tell Owen he was full of shit, but the words didn't come. "I'll see you soon," he said and hung up.

CHAPTER TWENTY-ONE

The first sight of Loughman land was a welcome relief to Wyatt. He wanted nothing more than to take Callie straight to the others, but he couldn't since it was still light outside.

He pulled up in between two live oaks and rolled down the windows before he shut off the engine. The chilly breeze ruffled Callie's hair. He touched her face, thankful that she wasn't running a fever.

His gaze slid out the window. It was a long walk to the barn where the base was located beneath one of the buildings. Even if Callie were awake, it would be a painful endeavor since she was so weak.

She wouldn't be the first person he'd carried over long distances, but she was certainly the lightest. Wyatt leaned his head back on the seat and closed his eyes. It was several miles to the house and barns with open pastures in between. That openness would be a prime opportunity for anyone to take a shot at him.

Wyatt would be carrying Callie as well as weapons. It would make it difficult for him to spot an enemy and fire, but it was doable.

He wanted to be out in the brush himself with a rifle and scope. No. He wanted to track down these fuckers and slit their throats with his knife.

The Saints had murdered his aunt and uncle and attempted to kill Owen and Natalie, as well as Cullen and Mia. He wanted them to come for him.

The longer he sat there thinking about it, the angrier he became. It turned into something taciturn, something deadly. There was only one other time he'd ever felt like this—when he'd found his mother.

He'd been too young to realize the emotion running through him then—and too young to do anything about it. The same couldn't be said for now.

For years, he'd trained his mind and body for just such an encounter. He was never more prepared than he was currently.

The minutes moved as slow as honey. He ate and drank, and managed to get more water down Callie's throat. He inspected her wounds then took out his bag of weapons and laid everything on the ground, checking each gun and rifle. He reloaded Callie's Glock and set it aside.

When the sun sank below the tops of the trees, Wyatt began to ready things. He knew exactly the route he'd take to the barn. Knowing Owen, he was most likely already there with his rifle, waiting.

Wyatt strapped three knives to his body—one in each boot, and one at his waist. He put Callie's Glock in the holster strapped to his left leg. Then he chose a rifle. The rest would stay until he could return for it later.

With the weapons in hand, he went for Callie. As soon as she was in his arms, he started toward the fence.

It was one of many he'd have to cross before he reached the barn. His gaze scanned the area, searching the clumps of trees for any movement. He chose to start his trek at dusk because it was difficult to see anything—for him, and for his foes.

He climbed the fence and threw one leg over the top rail. Then he sat and pulled his other leg over. When he jumped to the ground, Callie didn't even stir.

A bat flew over his head chasing mosquitos, while an owl hooted nearby. Every once in a while, he'd look behind him. He knew the Saints were out there, because it was exactly where he'd be.

With the vast area of the ranch, anyone with half a brain would expect the Loughmans to return by any means other than the main entrance. And the Saints weren't stupid. The leaders knew exactly what to do.

The same leaders he'd worked for his entire military career.

He reached another fence and crossed it. The hilly landscape aided in his bid to stay hidden. As did the night. The cloudy sky kept the half-moon hidden for long stretches at a time.

When the creatures of the night suddenly cut off their music, he knew danger was near. The sound of the retort reached him a second before the bullet slammed into his back near his shoulder, sending him pitching forward.

He turned as he fell to keep from landing on Callie. She rolled out of his arms when he hit the ground. Pain radiated out from the wound, making it hard for him to lift his right arm. He gritted his teeth through the pain and turned, raising the rifle.

Wyatt fired off one shot at the approaching attacker, stopping him dead in his tracks. Wyatt then rolled forward and came up on one knee, swinging the gun to the left where he'd heard gunfire.

The bullet landed in the dirt inches from Callie, right where he'd been. Wyatt quickly squeezed off two rounds, striking the man in the chest.

He felt blood, thick and warm, run down his back. His shoulder was on fire. The more he used the arm, the more the blood gushed. When the fingers of his right hand stopped responding, he switched the rifle to his left shoulder and took out another figure running toward him.

Then he was tackled from the side. His attacker kicked his rifle out of his hand while fingers dug into Wyatt's wound, pushing against the ripped flesh.

He bellowed his fury and punched the man in the face with his left fist. His attacker's hold loosened enough that Wyatt was able to knock him off. He rose up over the man and lifted his right arm, but the pain stopped him from delivering another hit.

That gave his foe time to get his hands around Wyatt's throat. With his good arm, he pushed against the man's face while he grabbed for the handle of his knife with his right.

But his fingers wouldn't obey his command. Wyatt looked over at Callie to see someone fast approaching. He fought harder against his attacker, frustration making him roar his fury.

Then—finally!—his fingers grasped the hilt of his blade. He launched it at the man coming for Callie, impaling him. Wyatt's attacker doubled his effort to choke him. With his air being cut off, Wyatt hit his foe with his injured arm and then immediately with his other.

In the few seconds that gave him, Wyatt grabbed for the pistol strapped to his leg. He brought it up to his attacker's head, but the man knocked his arm away, sending the shot into the air.

Dark spots appeared at the edges of Wyatt's vision. He bashed the barrel of the gun against his foe's temple twice. As soon as the man's fingers loosened, Wyatt drew in several gulps of air.

He sat up and turned the gun on the man and got off a shot. The Saint grunted as he climbed to his feet. Wyatt tried to do the same, but he was a second too slow, giving his attacker time to knee him in the chin.

The impact dazed Wyatt for a second as he fell backward to the ground. He turned the gun to the man, firing three shots, two of which hit his foe in the chest.

The Saint kicked the gun out of Wyatt's hand. They were wearing body armor. The sound of other weapons firing warned Wyatt that there were more Saints on the way. He hoped none of the bullets had hit Callie, but he didn't have time to look.

As he fought the Saint from his back, Wyatt managed to roll the man over and get off several good hits. When his foe reached for his gun, Wyatt hastily knocked it out of his hand and punched him in the throat.

While the Saint gagged and struggled to breathe, Wyatt dove for the pistol. He jerked around when a gun fired.

The Saint kneeled over him with a knife in his hand before he pitched forward, dead from a bullet to his neck. Wyatt looked past him to find Callie on her side with her gun in hand. Her head dropped to the ground as her eyes closed. He crawled to her, grabbing weapons as he did, but she was already unconscious again.

It was the quiet that alerted Wyatt. He reached for his rifle and spun around to see a lone man walking toward him with arms raised.

"Stop," Wyatt demanded.

"I'd rather not."

Wyatt frowned, recognizing the voice. He stood. "Maks?"

"Yeah."

"What are you doing here?" Wyatt asked as Maks approached.

Maks shrugged one shoulder and adjusted his rifle. "I was in the area."

"Bullshit."

"I knew the Saints would be waiting for you, just as I knew that you or your brothers would return."

Wyatt snorted as he turned back to Callie. "I'm glad you're here."

"You're bleeding."

"I'm fine," Wyatt said and knelt beside Callie. He hid his wince as he picked her up and stood. Then he began walking as Maks fell into step beside him. "How long have you been here?"

"Ever since I left Virginia."

"I suppose you scouted the entire ranch?"

Maks nodded. "Those were the only Saints watching tonight. More will come at noon to relieve them."

"Then we need to be here to kill them."

"After you see to that wound," Maks stated. "What happened to her?"

Wyatt gazed down at Callie, wishing her blue eyes were looking back at him. "The Saints."

"The fact that both of you are still alive attests to your skills. The Saints only recruit the best."

"Are you saying they came for you?"

Maks smiled as he cut Wyatt a look. "They might have shown interest, and I might've taken an undercover job in Russia."

"The Saints are there, too."

"I let them know I wasn't interested."

"This was while you were on my team?"

Maks glanced at him and nodded. "I wanted no part of them."

Wyatt glanced sideways at him. "You could be lying."

"I could be, but if I was, I'd have already killed you."

When they reached a fence, Wyatt let Maks go over first before handing him Callie. Once Wyatt jumped over, he reached for Callie.

"Let me carry her awhile," Maks said.

Wyatt shook his head. "I've got her."

They repeated the process another six times until the lights from the house came into view. Wyatt actually felt joy at seeing it.

How Callie would love to rub that in his face. All those years of refusing to return home, and now it was the only place he wanted to be.

Wyatt led the way through the gates to the barn that had the base beneath it. The back of the building was open. A moment later, Owen came striding out.

His smile faded when he saw Wyatt carrying Callie. He ran to Wyatt and tried to take her, but Wyatt kept walking. He saw Owen and Maks exchange a look.

"Maks, meet my middle brother, Owen," Wyatt said. "Owen, Maks."

The two shook hands as they walked inside the barn to the stairs that led to the base.

"You're the same Maks who helped Cullen and Mia," Owen said. "Thank you for that."

"Just doing my job," Maks replied.

Wyatt hid his pain as he maneuvered down the narrow steps with Callie. Natalie was standing near the back entrance to the bunks. Her face fell when she saw Callie.

"I'll get the supplies," Owen said and hurried off.

Wyatt knelt next to a bunk and set Callie down. He lifted her shirt to exam the wound and saw fresh blood staining the white bandages.

Wyatt dropped his forehead onto Callie's hip. Blood trickled down his arm to his fingers to drip onto the floor. He lifted his head to Natalie and said, "She needs fluids."

"There's so much blood," Natalie said. "I thought her wounds were stitched."

Owen stopped beside him. "That blood isn't Callie's. It's Wyatt's."

CHAPTER TWENTY-TWO

Andrew Smith held the cell phone to his ear, waiting for an answer as he stood outside the room where Konrad Jankovic currently worked.

"Well?" he asked impatiently.

There was a pause before one of his subordinates replied, "I'm sorry, sir, but I can't reach anyone we have watching the Loughman Ranch."

"Send out another team immediately," he ordered.

"Sir?"

"One of the Loughmans has returned and killed everyone, you idiot," Andrew stated before ending the call.

He spun to look at the closed door to what was once the kitchen. Everything Jankovic needed to make another batch of Ragnarok had been brought in days ago, but the scientist was dragging his feet.

Andrew busted through the door to find Konrad standing by the kitchen sink, staring out the window. "What are you doing?"

"I want to walk outside," Jankovic said in his thick Russian accent.

"That's not going to happen until you make the bio-weapon. It was our agreement before we helped you defect."

Konrad looked at him with his green eyes and shrugged. "I have changed my mind. We need to rene-gotiate, yes?"

"No."

The scientist turned to face him, leaning back against the sink. "You need what I have in my brain. I do not think you will fight me on what I want."

Andrew took a deep breath and slowly released it as he put his cell phone in his front pant's pocket and walked toward Jankovic. "While it's true we've gone to a great deal of trouble to acquire your . . . skills, don't mistake thinking you have control."

He didn't stop until he was a foot away from the Russian. "I have the control. Me. It'll be quicker for you to make the bioweapon of your own accord, and you'll be richer—and freer—because of it. But . . . if you make me hurt you, you'll be working with only one arm. I'll take away the money promised as well as your freedom."

"Y-y-you cannot do that."

"Try me," Andrew dared him.

Jankovic visibly swallowed before he scooted to the side and hurried to the island where all his equipment was set up. Andrew watched him until he was sure the scientist was actually working.

He walked from the kitchen and motioned one of the guards to him. "I want someone with him while he's working, and I want him working every day from now on. Limited breaks. An hour for meals."

"Yes, sir," the guard said and pointed to two men who strode into the kitchen.

At least Andrew didn't have to worry about the house being discovered. With his organization keeping the Loughmans on the run, they were more concerned about their own lives than anyone else's.

Too bad that would be their downfall.

Andrew checked the time, realizing that he was going to be late for his dinner reservation. He took out his cell to call and cancel. He was nearly to the door when the sound of breaking glass sounded on all four sides of the house. Spinning around, he raced toward the kitchen and Jankovic as gunfire erupted.

He slammed open the door and slid to a halt when he saw Orrin Loughman standing over Jankovic who had a single bullet wound to the center of his head. Andrew had but a second to duck out of the room as the eldest Loughman opened fire.

There were shouts, screams of pain, and gunfire all around him. Andrew plastered himself against the wall outside the kitchen. He drew his gun and turned to shoot into the room. When there was no return fire, he peeked around the corner, but Orrin was gone.

Andrew straightened and walked into the kitchen to stare at the dead bodies of his men and Jankovic. Had he remained a moment longer, he'd likely be dead with the others. How had Orrin found him? And though Andrew guessed it was Yuri with Loughman, who else had joined them?

"Sir?" came a voice behind him.

He closed his eyes and sighed. "Yes?"

"We lost seven men."

"Make that nine," Andrew said as he opened his eyes and turned to the guard. "How did they get in?"

The guard shook his head. "I don't know yet, but I'm going to look into it. Shall we go after them?"

"They're already gone. Get this mess cleaned up."

"Yes, sir."

Andrew stalked out of the house. Once outside in the night, he walked to the street and looked up and down it. "I know you're out there, Orrin. You miserable son of a bitch. I should've put you down a long time ago. You've been nothing but trouble for me."

Orrin stood hidden behind the Suburban as he stared at the man in the black trench coat across the street. Whoever he was, he knew Orrin. The flare of recognition in his eyes in the kitchen had been obvious.

What wasn't obvious was how? Did the man know him because the Saints were after him? Or was it something from Orrin's past? If only Orrin could place him, he might have some answers. There was a memory there, just out of reach that might answer so many questions.

"Dad."

He held up his hand, telling Cullen to wait. Orrin remained until the man turned and got into a car that drove off. Only then did Orrin face the others.

Yuri was smiling as he held his left arm that had been shot. "We did it."

Mia grinned at all of them. "Damn, but that felt good. It was time we put a hurt on the Saints. I want to do it again."

"Slow down there," Cullen said as he gave her a quick kiss.

Orrin started walking to Cullen's SUV that was parked down the street. "We got lucky. They weren't expecting us. We won't get that chance again."

"But we killed Jankovic," Yuri said.

"That's a win for sure." One Orrin knew they desperately needed.

Cullen stepped in front of Orrin, halting everyone. "One thing you haven't told us is what Ragnarok does."

Yuri looked to the ground, but Orrin met his son's gaze. "Once released into the air, it will sterilize women."

"Are you telling me that I'd never be able to have children?" Mia asked, her face slack with shock.

Orrin nodded. "That's exactly what I'm saying."

"How far of a reach does the weapon have?" Cullen asked.

Yuri swallowed and looked up at Cullen. "I never discovered, but I do know the Saints planned to release Ragnarok over certain areas, so it must be contained to a particular vicinity."

Orrin saw the impact the news had on Cullen and Mia. It was obvious the two were in love, which pleased him greatly. The pair was perfect for each other, and their love would only strengthen them.

Two of his sons had found love. Now, if only Wyatt could give in to his feelings for Callie.

"After this, the Saints will come for us with all they have," Orrin said. "Not only do we have Jankovic's formula, but we have Ragnarok. The Saints want this badly in order to cut down the Earth's population and take over."

Mia made a noise in the back of her throat. "For what?"

"Food? Climate? Money? Who knows?" Orrin said. "It doesn't matter why. It just matters that we stop them."

Yuri slapped Orrin on the back with his meaty hand. "I will not rest until the Saints are stopped."

Cullen looked at Mia before he said, "Count us in. They started all of this."

"So, let's finish it," Mia added.

Yuri asked, "What is next?"

"Hewett," Orrin stated.

Cullen nodded in agreement. "I'll be happy to get information out of him."

The buzz of a phone drew everyone's attention. Yuri pulled the cell phone out of his pocket and frowned when he looked at the number. "*Da*?" he answered.

Orrin watched as Yuri's face went slack and his gaze darted straight to him. Orrin knew then that something had happened to either Owen or Wyatt.

"*Spasibo*, thank you," Yuri said before ending the call.

Orrin squared his shoulders. "Just spit it out."

"That was Maks," Yuri said. He looked at Cullen and Mia. "He is the one who remained behind at the warehouse to help you two."

"Yuri," Orrin urged.

His old friend swung his blue gaze back to him. "It seems Wyatt and Callie decided to return to the ranch. On the way, some Saints stumbled across them. Callie was shot twice, but Wyatt patched her up."

"Thank God," Mia said.

Orrin waited because he knew Yuri hadn't finished yet.

Yuri wiped his good hand down his face. "When the two reached your ranch, more Saints were waiting."

"Is my brother alive?" Cullen demanded.

"He was shot in the back of the shoulder and lost a lot of blood, but he is," Yuri replied.

Orrin dropped his chin to his chest. "How bad is the injury?"

"Maks said Owen is tending to it now."

Cullen asked, "What was Maks doing there?"

Yuri shrugged and said, "You would have to ask him."

"Oh, we will," Mia stated.

Orrin lifted his head and continued walking to the SUV. His mind was stuck on a loop of knowing that both Callie and Wyatt were injured. It wasn't the first time Wyatt had been wounded, but this was the first time Orrin knew immediately after it had happened.

At least his son was somewhere with others to help care for him. And Callie.

The Saints would know by now that two Loughmans were at the ranch. How long before they attacked? Whatever time they had, it wasn't nearly enough.

"What are you thinking?" Cullen asked as he came up beside him.

Orrin glanced his way. "That we should return home."

"You'll give them what they want," Mia pointed out. "All of you in one place."

"She is right," Yuri said.

Orrin looked at Cullen. "What do you think?"

"I think my brothers are going to need us, but the Saints will expect us to head there."

Orrin smiled as they reached the vehicle because he realized what Cullen was thinking. "What do you suggest then?"

Cullen's lips twisted as he shrugged. "Oh, I don't know. Perhaps a visit to Hewett."

"Yes," Mia said and opened the back driver's side door to climb into the SUV.

Yuri nodded, smiling as he got into the back passenger side.

Orrin met Cullen's hazel eyes. This was what he'd always wanted—to work with his sons. He hated how it had come about, but he was going to enjoy every minute he had.

The past would still need to be discussed, but for now, he had his youngest with him. He would bask in every second of it while they took down as many Saints as they could.

"How long do you think we have until the Saints attack the ranch?" Yuri asked once they were on the road.

Cullen's lips flattened. "A day. Two at the most."

"Every second we're here will mean added time on the way to Texas," Orrin said. "But Cullen's right. We need to do damage while we can."

Mia said, "I can get us there in half the time. Provided you can find me something to fly."

Orrin smiled as he turned to look at her. "Then we'll find you something to fly."

"I think I know someone who can help," Yuri said.

CHAPTER TWENTY-THREE

"Dammit, Wyatt, stay still," grumbled a male voice.

Callie tried to open her eyes, but the harsh light blinded her. Pain shot through her, and all she wanted to do was go back to the blessed darkness and escape it.

But there was Wyatt.

"Just pull the fucking thing out," Wyatt snapped.

Pull what out? Callie heard the agony in his voice.

"Perhaps I should knock your ass out. It'd make my life easier."

Owen. That was Owen's voice. So, they'd made it to the ranch. She was relieved. Though she didn't know how they had gotten there. The day was a blur of pain and Wyatt forcing water down her throat.

Then the attack. It was the sound of bullets that had jarred her back to consciousness. When she'd come to and found Wyatt in a struggle with another man, she'd tried to call out a warning. Then she'd seen the pistol.

Grabbing it and lifting the weapon to shoot had cost her a great deal of energy. She'd tried to remain awake to talk to Wyatt afterward, but her body hadn't listened.

"If you don't take it out now, I'm going to punch you," Wyatt complained.

Owen ground out between clenched teeth, "Then be still."

Callie turned her head in the direction of their voices. She cracked open her eyes to see Wyatt sitting backward on a chair with Owen peering closely at something on his back.

"You should tend to Callie first," Wyatt said.

Owen shook his head. "Her bleeding is controlled. Yours isn't."

"I don't care about mi—" Wyatt began.

She licked her lips and said, "Wyatt."

It came out as more of a whisper than a shout, but it must have been loud enough because, suddenly, his gold eyes were focused on her. She saw cuts and bruises from the fights all over his face and hands, but he looked gorgeous to her.

"Hey, Callie," Natalie said as she came to sit on the edge of the cot. "How are you feeling?"

Like shit, but she didn't say it. Callie kept her gaze on Wyatt. His hands were fisted, and a muscle jumped in his temple. He was hurting. She wanted to help him, to ease him.

"Callie?" Natalie repeated.

She finally nodded, hoping that would be enough for Nat because talking was too much trouble.

"Son of a bitch!" Owen bellowed as he straightened and wiped the back of his arm across his brow.

Another man appeared. He was in black tactical gear and had the look of military about him. But that was all

Callie noticed because she refused to look away from Wyatt.

The new guest stood at Wyatt's head and put his hands on Wyatt's shoulders, pushing down at the same time Owen bent and returned to his work. There were tense seconds of silence. Callie watched sweat roll down the side of Wyatt's face, and his knuckles go white, as he held her gaze.

But he didn't move.

Finally, Owen held up the long tweezers and showed off the bullet "It's out."

"Good," Wyatt snapped. "Now, get it stitched and bandage it."

"You should rest," the guest said.

In response, Wyatt shrugged off the man's hold. Then he gave her a nod. It was his small way of letting her know he was all right. Callie gave him a smile in return.

As soon as the stitching was done and a bandage in place, Wyatt rose and walked to her. Natalie quickly got out of the way. To Callie's surprise, he took her hand. She hadn't even realized she held it out to him, but the instant his warm fingers wrapped around hers, she was able to breathe easier.

"You finally decided to wake?" he asked, a teasing glint in his eyes.

Since when was Wyatt playful? Never. But she liked it—and the crooked smile that accompanied his words. "I thought you could use the challenge."

"I was up for it." His smile faded, replaced by a small frown. "Don't ever do that to me again."

"I won't."

He squeezed her hand and cleared his throat before raking a hand through his hair and glancing over his shoulder. "Callie, I'd like you to meet Maks. He helped us against the Saints."

"Hi, Maks," she said, smiling up at him.

He gave a tilt of his head. "Ma'am." Then Maks looked at Wyatt. "I'm going to take a look around outside."

After he departed, Owen came to the other side of the cot while wiping his freshly washed hands on a towel. "I can check your injuries now."

"I'll do it," Wyatt said.

Owen shook his head at his brother in frustration. "It's nice to see you, Callie. Let me know if you get tired of his bossy ass."

Natalie gave a wave before following Owen out of the room, leaving Callie alone with Wyatt. Her gaze lifted to his to find him staring at her.

"You scared me."

His admission surprised her. "I didn't think anything frightened you."

"You did."

"So you do feel things."

"I feel everything."

She wasn't sure what to think of that confession, especially given what she knew of him. She'd been sure nothing got past the thick walls around his heart. Had she been wrong all these years?

He swallowed and glanced at their joined hands. "I should change your bandages and look at the wounds. I did a hasty job of stitching you up. I'm afraid you'll have some ugly scars."

"I'm alive. Scars will be a reminder of what we fought—and won."

She wished she knew what he was thinking. She couldn't read those gold eyes as he stared at her for a long, silent minute. Then he rose and turned to gather supplies.

That's when she got her first good look at his back. There was still dried blood on his skin and arm and a large, white bandage over his right shoulder blade.

He didn't bother with a shirt as he returned to her and spread out clean bandages and tape. It wasn't until he pulled down the blanket that she realized her clothes were gone and she was in nothing but her bra and panties.

Then she noticed the bag hanging on the other side of her, feeding her saline to battle her dehydration.

She watched as Wyatt gently peeled back the bandage on her right side and began to clean it before inspecting the wound. His touch was soft, tender. Just as he'd been when they made love.

"What are you thinking that has you looking at me so?" he queried.

She blinked and quickly looked away at having been caught. "How was I looking at you?"

"As if you don't know me."

"I don't."

His hands paused as he met her gaze. "You do."

"Do I? I thought I did once. You proved I didn't."

"You know me," he insisted.

She mulled his words over for a moment. "I think I've only known a part of you. Have you ever let anyone in to know your deepest secrets?"

Wyatt was silent for a long time as he finished bandaging her. Then he said, "Yes."

The jealousy and resentment that filled her were swift and instantaneous. Who was this woman who had gotten inside his heart when she couldn't? Callie wanted to meet her so she could find out what it took.

"It was you."

His words knocked the breath from her more forcefully than if she'd been kicked by a horse. She slowly lifted her gaze to him and shook her head.

Their conversation was halted when Owen called out to them before he entered the back room. She turned her head away when Wyatt moved around to her other side to check her neck.

Owen whistled as he came to stand beside the cot and saw the wound. "That one could've killed you, Callie."

"Yeah," she mumbled.

Wyatt's fingers grazed her skin, sending chills over her. "She's too quick for that."

Callie saw Owen's confused looked as he frowned at Wyatt. She was just as puzzled by Wyatt's odd behavior. The curt, angry Wyatt seemed to have been shut away in a closet.

But she'd seen this side of him before. It was always pleasant while it lasted, but it never stayed around long. She knew full well how much it hurt when his brusque nature returned, and how he could cut someone in half with just a look.

She winced when he pressed too hard on her wound.

"I'm sorry," he whispered.

It wasn't his words that caused her stomach to clench.

It was the way he caressed down her neck. It was a lover's touch, one that struck her right to her soul.

Owen scratched the side of his nose as he looked between the two of them. "I thought you both should know that more Saints are arriving. Those cameras you had us install have done wonders, Callie."

"I'm glad," she said.

Wyatt asked, "How many Saints?"

"Twenty," Owen replied.

"Four for each of us," Callie said as she tried to rise.

But Wyatt kept her in place. He gave her a stern look. "You're not doing anything but staying in bed and resting."

"I can still shoot. If you forget, I saved your ass out there," she argued.

"I've not forgotten. But I was also the one who carried you around the entire day because you were unconscious."

Owen twisted his lips in regret before he said, "Wyatt's right. You should remain here."

It was the last thing she wanted to do. Yet she didn't have the strength to shove off Wyatt's hand. Which meant she would be confined to the bed for a little while longer.

"Are they making any approach to us?" Wyatt asked.

Owen shook his head. "Not yet. It's only a matter of time though."

"Everyone needs to get to the house," Callie said. "If they see any of you remain in the barn, they're going to guess the base is here."

Wyatt sat back as he finished with the dressing. "I

hate to say it, but she's right. This base has to remain secret because of Ragnarok."

"That damn bioweapon," Owen said angrily. "I want to destroy it."

They all did, but until they learned how to find a cure for whatever it did, they had to keep it—and make sure it stayed out of the hands of the Saints.

No small order.

Callie liked that Wyatt remained near her. She listened as he and Owen talked about the various ways they could battle the Saints from the house—a residence that was still torn up from the last time they'd defended it.

She didn't pull away when Wyatt's fingers touched her arm as if by accident. But he didn't move away. Then his hand shifted closer to hers so gradually that she thought it was her imagination until their fingers made contact.

Her gaze jerked to him, but Wyatt's focus was on Owen. Maybe he didn't know what he was doing. Owen certainly hadn't noticed.

Or maybe it was all in her head.

She felt her eyes growing heavy, but she fought against it. There was so much she'd missed while unconscious. She didn't want to miss out on any more.

"Don't fight it," Wyatt's voice whispered in her ear.

When had her eyes closed? She forced them open to find that Owen was gone. Wyatt's hand was stroking her hair in a soothing motion that had her drifting off to sleep once more.

Even as she entered the dream world, she felt his lips on her forehead.

CHAPTER TWENTY-FOUR

Wyatt watched Callie for a few more minutes before he rose and left her to sleep. When he walked into the main area of the base, Owen was waiting for him.

He walked past his brother without pausing. There was no need. Owen wanted to talk about Callie, and Wyatt didn't. It should be the end of it. Except that was never the case with Owen.

"Walking away won't stop my questions," Owen said.

Wyatt made his way to a locker of tactical gear. He grabbed fresh clothes and turned on his heel toward the bathroom.

"Go take your shower," Owen called. "I'll be waiting. Wait. Wyatt, your bandage."

The bandage could be replaced. He needed a shower. Wyatt closed the door and turned on the water. Steam began to fill the room as he hurriedly took off his clothes coated with blood and dirt. Once beneath the spray, he closed his eyes and let the weight he'd been carrying fall from his shoulders.

Callie was now getting the treatment she needed. He'd feel better if she was at a hospital, but he didn't trust anyone there. Thank God his father had stocked the base with everything needed for bullet and knife wounds.

All he could do now was pray that Callie didn't have internal bleeding.

He pulled off the bandage and scrubbed the grime of the past hours from his body. The pull of his injury reminded him that he'd be going into battle less than healthy. If he showed the Saints any hint of weakness, they would take advantage of it—just as he would if the roles were reversed.

Once he was finished washing up, he shut off the shower and dried off. He put on all the clothes except the shirt. When he opened the door, Owen was there, holding a fresh bandage in his hand.

Wyatt sighed and turned his back to his brother so the bandage could be applied.

Owen left his hand over the bandage, applying just enough pressure to cause discomfort. "I saw the way you looked at Callie."

He stepped away from Owen and put on his shirt, facing his brother. His gaze landed on Owen, his expression full of annoyance. "I thought you had a question, not a statement."

"I could tell something happened between the two of you years ago. Am I wrong?"

Wyatt glanced away. "No."

"What happened?"

"She got too close."

Owen's jaw went slack. "Are you saying you fell in love with her?"

"No," he stated. No one could know how deeply he'd

fallen for Callie. If they did, they would hound him relentlessly.

He wanted to stay with Callie, to hold her in his arms every day for the rest of his life, but it wasn't part of his destiny. The course for him had been set the day his mother had been murdered.

There was no room in his life for softness—or for anyone that could destroy him if taken away violently as his mother had been.

"You came close," Owen said. "Admit it."

Wyatt walked around him to the steps up into the barn. "Let it go."

"Why, after what I saw? There is something between you. I always said there was a thin line between love and hate." Owen chuckled, following.

Wyatt met Maks's gaze as he walked toward his friend. He hoped that Owen would stop with his inane talk with Maks there. Wyatt should've known better.

"There's some serious chemistry between you two," Owen said.

Maks then added, "He wouldn't let me carry Callie despite his wound. Walked the entire way here, bleeding with her in his arms."

Owen raised a brow as his gaze shifted to him. Wyatt shook his head at both men and tried to ignore them as he turned to look out the door. If he didn't answer, maybe they would give up.

"That says a lot, brother," Owen stated.

Maks nodded. "Mmmhmm. It sure does."

"I think he cares more than he wants to admit."

"Definitely. He nearly took my head off when I offered to carry her."

Wyatt had heard enough. He faced them as he fought to keep his voice even so they wouldn't know how much their words had riled him. "She was my responsibility. I'd gotten her this far, I wanted to bring her all the way in."

"It's more than that," Maks said, all of the teasing gone from his voice.

Owen crossed his arms over his chest, serious, as well. "Why can't you just admit it?"

"Let it go. For everyone's sake, especially Callie's, let it go." Wyatt walked away from them to the paddock where some horses were being kept. He slowly climbed over the fence and walked to one of them.

Being forced back to the ranch reminded him of his love of horses. He held out his hand and waited for one of the animals to come to him.

A paint with a black and white coat was the first to approach him. The paints had always been his mother's favorites, and he was happy to see that Orrin still kept some around. He rubbed the filly's neck, scratching behind her ears while she stood patiently.

Horses had always soothed him. Whenever he'd been angry about something, Orrin would send him to the barn to muck out the stalls, feed the horses, or brush them. And by the time Wyatt was finished, whatever problem plagued him was gone. After that, he began to go to the horses on his own.

Except the problem he had now couldn't be fixed. It had been with him for years. Fifteen lonely years, dreaming of a woman he could never have.

He remained with the horses, petting them, as his mind drifted through the various ways the Saints might attack. He opened the gate and let the horses out into the pasture instead of bringing them to their stalls.

Wyatt wasn't surprised when Maks joined him. The CIA operative stood silently beside him for several minutes as they watched the horses snatch bites of grass as they walked away.

"I couldn't imagine returning home," Maks said.

Wyatt blew out a breath and closed the gate. "I never thought I would."

"But here you are. Defending it."

Wyatt turned slowly, taking in all the buildings while memories of his youth stole through his mind. "That I am."

"Even if we win this battle, the war with the Saints will continue."

"I know." It was all Wyatt had been thinking about.

"That means time away from your Delta team."

He turned his head to Maks. "What are you getting at?"

"That I can see why you got mixed up with Callie."

He walked out of the paddock and across the yard to the large oak tree on a hill to better look out over the land. If he thought Maks was done with him, he was wrong.

Maks scratched his cheek and adjusted the rifle he carried. "I came from a shit hole that I never want to see again, but this place is beautiful."

"There's no denying its beauty, but what happened here keeps me away."

"Your mother."

Wyatt drew in a deep breath and slowly released it. His mother. Yes, it was her murder that had changed him from a boy to a man in one heartbeat. That was the day he learned life didn't give a shit about anyone or anything. That bad things happened for no reason.

That it didn't matter how good of a person you were, destiny or fate or whoever the fuck it was, happily flipped you off, laughing as you fought to claw your way out of the grief that dragged you into the darkest parts of yourself.

Wyatt had been giving fate the finger ever since.

And now look where he was. At the last place he ever thought to be, fighting alongside brothers he didn't think to meet again, looking for a father he never wanted to see, and making love to a woman who shouldn't give him the time of day.

Fate was having the last laugh now.

"Do you think it was the Saints or someone else who sent you three back here?" Maks asked.

Wyatt leaned a shoulder against the tree. "I've long since decided it wasn't the Saints. They would know it was better to keep the Loughmans apart."

"True, but who else would find your father?" Maks pointed out. "They need Ragnarok."

"So you think it *was* the Saints?"

Maks nodded slowly. "I suspect they're regretting their decision now."

"They won't try to send us back to our teams."

"They'll kill you."

Wyatt glanced back at the house where Owen and Natalie were. "They'll have a hard time doing it."

"It won't change the outcome."

He looked at Maks. "What's your point?"

"Your brothers, while living dangerous lives, are

nothing like us. They can have a relationship. You and I know that to bring anyone into our Hell is reckless and unwise."

Wyatt swallowed and lowered his gaze to the ground.

"We go out on our missions not expecting to come back," Maks continued. "We hunt the worst of the corrupted degenerates, the ones who take lives as easily as breath."

"We're not much different with the killing we do," Wyatt said.

"No. We aren't."

Everything Maks said reinforced Wyatt's decision to leave Callie all those years ago. But it didn't make what he currently felt any easier.

Maks cracked his knuckles and shifted his weight onto one side. "If I were in your place, I think I'd take as much time as I could with her. For however long I got, I'd pretend and live in that reality. But I wouldn't bring her into my world."

"You get to pretend that all the time in your undercover work."

Maks shrugged and shot him a quick smile. "I've become so many men that I don't know who I am anymore."

"Is that why you're here?"

"Partly."

Wyatt lifted a brow as he watched Maks. "And the other part?"

"I hate bullies, and that's exactly what the Saints are. Someone needs to put them in their place. I figured I'd help out."

"Well, I'm glad you did."

"Are you?"

That made Wyatt frown. "What does that mean?"

"If you had it your way, you'd be fighting the Saints alone."

"So?"

"Your feelings are all twisted around inside you, Wyatt. About Callie, about your father, about returning home. Even about your brothers. You need to get it sorted."

Wyatt asked, "Is that what you've done?"

"Fuck, no. I'm telling you not to make the same mistakes I have. You've got a good, strong family. Hang onto them." Maks started to turn away, then stopped, looking back at Wyatt. "You hide your feelings about Callie very well, but you let that mask you wear slip just enough when I found you earlier. If you haven't already fallen in love with her, then cut all ties now."

Wyatt remained silent, refusing to admit to anything.

Maks's lips compressed briefly. "If you have fallen for her, then you have my sympathies because you'll have to make a decision soon. And I think it's one you've made before."

He waited until Maks was gone before he briefly closed his eyes. Maks made it all sound so easy. It was just the opposite. How could he hang onto a family he hadn't been a part of for years?

They were working together now because they didn't have a choice, but would they accept him after? Did he even want to be included again?

The one thing Maks was right about—he was all twisted inside. Especially when it came to Callie.

CHAPTER TWENTY-FIVE

Callie had no idea what time it was when she woke again. The base was quiet, and she knew without looking that she was alone.

She reached over and pulled out the needle in her arm before attempting to sit up. The pain was severe, but she wasn't going to let it stop her. When she finally managed to get upright, she winced at the pull on her side.

"What are you doing?"

Her head whipped around to find Wyatt in the doorway. "Sitting up, in case you couldn't tell."

"Not funny," he said as he strode into the room. "Lie back down."

"No. You need my help."

"Rest until that time comes."

He lowered her back onto the bed. As soon as she was stretched out, the pain began to dull. She was much weaker than she'd thought.

"You might try listening to me every now and again. I'm actually right sometimes," he said.

She gave him a flat look. "Sometimes."

"You love busting balls, don't you?"

"Just yours."

She looked into his eyes as he sat on the cot next to her and ran a hand through his dark hair. His face was impassive, the façade in place that prevented anyone from seeing what he was thinking—or feeling.

"We're screwed, aren't we?" she asked.

He gave a single shake of his head. "No."

"The Saints will outnumber us."

"That doesn't guarantee their win."

She turned her head on the pillow toward him. "You were right, you know. I do spend most of my time in this base while the others are out on missions."

"That doesn't make your role any less critical."

A compliment from Wyatt? Was the world coming to an end? "Maybe not, but I was a hindrance out in the field."

"Not with me, you weren't. I sparred with you. I know how well you've been trained. I'll give Orrin that, he made sure you'd be prepared if anything did happen."

She licked her lips and pulled the covers up to her chin. "Perhaps, but none of my training can equal what you do."

"You held your own—wounded—against seven Saints. That's damn impressive in anyone's book."

"I just wanted to stay alive." And to find him, but she didn't say that.

He leaned forward so that his forearms rested on his knees. "You think you failed because you got injured?" he asked in shock.

"You didn't get wounded. I should've known what my attacker would do, but I was too slow."

Wyatt dropped his head down for a moment. "Part of training is learning in just those situations. You survived it and killed the man attempting to end your life. Now you know what to do next time."

"So you don't think I belong in the base?"

"I was raised that a man protects those around him. I'll always look out for you, and yes, I'd keep you down here if it were my choice. But you've also shown how competent you are."

She couldn't help but smile even as her lids grew heavy.

"What are you grinning about?" Wyatt asked.

"You gave me two compliments in a span of five minutes. I think I might swoon."

He made a sound in the back of his throat. "You'd never faint. You have too much steel in your backbone."

Was that another compliment? What was wrong with him? Why was he being so nice? Callie was instantly on guard.

As if sensing her change, Wyatt sat up straight. "We're going to need you. I'd prefer to leave you as you are, but I'm prepared to tie your bony ass down to that cot to ensure that you stay in bed."

"You just said you needed me," she replied in confusion.

"We will. Just as soon as we get these assholes off the property. You're the only one who can work magic on the computer. To attack the Saints, we have to use brute force and brains. You're the brains."

She stared at him for several seconds. There was no doubt that he would tie her down. "Fine, but you will give me a gun. I won't be defenseless."

"The door to the base will be closed. No one is getting in here."

She simply stared at him until Wyatt blew out a breath and handed over her Glock. She tucked it under the blanket.

He was halfway out of the room when she said, "Thank you . . . for everything."

"You're welcome," he replied, keeping his back to her.

"You could've left me."

He gave her a shuttered look over his shoulder. "Is that what kind of man you think I am?"

"No."

"It must be for you to say something like that."

She held his gaze, refusing to look away. "I was merely stating a point. Some men would've left me to get away from the Saints."

"I'm not some men."

"I know."

He turned to face her once more. There was a hard edge to his words when he asked, "Do you really?"

"I think I know you better than anyone here."

His gold eyes darted away for a second.

She fisted her hand around her gun beneath the blanket. "You hate that, don't you?"

"There are many things about this world I hate, Callie, but that isn't one of them."

She could no longer look him in the face. All those years she had thought horrible things about him, and yet he had gone above and beyond to get her back home.

He walked to her slowly as he said, "Do you know one of the things I've always liked about you?"

"What?" she asked breathlessly.

"You always tell me the truth. You don't hold anything back."

Her eyes lifted to his. "Most of the time, I did it because you pissed me off."

"I know. While others keep away from me, you put yourself in my way. You challenge me and force me to see things I don't want to."

"Again," she said, swallowing. "Because you pissed me off."

He rubbed a hand along the back of his neck. "My whole life people have been afraid of me. But not you. Never you."

"You never gave me reason to be afraid."

There was a ghost of a smile on his lips when he turned on his heel and walked away. Long after he was gone, she stared at the doorway.

Wyatt was different. She didn't know what it was exactly, but something had changed. The obvious answer was them making love, but she refused to be that foolish and believe she had anything to do with it.

Most likely, it was the force of the Saints and how well connected they were. Wyatt was now learning that this wouldn't be a quick battle, but a long war.

She hated the sadness that filled her because she wanted to be the reason he'd changed. She wanted him to have feelings for her other than responsibility.

Callie wiped at the tear that escaped. The only person she could blame was herself because she'd given in. She'd wanted to feel alive on what she thought was the last night of her life. Now, she had to deal with the fallout.

They were alive—barely. And the Saints were coming for them again. She wouldn't repeat her mistake, even though she wanted him. Once would have to be enough.

If she hadn't turned to him that night, Wyatt wouldn't have done anything. They would've remained just as they were. Instead of tangled in this web of passion and unease.

Why couldn't she have been stronger?

But she knew the answer. Wyatt. She'd always had a weakness for him, and there had been a perfect excuse to give in.

Recognizing her problem didn't solve it, however. At this rate, she was bound to repeat the same blunder again and again. Worse, her body heated at the thought. She *wanted* that mistake, hungered for it.

If only Wyatt would be an ass again.

She snorted because not even that could cause her body to reject him. He'd walked back into her life without so much as a hello and began ordering her around.

Her years working at Whitehorse had prepared her for just such an encounter, and she didn't hesitate to put Wyatt back in his place.

Except the stubborn ass didn't stay there.

Because he was a natural-born leader, a man who always took charge and was ready to walk into a deadly situation without hesitation.

Damn him. Damn him, damn him.

She wished she hated him. She wished she felt nothing for him. But that's all it was, wishful thinking. The truth was that she saw that he was a good man who carried the weight of the world on his shoulders.

Funny how being around him recently had shown her that the cold indifference he projected was a way for him to protect himself. If only she'd have seen that when she was younger. If only . . .

All the Loughmans suffered after Melanie's death—but the worst was Wyatt because he'd been the one to find her and stay with her until the authorities came.

The part of Callie that always rose to the surface whenever Wyatt was near craved to wipe away his pain and comfort him.

It was foolish. Wyatt didn't want or need her comfort, nor would she attempt to give it to him. He was, after all, a Loughman. Loughman men buried their grief and hurt deep, quietly suffering with it every day until it eventually became bearable.

That wasn't the case with Wyatt. She feared he would always carry his suffering with him, using it as a shield to keep others away.

Callie heard a vibration. She looked over the side of the cot to see her burner phone on the floor. It took some doing, but she managed to reach over and grab it without causing herself too much pain.

As soon as she saw Orrin's name, she smiled and answered. "Hey, you."

"Callie," Orrin said, relief in his voice. "You sound tired."

"I'm all right."

"You were shot."

She wrinkled her nose. "Wyatt stitched me up and got me to the ranch."

"He saved you."

"Yes," she said softly.

Orrin cleared his throat. "Is he near? I'd like to talk to him?"

"He, Owen, and Maks are preparing for an attack."

"I see."

She frowned when Orrin didn't ask who Maks was. "How did you know I was shot? Was it Wyatt?" she asked hopefully.

"Maks called Yuri."

Callie shook her head regretfully. "Tell me what you need Wyatt to know, and I'll pass it on when I see him."

"We killed Jankovic."

"*You* did," came a faint voice.

Callie was instantly on alert. "Was that Cullen?"

"It sure is," Owen said with pride in every word.

She smiled, happy for him. "So the scientist is dead. That's great news."

"Not when it means the Saints will focus on all of you there."

"Are y'all coming?"

Orrin hesitated. "Not yet."

"What are y'all planning," she demanded.

"Stay safe. We'll check in soon."

She pulled the cell phone away from her face as the line disconnected.

CHAPTER TWENTY-SIX

"Well?" Cullen asked as he watched his father put the cell phone back in his pocket.

The four had returned to the empty office in DC to watch for Hewett. There was a surprise for Orrin that Cullen and Mia decided to keep to themselves for just a little while longer.

Orrin blew out a breath as he leaned back against the wall. "Maks wasn't lying about Callie's injuries. I can hear it in her voice."

"And Wyatt?" Mia asked as she turned her gaze from the window while holding the camera.

Yuri lowered the binoculars and looked at Orrin.

"He was with the others, getting ready for the attack," Orrin explained.

Cullen finished off his bottle of water. "Let's get Hewett taken care of quickly. We're needed in Texas."

"We must not be hasty," Yuri said.

Mia shot him a harsh look. "We've been watching Mitch for several days. We're not being hasty."

Orrin started to reply when the door opened, and

Kate Donnelly walked in. Cullen watched the way his father quickly straightened from the wall.

"Kate," Mia said as she hurried to her.

While Mia helped Kate with the bags of food, Orrin asked, "What is she doing here?"

"She wanted to help," Cullen explained.

Yuri shook his head, a frown upon his brow. "She should have returned home."

"Yes," Orrin agreed. "She doesn't belong in this war."

"Speak for yourself," Kate stated. Her gray eyes swung to Yuri. "Someone decided to pull me into this. So, now I'm here. Get used to it."

Cullen quite liked Kate. He also saw the way Orrin watched her. There was something between the two of them that, if allowed to grow, could be something significant.

"Doc, you don't want to be here," Orrin said as he took a few steps toward her.

She shoved her shoulder-length, red hair out of her face and smiled. "It wasn't by luck that I stumbled upon Cullen and Mia. I was meant to help you."

"And your son?" Orrin asked.

A sad look crossed Kate's face. "With his father."

"I am afraid not even that will keep him safe if the Saints want him," Yuri said.

Mia said, "None of us are safe. Not in this room, not out on the street, not in our own homes. It's going to be people like us—those who stand up and fight—who will win."

"I know what I'm risking," Kate said to Orrin, their gazes locked. "Your son gave me plenty of opportunities to change my mind. Now, let me look at your wounds."

His father followed her to a far corner where she pointed to a chair and told him to remove his shirt. Cullen watched it all with interest. Especially the way Kate kept touching Orrin.

"She cares for him," Mia whispered as she walked up.

Cullen had to agree. "And I think Dad might feel an attraction himself."

"It's about time. He's been alone for too long."

Cullen's gaze moved to Yuri, who also watched the couple. He made his way to the Russian. "Did you know my mother?"

"*Da.* I met her once. A beautiful woman," Yuri said, turning his attention to Cullen.

Cullen crossed his arms over his chest. "What do you know of her murder?"

"Nothing more than you or your father."

"But you have theories," Mia said as she joined them.

Yuri shrugged one shoulder. "Perhaps."

Cullen lifted a brow and said, "I'd like to hear them."

"Please," Mia added.

Yuri glanced at Orrin. "I think the Saints instigated the entire thing."

"Why?" he asked.

"Who knows," Yuri said. "Orrin always followed orders, but he would also do everything he could to save his men. That did not always sit well with others."

There was a deep furrow on Mia's brow. "So Orrin could've saved someone who was supposed to die?"

"It could be anything," Cullen said.

Yuri said, "You might never know the cause."

"Or the killer."

A fierce look filled Mia's black gaze. "I refuse to believe that."

"One fight at a time," Yuri cautioned.

Cullen looked out the window at Hewett's office. "Or two birds with one stone."

Mitch hung up the phone. There were times he liked that his offices weren't at the Department of Defense because it kept him out of sight of others. Then there were times when it would be easier if he were at the DOD.

He walked out of his office to look at the people working for him. Every available piece of technology was set to looking for Orrin Loughman and Yuri Markovic, but so far, there had been nothing.

They had gotten a glimpse of Cullen Loughman before losing him again, and they had gleaned nothing on the eldest son, Wyatt. Which made everyone in the Saints organization more than uneasy.

Results were wanted immediately. What none of them realized was that the US government had trained these men to blend in, to stay hidden when needed.

No matter what that shitbag Andrew Smith said, Mitch wouldn't stop searching until he saw Orrin's dead body with his own eyes.

"We have all the technology in the world at our disposal, people," he said from the doorway of his office. "And none of you can find the Loughmans?"

"Owen hasn't left the ranch," one of the team said.

Mitch laughed wryly. "That's not new news since he hasn't left in days. I need Cullen, Wyatt, and Orrin Loughman. And Yuri Markovic. We should be able to find a fucking Russian on our soil!"

His attention was diverted to the door to his left as it opened. As soon as he saw Schenck, he let his distaste show. The tall, skinny Airman was out of uniform as he saw Mitch and smiled smugly before making his way over.

"What do you want?" Mitch demanded.

Schenck tsked. "You should be nicer to me."

"Because you're a killer? Guess what, asshole, we all are."

Schenck crossed his arms over his chest. "I killed a general. Can you say the same?"

For some reason, someone in the Saints' higher tier had taken a liking to Schenck. For the life of him, Mitch couldn't figure out why. Schenck was a singularly dislikable fellow, who rubbed everyone raw.

"Obviously, you came for something. Spit it out," Mitch demanded.

"They're sending me after Mia Carter."

Mitch knew that the Saints taking such a drastic approach meant they were tired of not getting results from him. But he wasn't worried. He knew exactly what type of people he searched for, and they were going to be almost impossible to find. He'd done this kind of work his entire life.

Schenck had only begun recently. The odds of him succeeding were slim. And he was going to enjoy the little shit failing.

"Good luck with that," Mitch said.

Schenck laughed. "You don't think I can find her. Well, let me tell you that she liked me. She went out of her way to talk to me."

"Good for you." God, how he hated the fucker.

"She believes I was close to General Davis," Schenck continued. "As soon as she sees me, she'll want to comfort me for the loss."

It was all Mitch could do not to roll his eyes. "Are you just going to stand out in the open and wait for her to find you?"

"Of course, not. She's not far."

"Do you have any idea how many people are in this city alone?"

Schenck smiled as he turned his head to him. "Worried?"

"Not in the least. Even if Mia sees you, she won't go to you."

"I beg to differ."

Mitch faced the arrogant jackass. "If you see her, watch your back. They'll have figured out someone in Davis's office betrayed him. Cullen will sooner slit your throat than take the chance that you're a spy."

"Guess only time will tell which of us is the winner. Oh," Schenck said, holding up a finger. "I almost forgot. I was sent to give you the news. Jankovic has been killed."

Mitch balled his hands into fists he was so angry. "You're just now telling me this?"

Schenck's smile grew. "The most interesting part is who killed him. Orrin Loughman."

"Impossible," he stated.

Schenck shook his head. "Smith saw it."

The realization that Orrin had taken the key to their greatest weapon was dimmed by the fact that Orrin had found one of their secret locations.

How? The question ran through Mitch's head with the speed of a bullet train, but there was no answer.

"They aren't pleased."

Schenck's words sounded as if they came through a tunnel. Mitch's heart thumped irregularly against his ribs. If Orrin could find a secret location, he could find him.

And if that ever happened, Mitch knew his life was over. Orrin was smart. He'd have figured out who betrayed him.

Mitch ran a hand down his face and turned away from Schenck. Orrin was in the area. Was he even now waiting for Mitch to make a mistake or show himself?

"You really should step up your game," Scheck said before he walked away.

Mitch noticed that his team was staring at him. He motioned for them to get back to work as he walked into his office. Once seated at his desk, he looked at the phone. None of his calls or emails to Callie had been answered.

He might as well write her off. No doubt she suspected him as well. There would be no help from that corner. He'd have to kill Orrin.

And if he couldn't do that, then he'd have to convince Orrin that he hadn't betrayed him.

Mitch believed in everything the Saints were doing. He'd been a part of the organization since he was in college. Over the last twenty years, the Saints had more than doubled in size and now invaded every government in the world, no matter how big or small the country was.

He feared the Saints. Always had.

But he knew what Orrin Loughman could do, and he

was prepared to give up a name in order to live. There was one name Orrin would be most interested in—and it would definitely work to keep Mitch alive.

If Orrin believed him. And if he got a chance to talk to Orrin. Those were the two problems Mitch could foresee.

He pulled open his bottom right drawer. He paused, looking through the open blinds to the team beyond, and took out the gun. Mitch rubbed his thumb over the metal of the weapon.

There was much he was prepared to do for his country. Even more for the Saints. But when it came to facing Orrin, Mitch knew he was outmatched.

He put the holster on and slid the gun inside. Then he grabbed his coat. Mitch didn't say a word to his team as he walked out of the room and then left the building. He paused out on the street and looked up at the surrounding buildings.

"I'm here, Orrin," he said. "Come and get me."

CHAPTER TWENTY-SEVEN

Wyatt slowly chewed a piece of jerky as he stared into the night. Dawn was less than an hour away. The Saints were out there, watching. None had made a move toward the house or barns yet.

It was a waiting game. Each side was seeing who would make the first move. And it wouldn't be Wyatt's side.

The lights were off inside the house with the porch lamp the only one remaining on. Natalie was upstairs in the house with a rifle.

Owen was inside the barn where he'd placed weapons in various places throughout the structure in case he needed them.

Maks had taken the left side of the property. Wyatt had no idea exactly where the CIA agent was, but he had no doubt Maks would be there to help.

Wyatt had chosen the dense underbrush on the right side of the barn and house. He'd lain on his stomach for hours, waiting for the Saints. The slightest movement made his wound pull, but the pain wouldn't stop him.

He wondered how Callie was faring. It had been difficult not to go see her, but he hadn't wanted to give up his location. So far, the Saints had no idea where any of them were. That was to their benefit, and with the numbers on the Saints' side, Wyatt knew they needed every advantage they could get.

The stillness of the early morning hours was deceptive. The horses were staring in the direction of the Saints, their tails swishing. Even the cattle that were in one of the front pastures were restless as they gathered together.

Tension kept building. The birds were silent. The wind was still.

Wyatt looked through his scope. His rifle was trained on a Saint who thought he was hidden among the trees. Wyatt could take him out now, and he knew Owen and Maks had their sights on someone as well.

But each waited.

Let the Saints think they had the element of surprise. Let them believe that all of them were in the comfort of their beds. Let the Saints assume all of that and more.

Wyatt tossed away the remaining piece of jerky when he saw three of the Saints walk from their hiding spot. They were bent low, rifles up. They had gone about twenty feet before they suddenly stopped and looked over their shoulder to the others. Then the three turned and hurried back to cover.

Concerned, Wyatt looked through his scope. All he could see was the back of a Saint. The group wasn't moving, so they hadn't decided on another approach point.

That meant something else made them retreat.

Or someone.

Wyatt looked to the barn. A churning started in his gut. The troubles of Austin had most likely found their way north. If Ahmadi's men and the Reeds joined up with the Saints, then they were in big trouble.

There was a soft hiss through the COM in Wyatt's ear before Maks's voice said, "We have a problem."

"What do you see?" Owen whispered.

"They're retreating," Wyatt said as he saw the Saints move off.

Natalie then asked, "Why is that a problem?"

"Reinforcements," the three men said in unison.

And Wyatt knew just who was coming. He waited until the last of them were gone, and the horses went back to grazing. Then he jumped up and walked to the barn. He glanced upward to see the pink and yellow streaks of the sunrise in the partially cloudy sky.

He waited with Owen at the barn entrance for Maks. Wyatt didn't want to tell Callie about her family, but there would be no use keeping it a secret.

Callie needed to rest, not be anxious about her kin. Because Wyatt wasn't going let them anywhere near her. Ever. He'd told them what he would do if they ever bothered her again. Now, he would show them.

And Ahmadi. Those men would kill everything— man or beast.

He blinked and looked over to find Owen silently regarding him. Wyatt spotted Maks jump the fence and cross the yard toward the barn.

"It's been a long time since I've seen that look."

Wyatt frowned and looked at his brother. "What look?"

"That one," Owen said with a nod of his head. "The one that gives the impression you're detached from a situation when really it's the opposite."

Maks halted before them and looked from Wyatt to Owen and back again. "You know why the Saints left."

It wasn't a question. Wyatt nodded and took out his ear COM. The two men did the same. Then he said, "I thought we'd have a day or two before the troubles in Austin found us."

"Ahmadi," Maks said.

Owen's eyes went hard. "And the Reeds."

Wyatt nodded. "We'll soon be fighting all three groups."

"We're going to need more guns," Owen said.

Maks slipped the strap of his rifle over his arm. "That means trusting others."

"I'm not sure we can," Wyatt pointed out.

Owen ran a hand over his jaw. "Four against twenty was one thing. Four against forty, fifty, or sixty, is another."

"I say we call Orrin and Yuri," Maks said. "They're already aware of your injury and that the Saints were coming to attack."

Wyatt glared at him. "You called Orrin?"

"I called Yuri. Orrin just happens to be with him," Maks pointed out.

Wyatt met Owen's dark eyes. "What do you want to do?"

"We tell the girls and get their opinion," Owen said. "This involves them. Especially Callie."

Wyatt moved his eyes to the entrance of the base as Owen walked off to get Natalie.

"You could always give up the life," Maks said. "Stay here herding cattle or whatever it is you do on a ranch."

The idea took root in Wyatt, but it was swiftly killed. "I'm not suited to ranch life anymore."

"It was just a suggestion."

"Yeah." Wyatt walked to the hidden button that would slide back the portion of the floor that kept the stairs down to the base hidden, but he didn't touch it.

Maks raised a brow. "Do you want me to push the button?"

"I've got it."

"Do you? Because you look more twisted up than earlier."

Wyatt met Maks's blue eyes. "I swore to Callie's family that I would kill them if they didn't leave her alone."

"Seems like they didn't take your threat seriously."

"They did until the Saints backed them."

Maks nodded at that. "And you're having a problem putting an end to these evil bastards why?"

"Blood is blood. They're her kin."

"Have they ever hurt her?"

Wyatt thought back to finding her bloodied and unconscious. "They beat her."

"Then think of how she looked after they hit her when you see them."

"That won't be a problem."

Maks smiled. "Family or not, no one should be treated like that."

"No."

"You found her, didn't you?"

Wyatt frowned at him. "Why do you ask that?"

"Because whenever the Reeds are mentioned, there is anger in Owen's eyes, but when you talk about them, there is murder in yours."

Wyatt hit the button, cutting off anything else Maks might say. As if knowing what he was about to do, Maks simply smiled and followed Wyatt down the steps.

Maks went to the armory while Wyatt made his way to the sleeping quarters. When he looked inside, Callie was sleeping. He was just about to close the door and let her rest more, but Natalie and Owen came down to the base, talking loudly enough that it woke her.

Her gaze met his. How he loved the color of her eyes. He'd told her that once after their first kiss, and her smile had lit up her face.

"What happened?" she asked.

Owen brushed past Wyatt. "Oh, good. You're awake. We need to talk."

Wyatt shifted to the side so that Natalie could enter. He was going to remain in the doorway until Maks walked up and lifted a brow. Wyatt then strode into the room and stood against the wall while Maks remained by the door.

"Someone better tell me what's going on," Callie said.

Natalie grabbed some extra pillows as Callie struggled to sit up. Wyatt set his rifle against the wall while Callie got propped up. When he lifted his gaze, she was staring at him.

It was like a punch to his gut. It had been the same the first time he'd seen her looking at him. She'd been timid, but in her eyes, he saw someone who was willing to break free of the cage she was in, someone who was wild at heart.

Someone who hungered for the wide open spaces just as he did.

Their connection had been instant, even if he had tried to ignore it for another week. But there was no disregarding a girl like Callie. Her presence pulled him to her like an unseen force. It wasn't until he'd quit fighting it that he realized how good it felt.

She deserved the life that she wanted, the life that she'd worked so hard for. She deserved happiness and laughter.

And he was damned determined to see that she got it.

"They're here," he said.

There was no clarification needed. Callie understood that he referred to her family. She let out a breath, her shoulders slumping. "They're not fighters. Beating them should be easy enough."

He nodded, knowing she was right. As much as he hated the Reeds, he didn't want her to look at him differently when he had to kill them—and he feared she would.

The frown deepened on Callie's brow. "Ahmadi's men are coming, as well. Aren't they?"

"Yes."

Natalie asked, "Who is Ahmadi?"

"A man who leads a terrorists group," Maks explained.

Wyatt bent his knee and propped one sole against the wall behind him. "My team has been after them for years. They've had a bounty on my head for some time."

"And now the Saints have given Wyatt to them," Callie said.

Owen sighed loudly. "No doubt the Saints will come

back with more numbers. So we're looking at fifty or more attacking."

"We need more men," Callie said.

Natalie looked around the room. "But can we trust anyone to help?"

"That's why we're talking about this," Owen said. "Everyone gets a vote."

Callie scoffed at him. "This isn't the time for democracy. This is war."

Wyatt hid his smile and saw Maks doing the same.

"Callie, this is your blood," Owen said.

She shook her head as he spoke. "No. My family is in this room. My family was murdered by the Saints in that house a few weeks ago. My family was kidnapped and run off the road. I may carry the last name of Reed, but I stopped thinking of them as my kin a long time ago. The Loughmans are my family."

Wyatt stopped breathing when her gaze turned to him.

"They aren't my family," she repeated.

It was her way of telling him to do whatever he had to in order to remain alive. And he wouldn't hesitate. The Reeds had had their chances with Callie over the years, but they continued to blow it.

Natalie threw up her hands in frustration. "So, what are we doing?"

Callie smiled at her. "You're going to help me to my desk where I'm going to start monitoring the cameras on the perimeter. While I'm doing that, Wyatt, Owen, and Maks will determine who they think we can trust and call them in."

"Are you in charge now?" Owen asked with a grin.

Callie shrugged, her gaze meeting Wyatt's again. "That duty falls to someone else. Take it. It's yours."

Wyatt straightened and grabbed his rifle. She was all but daring him to assume command, and he found he was more than willing. "I'm bringing in my team," he stated.

CHAPTER TWENTY-EIGHT

Callie did her best to hide the pain that moving caused. It was Wyatt who lifted her and carried her to the desk. She could only imagine how his wound must smart, but he didn't so much as bat an eyelash.

"You shouldn't be carrying me. You're wounded."

He cut her a disgruntled look. "My gun weighs more than you."

She liked the feel of his heat against her. Beneath her arm slung across his shoulders, his muscles moved, reminding her of how he'd felt as they made love.

Unable to help herself, her eyes went to his mouth. Her fingers widened on his shoulder as she flattened her palm against him. Pure, unadulterated lust ripped through her with such force that it stole her breath.

She wanted to cry out when he set her in the chair and backed away. With his heat gone, she began to shake. Not even the blanket Natalie wrapped around her helped. Only Wyatt could.

Owen rolled the chair to the desk, shoving her stool aside as he did. She smiled her thanks up at him as she reached for her laptop—but it wasn't there.

"I stashed it," Wyatt said. "I'll return shortly."

Owen quickly followed him, saying, "I'm coming with you."

Callie was actually glad for the time alone with Maks, and apparently, so was Natalie because she took the stool and faced him.

Maks gave a shake of his head as he chuckled. "They won't be gone long, so whatever questions you have, ask them quickly."

"How do you know Wyatt?" Callie asked.

His smile grew. "I knew you'd ask that first. I met Wyatt about ten years ago when I was added to his Delta Force team. He's one of the best men I know."

"Is that why you came to help?" Natalie asked.

He straddled another of the stools. "I came because I wanted to help and because I knew it's what Wyatt would do in my place."

"So he's your friend?" Callie questioned.

"Wyatt is his own man, but he commands respect like I've seen few do. He'd give his life for any of his men, and that kind of dedication results in unflinching loyalty. If you ask Wyatt, he'll tell you he doesn't have any friends. But if you ask any of his team, they'd all say he's their friend."

That made Callie smile. "So he hasn't changed all that much since leaving here."

"I can't answer that, ma'am," Maks said. "What I do know is that Wyatt rarely shows emotion. He keeps it locked inside."

Callie wrapped the blanket tighter around her. "Why did you leave Delta Force and join the CIA?"

"I thought I could do more good. Besides, growing

up with a Russian father gave me an edge since I could speak the language. I didn't know how big of a shit storm I'd walked into until I saw Orrin."

Natalie said, "So I imagine there are Saints in the CIA."

"I didn't stick around to find out," he replied.

Callie gave him a hard look. "They'll be looking for me."

"Let them," he stated. "Now, let me ask you a question."

She was shocked to find it directed at her. Callie glanced at Natalie before she said, "All right."

"Was there something between you and Wyatt long ago?" Maks asked.

Callie could only stare at him. No one had ever actually come out and asked her. It felt odd to talk about what had been a private affair.

She licked her lips and said, "Yes. Briefly."

"That's what I suspected," Maks said.

Natalie quirked a brow. "Why do you say that?"

"He's protective of her."

Nat smiled as she turned her head to Callie. "That he is."

"He feels responsible, is all," Callie said.

Maks shrugged. "I beg to differ."

"What do you know that we don't?" Natalie asked.

Callie didn't like the turn the conversation had taken. She shook her head and said, "Enough. I don't want to hear any more."

"You don't want to know if Wyatt cares for you?" Natalie asked in surprise.

Callie felt Maks's gaze on her as she said, "I know

where I stand with Wyatt. We had something once, but it's over. We've partnered up again to find Orrin. That's all."

Flashes of their lovemaking replayed in her head, laying waste to her claim.

"Callie, you can't be serious?" Nat declared in shock.

"I know what type of man Wyatt is. I know where he belongs, and it isn't on this ranch."

"You're being nonsensical."

Callie lifted her chin. "I'm being practical."

"What are you being practical about?" Owen asked as he and Wyatt descended into the base.

Callie knew she had to speak before Natalie. "Programming the cameras for a wider angle to give us a better look."

"Sounds good to me," Owen stated.

It was the way Maks had silently watched her during her exchange with first Natalie and then Owen that made her uncomfortable. It was as if he knew that she and Wyatt had been together recently.

Wyatt handed Callie the laptop with a nod. She accepted it, her breath hitching when his hand brushed hers. That small contact sent heat skating through her seductively.

"We need to turn up the heat," Maks said. "Callie hasn't stopped shaking."

Wyatt frowned as he looked her up and down. "You are shaking."

Callie rolled her eyes. "Stop fussing. I'll be fine."

"It's the blood loss," Owen said.

She opened the computer and quickly went to her files to connect back to the cameras. Callie hoped by ignoring them that they would see she was only mildly chilled. Except her hands trembled as she typed, causing her to have to backspace and try several times to get the correct letters input.

A second blanket was put around her as she felt the heat kick on. But it was the steaming, giant mug of coffee that made her smile.

She looked up to thank the person responsible and found herself staring into gold eyes. "Thank you."

"Are you hungry?" Wyatt asked.

Natalie jumped off the stool. "Lord, I can't believe I didn't even ask. Callie, I'll make you anything you want. Say the word."

"Some soup," she said, thinking of the warm liquid in her belly.

Natalie gave her a wink. "I'll be back soon."

Callie pulled up the map of the ranch and motioned the three men to her. She pointed to where the red dots were blinking. "These are all the cameras that have been installed. Unfortunately that still leaves a lot of acres we can't see. The Saints could be out there now."

"I can fix that," Maks said.

Owen asked, "How?"

Maks took out his phone and put it on speaker before dialing a number. It wasn't long before a female voice answered.

"Hey, darling," Maks said.

"Maks," came the startled reply. "You know you're not supposed to call me while I'm at work."

He smiled at them. "Sally, do you remember that favor you owe me?"

She groaned aloud. "You're not going to call it in now, are you?"

"Yep. I am."

"I knew it," she snapped. Then she let out a loud sigh. "Well, go on. What is it?"

Maks looked at Callie as he pointed to her screen. "I need satellite imagery over these coordinates."

Callie hastily wrote them down and handed them to Maks, who read them to Sally.

"Where do I send these?" Sally questioned in a hard tone.

Once more, Callie scribbled, but this time, it was the secure email address.

After Maks read it off to Sally, he said, "If you do this, your debt is paid."

"I could get fired for this," Sally said.

They all waited as she determined what she would do. Finally, she said, "The satellite won't be over that part of the globe for another hour. As soon as it is, I'll send what we see."

"Thank you," Maks said and disconnected the call.

Callie gave him a thumbs up. "That was nice going. Thanks."

"It won't do us much good for another hour," Owen said. "Why don't we take a walk out there and see for ourselves?"

Wyatt shook his head. "We stay close to the base and house. What we do need is to move all the cattle and horses."

"Where?" Callie asked.

Wyatt glanced at Maks. "As far from us as possible."

"Ahmadi's men will slaughter everything," Maks explained.

Callie was appalled. "Over my dead body. I'll kill all of the terrorists myself if they even think about it."

"Maybe we should just let Callie loose on them," Owen joked.

Everyone laughed but Wyatt.

Callie tucked her hair behind her ear. "There are several herds in the back pastures. We'll never get to them in time."

"Then we move the ones we can," Wyatt said.

Callie pointed to a piece of land adjacent to Loughman Ranch. "There's a small pasture there that belongs to the Deckers, but we use it sometimes."

"I know the place," Owen said. "I'll start moving the animals."

Maks said, "I'll give you a hand. That way, I can see what you do on a ranch."

Their laughter faded as they left her and Wyatt alone. He took the stool Natalie had vacated and held his phone in his hand. He stared at it as if he were unsure about something.

"What is it?" she pressed.

He looked up at her and lifted the cell phone. "If I call the team, they could very well save our bacon."

"But you're worried that they're part of the Saints."

"While I carried you here after I was injured, Maks told me how Orrin's entire team was part of the Saints. That's why Yuri killed them."

Callie shook her head. "That's not possible. I helped Orrin vet those men."

"Maks seemed sure of it."

Well, hell. No wonder Wyatt was hesitant. She leaned to the left to ease her right side some. "We agreed to follow our gut in this. What is yours saying?"

"Nothing. Not a fucking thing. If I call them and they're Saints, I've killed us all. But if I don't ask for their help, we'll probably die anyway."

The sight of Wyatt so conflicted caused a myriad of emotions within her, and none of them good.

"What do your instincts say?" he asked.

Their gazes held for a long minute before she said, "Call them."

"Callie, I've known most of these men for years. I've been shot at for them, but I can't guarantee that they'll have our backs."

She shrugged. "We can say that about anyone, really. If it turns out even one of them is a Saint, then we do what we do."

"Fight."

"We fight. I'm not going to let any of them find this base and the bioweapon."

A soft smile tilted his lips. "You are vicious."

"I protect what I love."

The tension thickened as he rolled the stool to her. When he lowered his face near hers, he said, "I'm glad you're on our side."

CHAPTER TWENTY-NINE

Washington DC

"No," Orrin stated for the third time, but no one was listening to him. It was infuriating.

Mia rolled her eyes, while Yuri merely shook his head, smiling. Cullen didn't look up from cleaning his guns.

Only Kate bothered to meet his gaze.

"We've been over this," she said.

Orrin couldn't remember the last time he'd been so frustrated. "It's too damn dangerous."

"I'm the only one Hewett doesn't know."

"No," he said again.

Cullen finished with his rifle and stood. He turned his hazel gaze to Orrin. "You know it's our best option."

"She could die," Orrin said.

Mia walked to him and put her hands on his arms crossed over his chest. "The four of us will be nearby. Your plan is solid."

When he'd come up with it, he never intended for Kate to be a part of anything. Now it was out of his hands. Kate had already risked so much while Yuri held her captive, and she was doing it again.

Her strength and conviction surprised him. She hid her fear well, but he saw it in the depths of her fathomless, gray eyes. Kate had taken care of him, tending his wounds and offering comfort.

What was he doing? Shoving her right into the arms of their enemy, when he should be sending her somewhere safe.

"Here," Yuri said as he handed Orrin a pistol.

Orrin took it, his gaze looking over Mia's head to Kate, who finished putting on her coat. There was a fire inside Kate that matched her hair—and called to something within him. It was something he hadn't felt since Melanie.

"She's very pretty," Mia whispered conspiratorially.

He looked down at Mia and nodded. "Yes, she is."

"Nothing will happen to her. We're going to make sure of it."

"I'm going to make sure of it," he said.

Mia gave him a wink and walked to Cullen. When everyone had their weapons, they began to leave the office one by one until he was left with Kate.

"You can back out," he told her.

She gave a soft laugh. "You know, I hate anything adventurous. Just looking at a roller coaster gives me hives. But I have to do this."

"Why?"

She looked briefly at the floor before their eyes met once more. "You."

"Me?" he asked, confused.

She took a step closer to him and offered up a half-hearted shrug. "I'll never forget when Yuri brought me to that warehouse to tend to you. You were bleeding and unconscious with broken bones, but you kept fighting. You never gave up."

"I have a stubborn streak."

"Yes, but even when death was literally staring down at you, you never gave up. You inspired me."

He rubbed a hand over his jaw, feeling the day-old whiskers beneath his palm. "I wish I hadn't. I'd prefer you in the safety of your own home."

"And I'm happy right here. With you."

His arm dropped to his side. He hadn't gone through the last twenty-some-odd years as a complete celibate, but it was a rare thing indeed when a woman caught his attention. Even rarer when he wanted to do something about it.

"I bring trouble wherever I go," he warned her.

She tucked her fiery locks behind an ear. "You fight for what you believe in."

"Death follows me."

"You stand up for what is right."

"I live a dangerous life."

The corners of her lips tilted upward. "You are all those things, and it excites me. *You* excite me."

He wasn't sure what to say to such a comment. "Are you always so honest?"

"It's a flaw."

"It's refreshing." The way her eyes twinkled with pleasure made him want to kiss her.

Kate looked at her watch. "We should go."

When she turned to go, he grabbed her arm and

dragged her to him. Then he bent and placed his mouth over hers. Desire roared through him when her lips moved against his.

He raised his head, stunned at the feelings churning within him. While he could barely form a thought, Kate was smiling up at him.

"When this is finished, I want many more of those."

"Yes, ma'am," he replied, a grin forming.

He walked with her out of the office to the back service elevators that took them to the first floor. They exited via a back entrance that put them in an alley behind the building.

"I'll never be far," he told her, his hand on her back while leading her to Cullen's SUV.

"I know. It's the only reason I'm doing this."

Her faith in him was staggering. He didn't know what it was about Kate that made her so willing to trust him, but he was glad of it.

He opened the door for her and waited as she got inside. Her hand lingered on his arm. Orrin reached up and touched her face.

"Stay to the route," he told her.

"I will."

He hesitated, fighting the need to taste her lips again. It was Kate who pulled him down and pressed her mouth to his. The desire that went through him once more rocked him to his very core.

He leaned away, shocked at his primal reaction, but she merely winked at him as she fastened her seatbelt. When she started the engine, he closed the door and gave her a nod.

As soon as she drove off, Orrin made his way through

the buildings and away from cameras to set up in a secluded part of town. From the moment Hewett had
walked out of the building earlier, he'd known this plan
would work.

Mitch was waiting for him to make a move. What
Hewett wouldn't see coming was Kate, who would lead
him right to Orrin and the others. It would be a simple
snatch and grab, but the majority of the operation relied
upon Kate.

Orrin didn't doubt her ability. He worried that they
were throwing her to the wolves. Then again, they didn't
have a choice. Mitch knew everyone. It was either Kate,
or they ask someone else.

At least he knew he could trust Kate. He didn't know
why or how, but the moment he'd looked into her eyes,
he'd known. And he hadn't second-guessed himself
once over it.

Orrin looked at his phone where he could track Kate's
progress as he settled into his spot. She would drive
around until Hewett was in position. It all depended on
how quickly Mitch spotted Mia.

Cullen was tracking Hewett and acting as backup to
Mia. Yuri was on the roof above Orrin, waiting to take
out anyone who tried to interfere with them taking
Mitch.

The minutes crawled past. Orrin checked his phone
constantly to see Kate's progress. The group had no
COMs, so they couldn't talk to each other except through
their phones.

Just as that thought went through his head, his cell
rang. He saw Cullen's number and answered it immediately. "Yes?"

"The bait has been hooked," Cullen said.

The line disconnected. Orrin then sent the message to Yuri to alert them that Hewett was being led to them. Now, all he had to do was wait.

Wait to come face-to-face with the bastard Orrin had trusted who had betrayed him.

Wait to talk to the man who he'd shared meals with.

Wait to look into the eyes of a so-called friend, who had been willing to kill him.

Now that Orrin knew about the Saints, there were new questions he'd like to put to Hewett. Not the least of which was what he knew about Melanie's murder.

Orrin spotted Mia come around the corner and duck behind a car. A few seconds later, Mitch ran after her, coming to a halt as he looked around to find her.

While Hewett searched for Mia, Kate drove up and parked about fifty feet from him. She got out with her phone to her ear as she began talking frantically, pacing back and forth. As expected, Mitch turned toward the sound of Kate's voice. Kate lowered the phone and let out a loud groan before she shook her head at the vehicle.

Hewett was hesitant to go to her, but his curiosity won out. He kept looking around him as he approached Kate. "Ma'am? Is everything all right?"

"No," she said loudly. "There's something wrong with my engine, and I can't get a tow for another hour."

Mitch glanced behind him. "Did you see a woman with black hair come running this way?"

Kate shook her head. "Sorry. I've been on the phone and not paying attention. Do you think you could look at my vehicle? Don't men know how to fix these things?"

Orrin wasn't surprised that Hewett was on edge. He was cautious about getting closer to Kate.

"Let me see your hands," Mitch demanded.

Kate gave him a confused look and took her hand from the pocket of her jacket to show him. Only then did he walk to the driver's side of the SUV and pop the hood. He didn't take his eyes off Kate as he walked to the front of the vehicle and pushed the hood up. He was so concerned with Kate that he never saw Orrin approaching.

Orrin walked right up to Hewett's back and pushed the barrel of the gun into his spine. "Hello, Mitch."

Hewett hung his head and held up his hands. "I need you to listen to me, Or—"

"Shut the fuck up," Orrin ordered. "Walk to the right toward the alley."

The few cars that passed didn't pay them any mind, and then they were soon out of sight. Orrin gave a nod to Kate, who walked behind him.

By the time they reached the alley, Mia, Cullen, and Yuri were already there. Cullen walked up to Hewett and punched him in the face so hard that Mitch was knocked down to his knees.

"Get up," Mia demanded.

Mitch looked up at Orrin as he got to his feet. "You're going to want to hear what I have to say."

"First, you're going to answer some questions," Orrin said.

"Then ask."

Yuri was the first. "How long have you worked for the Saints?"

"Twenty years," Mitch answered.

Orrin suspected as much, but to hear it was like a punch to the gut. "You specifically chose me for the Russia job, didn't you?"

Mitch nodded.

"Why?" Cullen questioned.

Hewett shrugged and wiped at his busted lip. "I knew Orrin was the type who would figure things out. The easiest answer was to get rid of him."

"Who runs the Saints?" Orrin asked.

Mitch held up his hands and said, "I don't know. We aren't allowed to know their names or see their faces."

"How many lead the Saints?" Mia asked.

"I don't know that either."

Orrin saw Kate out of the corner of his eye. "We need answers, and you aren't providing them. Perhaps you aren't useful to us."

"I am," Hewett insisted. "I heard there's a book that lists all the names of every Saint and their rank."

"Where is it?" Yuri demanded.

Mitch shrugged helplessly. "I have no idea. My contact is Andrew Smith. He works for the CIA."

"One name?" Yuri asked with a snort. "We should just kill him."

Hewitt shouted, "No! I've got information you want, Orrin."

Orrin cocked his head to the side. "Really? What might that be?"

"I've lied to you all these years."

Cullen scoffed. "Of course, you have. You lied about everything."

Hewett shook his head. "No. About Melanie."

"What did you say?" Orrin asked. He was deadly

calm, the anger coiling within him like a snake ready to strike. Mitch was going to give him information without being asked? How . . . interesting.

Mitch swallowed nervously and shrugged. "I had my orders."

"What did you know?" he demanded.

"Everything," Hewett admitted. "I knew everything. I knew when it was going to happen, how it would happen."

Cullen took a menacing step toward him. "And who?"

"Yes. And who."

Orrin walked to Mitch and put the gun to his forehead. "Who murdered my wife?"

"Don't you want to know why first?" Mitch asked.

Mia said, "I do."

Hewett licked his lips. "The Saints were eyeing you as a recruit, Orrin, but then on that mission in Afghanistan, you went back to the village overrun with insurgents and rescued that British businessman. They needed him killed in action."

"Who?" Orrin bellowed. "Who killed Melanie?"

"Andrew Smith."

As soon as the name passed Hewett's lips, Orrin pulled the trigger.

CHAPTER THIRTY

Cullen stared at Hewett's dead body on the ground as the name of his mother's killer reverberated through his head. There was a chance Mitch had lied. But there was also a chance he hadn't.

Mia's hand slipped into his. Cullen squeezed it as he looked to his father. It had taken over twenty years, but they finally had answers.

The depth of betrayal against the entire Loughman family was staggering, but it was mainly done to Orrin—for following his conscience.

Kate was the only one who dared to approach Orrin, who still held his gun up. She lightly touched his right arm until he lowered it. Then she put her hand on his cheek.

Cullen watched as Orrin closed his eyes and turned to face Kate. There were no words between them as Kate wrapped her arms around Orrin and simply held him.

In all the years since his mother's death, Cullen had never wondered why his father didn't date. It never occurred to him that Orrin might be lonely. Until now.

Seeing his father with Kate brought it all to the surface. They looked good together. And despite that such a horrible thing had brought them together, Cullen hoped they could find comfort in each other's arms.

"I like her," Mia whispered.

Cullen smiled down at his woman. In many ways, she knew Orrin better than he did, so her opinion mattered. "I do, too."

"You should tell him that."

Cullen bent and gave her a kiss. "I will."

Yuri cleared his throat to get everyone's attention. "Who is Andrew Smith?"

"I've no idea," Orrin said.

Cullen saw how Kate's and his father's hands were entwined. "I doubt that's his real name. We should've gotten a picture."

"Callie can work her magic," Mia said.

Yuri looked to the sky. "We should get going."

"Going where?" Cullen asked.

"Mia did ask for a plane or helicopter. I said I knew someone. They are waiting for us," Yuri explained.

In seconds, they were on their way north of the city. In the fifteen-minute drive, no one said a word. They were all crammed into the small SUV with Mia, Kate, and Yuri in the back while Cullen drove and his father sat in the passenger seat.

There was much Cullen wanted to talk to his dad about, but Orrin was still coming to terms with how the government had killed his wife, thus destroying their family.

Cullen followed the directions that Yuri gave him as they drove until he pulled up to a private airstrip. Sitting before them was a gorgeous white and silver luxury helicopter.

He stopped the vehicle and put it in park as someone came around the chopper. Cullen recognized the black hair and walk as none other than Lev Ivanski. A moment later, Sergei Chzov appeared.

Mia was out of the SUV and walking toward the Russian don in the next second. Cullen watched as Sergei's smile lit up his face while his head of thick, white hair blew in the wind.

Cullen waited until they were all out of the vehicle before he turned to Yuri. "I didn't realize you knew Sergei."

"Everyone knows Sergei," Yuri replied and walked to the chopper.

Lev greeted Cullen with a nod. Cullen eyed the *Brigadier* because he knew just how dangerous a man Lev was. "So, we meet again."

"Unfortunately," Lev replied, his ice blue eyes watching Sergei like a hawk. As the captain in Sergei's mafia and most trusted, Lev was always by his side.

"Suck it up, buttercup," Cullen said and turned to Sergei.

Sergei smiled and held out his hand. "It is nice to see you and Mia again. You are healing well?"

"Very. We'll never be able to repay all that you've done for us."

Sergei waved away his words. "Bring Mia to visit me, and we will call it even."

"Consider it done." Cullen watched as Sergei went to Orrin.

Sergei held out his hand to Orrin. The two clasped

hands, smiling. "And you did not think we would meet again."

"I knew you would look after Mia," Orrin said.

Sergei laughed and clasped his hands behind his back. "Our pledge to each other. I believe that promise has now passed to your son."

Orrin glanced at Cullen and smiled. "It has. Let me introduce Dr. Kate Donnelly. Kate, this is Sergei Chzov. He has several businesses in the Dover area, and to be frank, he runs the docks."

"It's lovely to meet you," Kate told him.

Sergei took her hand and kissed the back of it, his gaze moving between Kate and Orrin. "I think it is good the Loughmans have a doctor with them, no?"

Kate's laugh lifted the mood. "Definitely," she replied.

"I think we have spent enough time talking," Sergei said. "Let us go."

Mia was already inside the chopper, readying it for flight when Cullen saw a muscle twitch in Lev's jaw. The Russian stood as still as stone as he looked with distaste at the chopper.

"Afraid of flying?" Cullen asked him.

Lev gave him a look that would've flayed him alive. "Of course not."

"Ah. Then you didn't know Sergei wanted to join the party."

"This isn't a party," Lev said, the hint of Russian accent coming through. "Sergei has no business in battle."

Cullen moved closer to Lev. "You might've been born and raised here, but you know the Russian culture better than most. Did you actually think you could keep Sergei out of this?"

"I'd hoped," Lev said tightly.

"Then we don't tell him that the two of us are protecting him."

Lev's ice blue eyes jerked to Cullen before narrowing. "Is this a joke?"

"Do I look like I'm joking?"

After a moment, Lev released a sigh. "No."

"Sergei did much for Mia before I arrived, and the two of you have saved our lives since then. Let me repay you in the best way I can."

Lev gave a nod and walked to Sergei's side.

Orrin then came up. "What was that about?"

"Sergei."

"I'm a little surprised he's coming."

Cullen jerked his chin to Lev. "That's putting it mildly compared to others."

"We can't land this chopper anywhere near the ranch."

"What are you thinking?"

Orrin glanced at Kate, who was being helped into the chopper by Sergei. "Those of us who can will rappel down when Mia flies us over."

"And the others?"

"Will stay with the chopper."

Cullen ran a hand down his face. "Mia isn't going to like that."

"This isn't a jet loaded with weapons for her to aid us," Orrin pointed out.

The one thing his father didn't bring up was Kate. The fact that Orrin didn't say anything proved how quickly the doctor was coming to mean so much to his father.

"I'll let her know," Cullen said.

Orrin slapped him on the arm. "Let's get this bird in the air, son."

Cullen took one last look at DC. They had accomplished much while there, but would it be enough? He had a feeling they'd only chipped away at a mountain instead of tearing down a hill.

The repercussions were likely to be extreme. And getting to the ranch was imperative. His brothers needed them and the skills each of them possessed.

Because this was just the beginning of a war.

Andrew Smith stood in the drizzling rain with his hands in the pockets of his trench coat as he stared down at Mitch Hewett.

"We can find nothing on any of the cameras in the area," one of his men informed him.

Andrew turned away from the body. "You won't. This was Orrin Loughman."

"Are you sure, sir?"

"Without a doubt."

Andrew didn't relish informing his superiors of this latest incident, but he wasn't surprised by Hewett's death. When Orrin wasn't killed, Andrew knew it was only a matter of time before he pieced things together and came for Mitch.

Not that it would matter for much longer. Orrin's options were slim, and he would never make it back to Texas in time to stop the slaughter of those at the ranch.

By the time the Saints were done with the ranch, Orrin would have nothing left. He'd have no choice but to hand himself over to the Saints.

And he'd do it gladly because Orrin would think it was to save his sons.

Andrew smiled. He couldn't wait to wipe every Loughman from the face of the earth. He'd wanted to kill the boys the same day as their mother, but he'd been stopped.

If his superiors had allowed him to get rid of the kids, none of this would be happening now. Orrin would've been a broken man.

But it was fine because Andrew would finally get his revenge.

He was on his way to his car when his cell phone rang. "Hello?" he answered.

"Well?" asked a deep voice.

"We found Hewett."

"Is he dead?"

Andrew paused beside his car. "Yes, sir."

"Just as you predicted. And was it Orrin?"

"Yes."

There was a brief pause. "You have proof?"

Andrew ground his teeth together. "Orrin never leaves any evidence behind. But he was here, in the city, sir. Who else would go after Hewett?"

"It's not like Hewett had a lot of friends."

"Neither do I, but I don't expect any of them to kill me."

A soft chuckle came over the line. "Because they're all afraid of you, Andrew. Your reputation precedes you."

"My reputation has served me well when I needed it to. If that is all, sir, I'll head to Texas."

"Not yet."

Andrew closed his eyes and counted to ten as he clamped down on the rage that threatened to explode. "I thought you wanted me to bring the Loughmans to justice."

"We have something else for you to do first. The eldest son, Wyatt, just placed a call to his team. The Delta Force group is now readying to go to him. We have a member there. Make sure he's up to date on what to do. Then, I want you to recruit another."

"Sir, I don't have the weeks that usually takes."

"Then threaten a family member. I don't care what you have to do, Andrew, but we want the Loughmans finished by dawn tomorrow. You've never failed us before. Don't start now."

Andrew opened his eyes, his mind already sorting through the various ways he could get to members of Wyatt's Delta team. "I'm on it, sir."

"Good. We're expecting a grand celebration. Not just because of the Loughmans' deaths and the destruction of everyone helping them, but because you will bring us Ragnarok."

His task had just become harder, but failing wasn't an option. Andrew knew what happened to those who didn't give the Saints what they wanted, and he wouldn't be one of them.

"Yes, sir."

Andrew disconnected the call and hurriedly placed another as he got into his car. "I need the names and information of everyone on the Delta Force team with Wyatt Loughman. You've got ten minutes to get it to me."

CHAPTER THIRTY-ONE

Wyatt brushed the hair from Callie's face. She stirred from her slumber bent over her desk and took a deep breath as she raised her head. Her wince contorted her entire face as she sat up.

In those few treasured moments before she realized he was there, he saw a woman who wouldn't let anything keep her down. No matter the pain in her body or soul, she kept her gaze forward, never looking back.

Callie was the type of woman who would sacrifice herself for those she loved. The type of woman who wouldn't think twice before rushing toward danger if it meant saving others. She was a fighter—both for herself and the innocent.

She was resilient, spirited, gutsy, and vibrant.

Simply put, she was everything he wanted and hungered for. If only his life had been different, then he could be the kind of man she needed.

But fate hadn't given him a smooth, easy road to travel. His path had been lined with blood, death, and betrayal.

Callie's head turned as she looked at him suspiciously. "How long have you been standing there?"

"Long enough."

"That's not an answer."

He held out the plate of food. "It's been hours since the soup. Nat thought you might want something more substantial."

"She was very right." Callie took the plate from him and hastily bit into the sandwich. Her eyes closed as she chewed, savoring the food.

Wyatt wondered if he'd ever found such pleasure in simply eating before. Since most of his meals were in a package that he prepared while in combat, he didn't allow himself to taste anything. Not when the food had to be scarfed down before they had to move positions or were locked in battle again.

Callie's eyes opened. Once more, she found him staring. This time, there was no derision on her face. "What is it?" she asked softly after swallowing.

"Nothing. I need to change your bandages."

"Right," she said and took another bite.

He started to help her up, but she stopped him with a look. Wyatt stood back but remained close in case she needed him. Callie moved slowly, but she stood and walked to the medical room.

While he gathered the necessary items, she sat on the table. He moved her hair aside to look at her neck first. Her skin was warm, her tresses soft. He held the strands in one hand, staring at it. Damp. Which meant she had taken a shower.

"I had to get the dirt and blood off me," she said. "It was everywhere, and I couldn't stand my own smell."

His gaze lowered to look into her blue eyes. "Tell me Natalie was with you."

"Everyone was busy."

"You could've fallen or passed out."

She put her hand on his chest. The connection slammed into him with the force of a grenade. Being this close to her, looking into her beautiful eyes, he yearned to kiss her.

"I was careful."

Her voice was low, breathy. She too felt the magnetism that drew them together. It was undeniable, irrefutable. It was irresistible. The hunger, crushing.

If he didn't press his lips to hers and taste her, he would die. He needed her warmth, her softness . . . her scent.

He released her hair and gently cupped the back of her head. Her legs parted, and he stepped between them, bringing them closer. Blood pounded through his body and went straight to his cock.

Her lips parted as her lids drifted closed. The moment his mouth touched hers, he released a tormented groan. She had no idea what she did to him, how she kept him aroused and aching for her.

How he would walk through the fires of Hell just to feel her skin beneath his palm.

For years, he'd kept the memory of a girl alive, but now, the woman was in his arms. A woman who stole his heart with a smile. A woman with a fiery spirit who laughed in the face of overwhelming odds.

A woman who matched him in every way.

Her tongue slid along his lips, making him burn. If it weren't for her injuries, he'd already be inside her. His tongue dueled with hers as the kiss deepened.

Desire roared as the flames of temptation licked

against them. The longing to be one with her again smoldered within him, driving their passion higher.

Her hands skimmed up his arms and around his neck. The feel of her palms along his body was glorious, but it was nothing compared to what her moans did to him.

"Hey, guys," Natalie called out as she entered the base.

Wyatt ended the kiss, but he couldn't make himself step away from Callie. He mourned the loss of her touch as she lowered her arms.

"There y'all are," Natalie said with a smile.

Callie turned her head to the side so he could get to the wound on her neck. "Wyatt wanted to change the bandages."

"I can do that," Nat offered.

"I got it." Wyatt inwardly grimaced when he heard the way those words came out more of a growl than he'd intended. He gently removed the bandage from Callie's neck.

There was a beat of silence before Natalie said, "Ah, okay. Is there anything I can do?"

He felt Callie's eyes slide to him before she said, "I could use your help since you can move around better than me."

"Sure. I'll wait for you by your desk," Natalie said.

Wyatt inspected the wound before putting on a new bandage. He then shifted to her right side and lifted her shirt. As he inspected the injury, he waited for her to hold up her shirt. When she didn't, he looked up to find her staring at him.

"Why did you kiss me?" she asked.

He knew nothing less than the truth would satisfy her. So he gave it to her. "I wanted to."

"That's all I get? You wanted to?"

It was so much more than that, but he couldn't tell her the rest. "Yes. You wanted it, as well."

"So I did." She drew in a breath and released it. "We never talked about our night together."

This was one area he wasn't prepared to discuss. "Do we need to?" he asked and turned to get the fresh bandage.

"Yes."

He briefly closed his eyes before he faced her again. "All right."

"I'll go first," she said.

He gave a nod and lifted her shirt once more. This time, she took it from him so he could have both hands to work. The fact that the side of her bare breast was within inches of his hands and face was a special kind of torture, especially after their frenzied kiss.

"I know we have a past," she said. "And we shouldn't have given in to desire. I had a weak moment because I wasn't sure if I would live through the night or not."

The more she spoke, the pit in his stomach that had been there since his mother died began to expand as a sinking feeling came over him.

Callie swallowed. "I wanted to feel alive. I just didn't want you thinking that there was something starting between us again."

To his horror, he saw that his hands were shaking. Everything she'd just said was exactly what he'd been telling himself. Why then did it hurt so fucking bad to hear it? Why did he feel as if the pit inside him was about to swallow him whole?

He glanced up at her since she was now staring at him. He was going to have to get some words out, something that let her know he understood and agreed.

There was a heartbeat of time where his mind went black. He couldn't come up with anything except for the bellow of loneliness and rage that threatened to break free.

"Of course."

Two words. Two simple words, but they cost him much more than anyone would ever guess.

Yet he couldn't figure out why. Hadn't he agreed with Maks about their lives being too complicated and dangerous to have any kind of relationship? Hadn't he told himself that Callie was better off without him?

Hadn't he intended to leave and return to his old life once the Saints were finished?

No matter how many times he told himself all of that, it didn't diminish the anguish within him. It was the first time he felt lonely—and came face-to-face with the solitary road that stretched endlessly before him.

"But you kissed me."

He paused in his tending and turned his gaze to her. As he looked into her blue eyes, he saw the truth as clear as day. She was finished with him. Even if she still felt the attraction, she was going forward—not backward.

And he was stuck holding onto a memory that was disappearing out of his hands faster than smoke.

"It won't happen again," he stated.

There was a second when he thought she might change her mind, but the pragmatic Callie gave a nod and faced forward. Wyatt took his time finishing with her because he knew it might be the last time he touched her.

All too soon, he was done. She flashed him a smile and carefully slid off the table before heading out of the room. He remained, wanting the silence and isolation.

He leaned his hands on the table and let his chin drop to his chest. Much to his dismay, he recognized that sometime between returning to Texas and now, his feelings had taken control.

While he'd been systematically attempting to justify his intention to walk away from Callie again, his heart had gone in another direction.

The career he had worked so hard and long to obtain no longer mattered. Nothing but Callie mattered anymore.

And he'd lost her.

The truly sad part was that he'd lost her years ago but hadn't comprehended it until now. He'd known of her love back then. Like a jerk, he'd expected that love to remain alive.

He'd wanted her to forget him , and he'd made damn sure he left her nothing to hang onto. The ironic part was that he was the one left holding onto something that had been dead for a long time.

The walls he'd constructed around himself—those indestructible barriers—had now crumbled to dust. With a few honest words, Callie had gutted him.

It was nothing less than he deserved.

"The satellite imagery is here," Callie called out.

Wyatt straightened and looked at the old bandages. Callie's wounds would heal, and as long as she remained in the base, their enemies wouldn't be able to touch her.

That alone gave him comfort.

He pivoted and stalked from the room and stopped beside Callie. "What do you see?"

"I see two distinct camps," she said as she pointed to the screen.

He nodded as looked. "The smaller of the two will be Ahmadi's men."

"I guess we should be grateful that they didn't bring more people," Natalie said.

Callie's lips twisted as she continued to stare at the computer. "Except the Saints brought in more. They have almost thirty in total. And none of this includes the Reeds."

Wyatt noted that she'd stopped calling them her family.

"I've got movement," Callie said. "They're coming in from different sides."

He watched as she switched screens to the small cameras placed around the ranch. He spotted the men. "It's my team," he said and grabbed his rifle on the way up the stairs.

As soon as he reached the barn, he pressed the button that closed off the base. He might need his team, but that didn't mean he trusted them enough to let them know about Callie or the base.

Maks looked down from the hayloft. "They're almost here."

Wyatt nodded. He'd been born for this type of work. It was the only thing he excelled at. No matter who or what came at them, he was prepared to die for the safety of the world—and for Callie.

"You all right?" Owen asked as he walked up beside him.

He'd never be fine again. "Yeah."

"You don't look it."

Wyatt turned his head to his younger brother. "We've got a bioweapon with unknown uses hidden below us with Natalie and Callie. We've got the Saints, Reeds, and Ahmadi's men coming. I'm in my element, little brother."

"Yeah," Owen said, his shuttered look saying he was unconvinced.

Wyatt walked from the barn to greet his team.

CHAPTER THIRTY-TWO

"Callie?"

She blinked and looked over at Natalie, who was staring at her. "Yeah?"

"You okay?"

"Sure."

Natalie raised a light brown brow. "You sure? Because I've said your name five times before you heard me."

"I'm just thinking about the upcoming battle." It was a lie. A boldface, outright lie. Her thoughts were centered smack dab on Wyatt Loughman.

Her stomach churned viciously. She knew that feeling. The one that said she'd done or said something she shouldn't. The feeling that alerted her that she'd messed up royally.

Or was it just wishful thinking.

Wyatt's kiss had sent her heart soaring. The same feeling of freedom and love that she recognized all too well from once before. Except she wasn't the same girl as before—nor would she be discarded so easily.

She wanted to be the one to let him know that she didn't need him, that he could leave any time, and she would be fine with it. It all went to plan. Even his reaction.

Yet it all felt so . . . wrong.

It was everything she could do not to cry. Her heart actually hurt, as if she could feel it slowly breaking into a million pieces.

"Callie? What is it?" Natalie pressed.

She shook her head, refusing to put her emotions into words. "In Orrin's office, there is a folder with Wyatt's name on it in the bottom right desk drawer. Inside the file is a piece of paper with the names of his team members. I need it."

Natalie hurried to do as asked and returned with the paper. "Do you think they're with the Saints?"

"I'm not going to take any chances."

"It's not like there will be something that says any of the men are Saints."

Callie shrugged as she typed. "I know, but the more I know about their home lives, family, and such, the better we'll be able to know them."

"Because you don't trust Wyatt?"

She stopped typing and looked into Natalie's green eyes. "I trust him completely. It's everyone else that hasn't sided with us I'm wary of."

"I wish Orrin, Mia, and Cullen were here."

"Me, too." Despite the knowledge that Orrin was alive, Callie still wanted to see him, to hug him and feel for herself that he was hale and whole.

The closer the Delta Force team got to the barn, the more frantic Callie's fingers moved over the keys. She looked up one team member after the other, scanning information and pictures as she looked for anything she saw as a weakness that could be exploited by the Saints.

As she read the files, she realized each of the men was more like Wyatt than she expected. Men with little to no families, lethal combat skills, and all of them with numerous commendations and medals for acts of valor and heroism that the public would never hear about because of classified missions.

She was about to give up on finding anything useful when she saw something that caught her attention. Her heart plummeted to her feet.

"Wyatt," she said into the microphone that led to his COM. "We might have a problem. Danny Mazza."

"What about him?" Wyatt whispered.

She licked her lips. "I looked into your team. I couldn't find anything that would cause me to think the Saints might try to use any of them until I found that a young girl from Kentucky just filed papers with the military stating that Danny is the father of her child."

"He's not dating anyone," Wyatt said.

"It was a one-night stand."

There was a beat of silence before she heard him murmur, "They could use her against Danny. Fuck."

"Nice work, Callie," Maks said through the COMs.

She wished she were up there with Wyatt to look each of the Delta Force members in the eye. After everything their group had been through and survived, it wouldn't be right for the Saints to get to them through Wyatt's team.

But it was a distinct possibility.

"I think I might throw up," Natalie said as she plopped down on a chair. "This constant state of my nerves being twisted as we try to guess what the Saints might do is horrible."

"Which is why they have to be ended."

Natalie gaped at her. "You sound just like Owen."

"You don't want them gone?"

"Oh, please," Natalie said with an irritated expression. "Those assholes put a hit on me. Of course, I want them gone, but you can't just take out a group like this in a day, a week, or even a month. Callie, this takes years, with a group big enough to make waves against the Saints. So far, it's just nine people against thousands or more."

Callie winced at the pull in her side. "Every uprising had to start somewhere. It was just a handful of people who stood against the British that began the American Revolution."

"I'm going to fight against the Saints," Natalie said. "I'm just saying that it isn't going to be easy."

"Nothing worthwhile ever is." As soon as the words were out of her mouth, Callie thought of Wyatt.

She wanted to be with him, to feel his presence beside her. To look into his gold eyes and see the determination and grit that made him who he was.

Natalie got to her feet. "What else can I do?"

Callie heard Wyatt greet his team. As she listened to them, she pointed to the back room full of tech gear. "There is a small device on the upper rack to the left. Bring it to me."

"What does this do?" Natalie asked as she handed it over.

Callie smiled. "It'll disrupt communications for the Saints."

"And us?"

Her grin faded. "And us."

For the next hour, Callie listened to Wyatt with his team, Maks, and Owen plan how they were going to defend the ranch. Wyatt was spacing the men from his team at wide distances to cover every angle.

She waited until he'd gone over the skirmishes each of the Loughmans had with the Saints before she said, "I have a jammer ready to use to disrupt the Saints communications, but it will also end ours."

"It'll be a last resort," Owen said.

"Sacagawea."

With that one word from Wyatt, she knew it was the code word for her to use the jammer. "Understood."

Maks's whisper came over the COMs, "Got it."

No sooner had that been taken care of than Wyatt gave his team the channel for their COMs. Now everything she said, the entire Delta Force team would hear.

"Say hello to Callie, men," Wyatt said through the COMs. "She's at a remote location, monitoring our communications and the cameras hidden around the ranch."

A myriad of greetings came at her. Callie put a smile in her voice as she said, "We're happy you've come to help."

"Nowhere I'd rather be," came a deep voice. "I'm Bobby Jennings, the only one Wyatt doesn't have command over."

Callie hurried and pulled up the picture of Bobby. He was about Wyatt's age with deep laugh lines around his eyes. "Wyatt believes he commands everyone," she said.

"Damn. She knows you well," Bobby said to Wyatt.

She couldn't help but smile. She wanted to like all the men, to trust them as Wyatt did. But she couldn't. Not when so many lives were at stake.

"Well, Callie," Bobby said through the COM. "Just so you know, we're epic at ass-kicking, and we plan to do a lot of that today. Especially with Ahmadi's men."

Another voice came through the line. "How is it we've never heard of these Saints?"

"Because they're a secret organization, Danny," Wyatt said.

Danny. He'd mentioned the name for her so she could recognize the voice. With a swipe of a finger, Callie had his file pulled up. She looked into his young face and eyes hardened by war and killing.

"We've been betrayed several times by people we thought we could trust but who were really Saints," Owen said.

Bobby asked, "Despite that, you called us in, Wyatt?"

"My aunt and uncle were murdered by this group, Natalie had a hit put out on her, Cullen and Mia were run off a mountain, and Callie was nearly killed by them. They will stop at nothing to take us out," Wyatt explained.

"Why?" came another voice.

Callie hoped Wyatt would tell her who it was. Being stuck down in the base was annoying, but she recognized she would only be a hindrance topside.

There was a beat of silence before Owen said, "Our father was sent to steal a bioweapon from Russia. It wasn't until he returned and was kidnapped that we discovered the Saints were behind it. They want the bioweapon for themselves."

"We know the Saints have infiltrated our government as well as Russia and Columbia," Wyatt said.

Maks then spoke up. "It's best to assume that they're all over the world. We've learned that most times, a Saint was standing right next to us and we didn't know it."

"You think one of us could be a part of this?" Bobby asked.

Callie was about to answer when Wyatt said, "No."

"Good, because I'm ready to get rolling on this." Bobby laughed loudly. "Let's get set up, men."

Callie looked to another monitor to see the men stealthily exit the barn and take their positions. Her head turned at the sound of the base door opening.

When she saw Owen, she almost didn't contain her disappointment. Her injury kept her sitting while Natalie gathered a few more weapons and headed back up with Owen.

Normally, Callie liked the silence of the base when she had it to herself. But now it was a reminder of her predicament and the situation they were in.

She glanced at the stairs and saw a pair of boots. Her heart kicked up, thinking it was Wyatt. Then Maks's face came into view.

"Not who you wanted, huh?" he said with a grin after taking out his COM.

Callie shook her head. "I don't know what you mean."

"You're a terrible liar." He walked to stand beside her. "If you want Wyatt, tell him."

"Why would I do that?"

Maks's bright blue eyes held her gaze. "Because you're in love with him."

"It didn't matter before. It won't matter now."

"That's probably true. Wyatt is a warrior. It's because of men like him that people in this country can take freedom for granted. He's meant to fight evil."

She looked down at her hands. "You're trying to tell me that I could never hold him and that I shouldn't try."

"I'm trying to tell you who he is, but I think you already knew that."

"I have. From the very beginning."

Maks sighed. "I don't think anyone knows him like you do."

"Every time I think I know him, I realize that I don't. When he walked away, he left everything behind. His memories, his family, his friends, and most especially me."

"I thought Wyatt said you were smart."

She gave him a hard look. "What's that supposed to mean?"

"If you really think Wyatt left you behind, you're very wrong."

"Until a week ago, it had been years since I last saw him. He doesn't care."

"If he didn't care, why did he keep tabs on your family to make sure they left you alone? Why would he visit your family to ensure they didn't overstep all those years?"

Chills raced over her as it dawned on her just what Wyatt had done. For her.

"Yeah," Maks said as he gave her a sad smile and turned to walk to the stairs. "I was with him a couple of times when he got those calls. You're the only thing that he held onto, Callie. Why do you think he did that? There's only one reason."

Because Wyatt loved her.

CHAPTER THIRTY-THREE

The brisk fall wind did nothing to cool Wyatt's anger. Less than an hour after his Delta Force team arrived, the truck full of Reeds drove up.

As he stared at the people who had made Callie's life a living hell, he wanted to release his pent-up fury on them. With his fists.

"You should let me ta—" Owen began.

But Wyatt was already walking from the barn. He knew this for exactly what it was—a diversion. No doubt there were more Reeds as well as Saints and Ahmadi's men already on the property.

The truck slid to a halt as men jumped from the bed and cab of the truck. Front and center was Melvin Reed. Wyatt glared at him. There was no need to hide his hate now. The Reeds had shown their true colors long ago, but now, they were waving those colors for all to see.

And Wyatt was more than ready to tear them down.

"We've come for Callie," Melvin said.

There was a crackle before Callie's voice came through his COM. "I'm on my way."

"Owen," Wyatt whispered. He knew his brother would

make sure Callie never made it out of the base. He then raised his voice for Melvin. "This is your last chance. Go home."

"Or what?" an older Reed asked insolently.

Wyatt took a deep breath and released it as calm came over him. It was always the same right before an attack. "You die."

There was a second of silence before they began to laugh. All but Melvin. He pulled out a handgun and pointed it at Wyatt's head.

Wyatt held out his arms. "Shoot," he dared Melvin.

"Stop!" Callie shouted in his ear. "Wyatt? Do you hear me? Stop this! You can't let him shoot you! Wyatt!"

He focused on Melvin, drowning out Callie's voice. The young Reed was overconfident, and he was holding the gun in the hand that Wyatt had nearly broken. The longer Melvin held the weapon, the more his hand began to shake.

It was slight at first, just a tremor. The fact that Wyatt didn't look at the gun, but instead stared at Melvin, unsettled the unseasoned thug.

"They're mine," Wyatt whispered.

Maks's voice came through the COM. "You sure? Because I could take out three right now. The stupid sons of bitches are lined up right in a row. One shot, Wyatt. One shot and three dead."

"Mine," he repeated.

Melvin lifted a brow. "Mine? What the fuck does that mean?"

"I'm telling the others that I'm going to kill all ten of you."

The Reeds laughed, but it wasn't as boisterous. And it held a thread of fear.

Wyatt dropped his arms as he counted the weapons the Reeds held. Ten men with five rifles, three pistols, and two machetes. He'd faced harsher odds.

Only one gun was pointed at him. The rest stood around waiting. Fools. Everyone should have their weapons on him. Because that was the only chance they'd have to kill him.

Callie held her injured side as she continuously pressed the button to open the door to the base, but it wouldn't work. Tears streamed down her face. The one camera she had facing the house only showed her a partial view of what was happening. But she heard everything.

"Wyatt! Damn you!" she bellowed.

If he died, she was going to . . . Well, she didn't know what she would do, but she would make him hurt, whatever it was.

She slipped on the stairs, landing on her bad side. Callie struggled to catch her breath through the pain. She slammed her fist on the metal stairs.

Wyatt might be a legend, but he wasn't invincible. She wanted to knock him upside the head for thinking he could stand against so many and come out unharmed.

"I'm going to kick his ass," she muttered to herself.

She gingerly pushed herself back to her feet and limped to her chair. With her laptop, she panned out as wide as she could on the camera and counted ten members of her family. Wyatt's back was to her so she couldn't see his face.

Her heart thumped against her ribs as the minutes

stretched out. When Wyatt sprang into action, it was with a quickness and agility that stunned her.

He got to Melvin first, snapping her cousin's wrist without even looking at him. Wyatt then turned to his left and punched one of her uncles in the face and grabbed his rifle before pivoting to shove the butt of the weapon into cousin Wilfred's face, knocking him out.

With three down, Wyatt leaned to the side as a knife was thrown at him. He fired the rifle before using it as a club, swinging it at the legs of another Reed.

In seconds, five members of Callie's kin were down. She didn't know if they were dead or unconscious.

Wyatt had moved on to the remaining five, with ease. He punched and elbowed his way through them, using hand-to-hand combat skills she'd never witnessed before. His movements were so fast that the Reeds couldn't keep up. And before she could blink, the remaining men were on the ground.

He stood in the middle of them and looked right at the camera—right at her. After a moment, his gaze shifted.

"Get up," Wyatt told Melvin, who was cradling his hand. "Get your family, and get out of here."

Melvin started to get to his feet, but something on the ground caught his eye. Callie screamed a warning when she saw her cousin go for the pistol.

Wyatt turned, firing off a quick shot. Callie heard four distinct weapons. She held her breath, waiting as Wyatt and Melvin both remained upright. Then Melvin tilted to the side before falling to the ground.

Callie dropped her face into her hands. How in the

hell was she going to get through the main battle? This precursor had about done her in.

Wyatt's head rang with the sound of Callie screaming his name. He stared down at Melvin's dead body before he turned to the barn to see that both Owen and Maks had fired shots.

"The next wave will be soon," Owen said.

Wyatt holstered his gun and turned on his heel to make his way back to the barn where he'd left his rifle. He knew who would come next.

"Listen up," Wyatt said. "When Ahmadi's men come, let them get close to the barn without revealing your positions. I want to box them in."

Owen asked, "Is that wise? Shouldn't we keep them out? With them close, it'll be easy for the others to get close."

"Wyatt's right," Bobby said through the COMs. "Let the bastards close. We'll keep the others at bay."

Wyatt looked at Owen, who still remained in the barn. His brother gave a nod of agreement before sneaking out to his designated spot to the right.

It was only Wyatt and Maks left in the barn. He looked at the hay bale that covered the entrance to the base. He wanted to go to Callie and tell her he was sorry for what happened with her family, but he couldn't.

He settled into his position near the back doors that were thrown wide. The silence of the COMs was an indication of how on edge everyone was. Wyatt looked to where Danny Mazza was positioned. He'd put Danny close to the barn so he could keep an eye on him, and he could only hope that none of the other members of his team were part of the Saints.

There was a crackle on the COMs before Callie's voice whispered, "Two dozen men coming in from the left. Another fifteen on the right. They're all in black with their faces painted. I can't tell who is with who."

"It doesn't matter," Wyatt said. "They came here to execute us. We kill or be killed."

Ten minutes later, Wyatt spotted the first of the men. The group approaching kept looking around, waiting for an attack. Wyatt smiled as he and the others remained motionless.

It was a battle tactic to allow the enemy so close, but he had to use everything to his advantage from the land to outthinking his opponent. He just prayed it worked.

As their foes closed in, he sighted down his rifle through the scope. They were within fifty yards of the barn, then forty, and then thirty. The second group was closing in fast.

"Fire," Wyatt whispered.

Shots rang out as men fell. Return fire was immediate. But the retreat of their enemies without anyone stopping them sent a warning through Wyatt. Had Bobby and the others all turned on him?

Just when he was about to accept that his team members were Saints, they began firing on the men. Those that had gotten past them ran faster to the trees, hoping to escape.

Wyatt stood and fired at three that rushed the barn. When the ammunition ran out, and he grabbed a semi-automatic rifle, he glanced to the trees and found men lying on the ground.

Wood splintered near his face as a bullet embedded in the side of the barn. Wyatt swung his rifle to the side and fired. He saw a shot ring out, hitting one of their enemies, nowhere near where he'd positioned anyone.

"Grenade!" came a shout through the COMs.

A moment later, a massive boom sounded to the left. Wyatt kept firing, moving from one gun to the other and shifting positions around the barn as needed.

In fifteen minutes, all but a handful of the attacking force lay dead. Those still alive were the ones who'd managed to retreat.

"Check in," Wyatt said as he grabbed a bottle of water and drank down over half of it before pouring the other half over his head.

"I'm good," Owen stated.

Natalie said, "I'm fine."

"Alive," Maks said.

Wyatt looked up at the loft to see Maks tying off a bandana around his arm with his teeth. Maks gave a nod and retrieved his rifle.

"Zeus," Wyatt said.

Bobby then responded by saying, "We lost two in the grenade. Another three wounded, but we're still able to fight."

"That trick won't work again. I expected Ahmadi's men to be the second wave, but I was wrong." And Wyatt hated being wrong.

Callie's voice then said, "There are more men waiting out there, watching. If any of you move now, they'll know."

"Not all of us," Bobby said with a laugh.

Wyatt began to quickly reload the rifles, looking up

often at the pastures littered with dead bodies. "This time, kill the fuckers as soon as you see them. If you have a shot, don't wait for my signal."

No sooner had he finished talking than Bobby said, "They're here, Wyatt. They're coming."

He didn't need to ask who his friend was referring to. Wyatt lifted his rifle, but it was the distinct sound of an RPG firing that had him looking upward.

"Incoming!" Owen shouted.

Wyatt barely had time to dive out of the way as the missile came right for him. The explosion sent dirt, wood, and hay upward.

He rolled over and sat up, firing at the men who had rushed the barn. The sound of a gun firing above him let Wyatt know that Maks was all right.

Another RPG came at the barn. Wyatt rolled out of the way and reached for a rifle only to have a bullet hit the dirt an inch from his hand.

He glared at the Middle Eastern man firing at him and started to get to his feet when there was a shot, and a hole appeared in the center of the attacker's head. A bead of blood ran down his forehead as he fell to his knees before falling face-first to the ground.

Wyatt turned around and came face-to-face with his father.

"Hello, son," Orrin said before firing off more shots.

CHAPTER THIRTY-FOUR

"No!" Callie cried out when another camera was shot. She was fast losing what little sight she had of the battle.

Without knowing what was going on, she felt disconnected from her team. She didn't know if they were winning or losing. Nor could she help them if she saw something they didn't.

"Dammit," she said and slammed her hand on the desk.

It sent a jolt through her, reminding her of her injury. She grimaced at the pain. She should be out there fighting with them, not holed up in the base, waiting.

A boom rocked the ground, halting her thoughts. She stilled, feeling the vibrations all around her. Callie looked up. Whatever had gone off had done so right above her.

A myriad of voices, gunfire, and screams were coming over the speakers. She didn't know which were from the enemy and which were her team's.

She searched the feed from the cameras for any sign of Wyatt. She spotted Natalie and Owen outside of the house, running toward the barn. She saw a few of the Delta Force team, but there was no sign of Maks or Wyatt.

The second explosion was louder, forcing her to grab hold of the desk to keep from falling out of her chair. She sat still until the shaking stopped.

Her heart pounded like a drum. At this rate, it would only be a matter of time before they got into the base. Callie jumped up and hurriedly limped her way to the armory. She grabbed an AR-15, extra ammunition, and a pistol before bringing it all back to her desk.

Sweat beaded her brow from that simple exertion, but she didn't stop to rest. There was no such thing in the heat of battle.

Callie quickly put her hair up in a ponytail. Then she slung the strap of the rifle over her shoulder and grabbed a crossbow, arrows, and the jammer—just in case. After, she walked to the back of the base where there was a hidden door.

She tried to run, but couldn't manage more than a few steps before she had to stop and rest. With no other choice but to settle for an awkward limp, she made her way out down the tunnel and finally outside, locking the door behind her at the foot of the hill.

The sounds of battle were so loud that it deafened her after having been underground. She took a few calming breaths, then began climbing up the hill. She gripped the grass with her empty hand to help her climb and remain unseen. Then she rolled onto her stomach.

Gritting her teeth against the agony, she lifted the rifle to her shoulder and took aim. Then she began firing, moving from one target to another and aiming for the largest part of their bodies.

She was able to get five shots off before she came under fire. Callie rolled twice to the left and took out two more before she had to slide down the hill, covering her head.

With no other choice, she moved to a cluster of trees where the hill was at a more manageable incline in her present state. She reached the trees and suddenly found herself pinned against one, looking into Arctic blue eyes and feeling a blade against her throat.

"Hey, Callie," Cullen said from behind the man.

She looked at Cullen and raised her brows. "Can you get this maniac off me."

The man lifted his lip in a sneer. "You're bleeding," he said before he turned away.

"That's Lev," Cullen stated. Then he looked at her side, a frown forming.

She didn't care who Lev was as long as he was on their side. "When did you get here?"

"A few minutes ago. Dad is in the barn with Wyatt and Maks."

"So Wyatt's alive?"

Cullen shrugged. "The last time I saw him, yes."

She set aside her rifle and lifted the crossbow to her shoulder, but she couldn't hold it steady. Lev threw a set of knives at two foes, then he came to her. He held out his hand, waiting. She grudgingly handed the weapon to him.

"You should take care of that wound," Lev said.

She heard a hint of Russian in his voice, but she didn't

have time to think about it as Cullen dropped down on one knee and began firing. The return shots had them both seeking cover while Lev snuck away to a better position.

"You shouldn't be out here," Cullen said as he reached for her rifle when his was emptied.

Callie took his weapon and began reloading. She could at least do that. "Where's Mia?"

"With the chopper. She's our best pilot."

Callie kept reloading the rifles, looking up for a glimpse of Wyatt, and taking note of how well Lev was using the crossbow.

"Who is Lev?" she asked.

Cullen grunted and fired. "A fucking badass."

For someone like Cullen to say such a thing, then Lev must be that good. "Then I'm glad you brought him."

"Damn. Do the fuckers never die?" Cullen ground out.

Callie had also noted how Ahmadi's men kept going straight for the barn where they knew Wyatt was. "Someone told them where Wyatt is."

"Looks that way. Come on," Cullen said as he grabbed her arm and hurriedly moved her seconds before bullets sprayed the area.

Callie felt blood trickle down her side. No doubt she'd busted a stitch or two, but she'd worry about that later. "We need to get to Wyatt."

"We need to keep thinning the assholes out so they don't swarm the barn."

She knew Cullen was right, but her heart was begging her to go to Wyatt. Just when she was about to give in, she caught the briefest glimpse of him. Her heart nearly burst from her chest in happiness. His face was covered in grime, and there was blood dripping down his face from a wound on his temple. But he was alive.

"See? Wyatt's fine. He's too mean to die," Cullen said.

Callie jerked her head to him, fury causing her to shake. "You don't know anything about your brother."

Cullen's hazel eyes met hers. "No, I don't. He made sure of that."

"You didn't exactly make an effort either."

Their conversation ended when another spray of bullets found them. Callie moved one way while Cullen went another. She found a gun lying on the ground and scooped it up as she dove for cover.

She began to crawl on her stomach to one of the paddocks. The other barns were being left alone. Everyone was focused on where Wyatt and Maks were located. It was no coincidence. Someone from the Delta team had told the Saints. Was it Danny as she'd suspected? Or someone else?

The fact that Maks was fighting for his life alongside Wyatt in the barn removed him as a suspect.

She ignored the blinding pain in her side and kept moving. Her intention was to come up at the front of the barn and get inside to fight alongside Wyatt.

After another twenty feet, she stopped and looked down at her side. The blood had soaked through the bandage and into her shirt. She refused to let that stop her, though. Wyatt needed her help—they all did.

And she wasn't going to let them down.

She made it to the front of the barn and looked around. The sight of her dead family made her sad. Not because she would miss them, but because they'd been so blinded by greed that they aligned with an evil group. They had left Wyatt no choice.

It boggled her mind that he had intervened on her behalf all those years. How had she not known? Had Orrin? Most likely. There was very little that escaped that man's attention. Why then hadn't Orrin told her?

What a fool she'd been. She looked at the house, the place Wyatt had grown up—and the place where he'd found his mother's body. A single act had forever altered his path. It had isolated him, closed him off to everyone, but inside, he was still the same man who loved deeply and cared greatly. He just refused to show it.

Yet he had shown her in so many ways. It hadn't been how she wanted or expected, but that didn't make it any less so. She had just been too blind and angry to see what had been before her the entire time.

And she wasn't going to lose him now. She would get to her feet and walk into the barn to help him fight against their enemies. Then she would watch him leave because she understood that he couldn't be on the ranch since it was too painful.

Besides, there were people who needed Wyatt.

All the while, she would wait for him. Because he would come back for her. She knew that now. She'd tasted it in his kiss, felt it in his touch.

He was the only one for her. She was willing to fight to the death for him, to have him any way she could—because he was the other half of her heart.

Callie used the side of the barn to help her get to her feet. She touched her side, hating the pain. Then she wiped off the blood from her hand onto her pants and walked around the corner.

Her gaze immediately landed on Wyatt and Orrin, who stood together fighting off a swarm of dark-skinned men. She glanced upward and spotted Maks using what was left of the roof of the barn as cover as he continued to shoot.

An enemy snuck around Wyatt and made to come up behind him with a knife raised. Callie fired the rifle from her hip since she couldn't lift it any higher.

Orrin glanced at her and winked. But it was Wyatt's gold eyes that she stared into. He gave a nod and went back to shooting.

Callie moved to the side, using hay bales stacked together as a shield. Her rifle was soon out of ammunition, but Maks dropped four guns at her feet and grinned before rushing off.

She discarded her empty rifle and picked up another. The battle continued for another hour before it finally grew quiet. She leaned back against the hay and saw the blood on her side.

"What the fuck are you doing out here?" Wyatt demanded.

She turned so he couldn't see her wound. "Most of the cameras were shot out, and you needed me."

"That we did," Orrin said. He came to her, bending to kiss her cheek. "It's good to see your face."

"It's about time you got home," she teased.

His eyes crinkled as his smile widened. Then he walked away to see to Yuri Markovic, who was with Maks.

Wyatt squatted down beside her. "Callie," he began.

"One of your team betrayed you," she blurted out.

He blew out a tired breath. "I know."

"Is it Danny?"

"I don't know. And this isn't over yet."

She swallowed. "I know."

"I wanted you below in the base so you'd be safe."

"While you're out here?"

He ran a hand through his hair and sighed. "This is what I do."

"You do it well."

"Go below. Please," he begged. His voice was soft, his eyes pleading. He was showing her his feelings again.

Wyatt didn't always say the words—in fact, he rarely said them. But he showed them. And this time, she knew what to look for.

"I'm not leaving," she told him.

"I knew you'd say that. How's your wound?"

"Not too bad."

Orrin called Wyatt's name before tossing over two bottles of water. Wyatt caught one at a time before handing a bottle to her. Callie drained it quickly.

When she lowered the now empty bottle, she found Wyatt staring at her with an odd look in his eyes. "What?"

"I'm sorry about your family."

"Don't be. They brought it on themselves, just as every person who joins the Saints does."

Orrin walked up to them. "I hate to interrupt, but there are some things I need to tell you."

"Like?" Wyatt urged.

Callie frowned when Orrin paused. She watched as he began reloading magazines.

Finally, Orrin said, "Ragnarok is a bioweapon unlike any other. Its main purpose is to render women unable to bear children."

She was too stunned to speak, but not so Wyatt, who said, "Population control."

"Yeah," Orrin said.

Wyatt handed Callie the rest of his water to drink before he stood. "The Saints won't get Ragnarok."

"I know, son." Orrin swallowed loudly. "I killed Mitch Hewett."

"Good."

Callie looked between father and son. There was something Orrin had to say, but he was having a hard time with it. The only instance when that occurred was when it involved Melanie. Callie's gaze snapped to Wyatt as realization dawned.

Orrin looked up into Wyatt's eyes. "The Saints had your mother killed because I saved a man they wanted dead."

There was a long minute of silence before Wyatt asked, "What was the name of the person who killed her?"

"Andrew Smith."

"Then I know who I'm going after when this is over."

Orrin started to say something, but his words were drowned out as the firing began again.

CHAPTER THIRTY-FIVE

A piercing, bitter rage filled Wyatt. The Saints had killed his aunt and uncle, they'd attempted to take Natalie's and Owen's lives as well as Cullen's and Mia's, and they'd nearly succeeded in ending Callie's.

The Saints had terrorized his family, disrupted all of their lives, and killed dozens of innocents.

And they had taken his mother.

"Wyatt," Orrin called.

But he wasn't listening. The Saints wanted him dead. Ahmadi had tracked him halfway around the world to find him. He was going to give them exactly what they wanted.

Maks grabbed his arm. "What are you doing? We've cut their numbers in half. Stay here."

Wyatt was done waiting. He was ready for action. "Sacagawea," he said into the COMs, knowing Callie would use the jammer.

A moment later, the COMs went quiet. With a gun in each hand, he walked out of the barn and began firing, each bullet aimed with precision.

Not one of them missed their mark. He could hear Callie shouting his name, but he was done playing it safe. The Saints needed to be wiped out. And it was time they realized who they were dealing with.

That's when he saw Bobby stand up and join the ranks of the Saints alongside Ahmadi's men. Wyatt didn't hesitate to turn his gun on his friend.

Bobby saw him and fired. Wyatt dropped down to one knee and squeezed the trigger, aiming for a debilitating wound instead of a kill shot. Because he was going to have a chat with his friend.

He didn't watch as Bobby tumbled to the ground. When Wyatt stood, each of his brothers was on either side of him. Maks and another man Wyatt didn't know soon joined them. The five stood against a seemingly unstoppable force. Then the remainder of the Delta team, including Danny, stood with them. Wyatt reloaded as he saw Orrin, Yuri, Natalie, and Callie join in the fray.

Their line held, even as bullets continued to shower down on them. But if they didn't stand firm, if they didn't prove their might, the Saints would win.

And the bastards had taken too much already.

He briefly thought of Callie and how different his life might have been had his mother not been murdered. There was a good chance he would have Callie in his life, and they'd be happy.

Wyatt loaded his last magazines into his guns and fired. Cullen was already out of bullets as he picked up a discarded enemy rifle.

The sound of a helicopter coming in low flooded the area with noise. Wyatt glanced up, expecting it to be their enemy. Instead, he saw a sleek white chopper with the doors open and a woman with vibrant red hair holding an RPG aimed straight at the enemy.

"Kate!" Orrin yelled.

But she couldn't hear him over the roar. Mia sat in the pilot's seat, maneuvering them easily. There was another man in the chopper with white hair, smiling as he fired his semi-automatic rifle into the enemy ranks.

Kate launched the RPG, sending the missle right into the heart of Ahmadi's men. Wyatt and the others never quit firing. They were able to take out more of their foes, who had to choose between those in the chopper and those on the ground to kill.

Wyatt smiled when Kate released a second RPG, causing even more damage. Within seconds, the tides had turned in the Loughmans' favor.

They were able to finish off the remaining men, who stood their ground instead of running off. Wyatt started after the cowards who ran, but his legs wouldn't move as fast as he wanted. It wasn't until he felt something drip into his boot that he looked down to find his leg bleeding from a wound near the top of his thigh.

That wasn't his only injury. His side and arm hurt, and the wound on his back was bleeding again. He blinked the sweat and dirt out of his eyes and bent to retrieve a weapon as he ran past.

His brothers were beside him, the three gaining ground quickly. But they weren't alone. Maks and the other man with the Arctic eyes were with them.

The five of them cut down the others viciously. There was no mercy, no quarter.

Wyatt sliced the throat of the last of Ahmadi's men.

He shoved the man away and looked around. The peace of the ranch had been shattered irrevocably.

"Well, shit," Cullen said. "We did it."

"Not quite," Wyatt said as he turned and made his way back toward the barn.

He found Bobby on the ground, surrounded by the Delta team. The men moved aside when Wyatt and the others arrived. Wyatt stared down at Bobby with disgust.

"Wyatt, you need to listen," Bobby began.

It was Maks who put the barrel of his rifle against Bobby's temple. "I think we're all done enough listening to you."

"Why?" Wyatt asked him.

Bobby's gaze moved around him before returning to Wyatt. "I didn't have a choice."

"You always have a choice," Danny said.

Wyatt stared at the young soldier. "The Saints approached you?"

"They tried to blackmail me," Danny admitted. "I told them to kiss my ass."

Owen gave a nod of approval. "That's how the Saints should be handled, Bobby."

"You don't know how powerful they are," Bobby argued.

Wyatt went down on his haunches beside his old friend. "Tell me."

Bobby licked his lips, indecision on his face. Finally, he said, "There is a council that runs the Saints."

"How many?" Cullen demanded.

Bobby removed his hand from his stomach wound and looked at the blood. "I don't know."

"We need a name," Wyatt said as he wiped the blood from his face with the back of his arm.

Bobby coughed, blood trickling out of the corner of his mouth. "Give me sanctuary, and I'll tell you."

"How about I give you another bullet?" said the man with the Arctic eyes.

Cullen shrugged, his lips twisting. "I'm siding with Lev."

Wyatt's gaze met Lev's, and he recognized another soldier. Wyatt returned his gaze to Bobby. "No."

"We've been friends for years," Bobby said. "Please."

"You didn't hesitate to give my position away to the Saints or Ahmadi. Our friendship never came into question."

Bobby coughed again. "I'll give you all the information I have if you'll spare me."

Wyatt looked up at his brothers first. They each reluctantly gave a nod. Maks was even less thrilled with giving his agreement. The Delta team was mixed, and Lev refused.

Information was what they needed, so as much as Wyatt wanted to get Bobby as far from the ranch as he could, he had to make a deal. "Fine."

"Thank you," Bobby said smiling.

Lev tsked and moved to stand at Bobby's feet. Lev's gaze held not an ounce of warmth. "You tell us what you know, now."

"But I'm bleeding," Bobby said.

Wyatt started to intervene, but Cullen put a hand on his shoulder and shook his head. Curious, Wyatt allowed Lev to continue to see where it might go.

"You get nothing until we're satisfied with the information you give us," Lev stated.

Wyatt shrugged when Bobby looked at him for help. "I think you'd better start talking before you bleed out."

"Smith," Bobby hurriedly said. "Andrew Smith."

That name had been mentioned earlier to Wyatt. Hearing it again sent his rage to near boiling, but he kept his emotions in check so his friend wouldn't know. "Who is he?"

"He's one of the top men in the Saints," Bobby said.

Owen asked, "On the council?"

Bobby shook his head. "Smith never fails to get a job done. Until today."

"Explain," Wyatt said, narrowing his eyes.

Bobby wiped at the blood from his lips. "He was here. He approached the Reeds when the Saints wanted their help. Smith also got Ahmadi's men cleared upon entering the country."

"Un-fucking-believable," Maks ground out.

Bobby looked up at Wyatt. "Smith hates your father."

"Who is this man?" Wyatt demanded.

"All I know is that he works for the CIA, but Smith isn't his real name," Bobby said.

Owen shifted his rifle to his other shoulder. "What else do you know?"

"I can get you to Smith," Bobby said.

Before Wyatt could respond, an arrow pierced Bobby's heart, and he took his last breath. Wyatt looked up to find Lev resting the crossbow on his shoulder.

"He'd told us all that he could," Lev said.

Cullen shook his head. "You don't know that."

"Lev's right," Maks said. "Bobby gave up everything he knew."

Owen let out a long whistle. "We won this battle, boys."

Wyatt stood as he watched his brothers hug, smiling and enjoying the moment. He wanted to join in, but he couldn't. He didn't know how—nor did he imagine they'd want him.

Owen looked his way. "What? Not even a smile?"

"This was merely the beginning," Wyatt said.

Cullen nodded, still grinning. "True, and the war stands before us, but we won. Enjoy it, Wyatt. You're allowed to."

"He's right," Maks said.

Cullen motioned to Lev. "Even Lev agrees, don't you?"

"I do," Lev said.

Wyatt looked between his brothers before he reached for each of them, pulling them toward him. The three stood together, locked in an embrace for several minutes.

This was a moment he never expected to have, hadn't dared to even dream about. Being at the ranch had been too painful, and since Wyatt didn't do anything in half measures, he'd cut all ties cleanly.

But he'd missed his brothers and the bond they'd shared growing up. He thought he could have it with his team, but it wasn't the same and never would be. Whether he liked it or not, he needed his brothers and the ranch in his life.

Wyatt stepped back and rested his hands on each of their shoulders. "The Saints tore our family apart years ago, and we let them. But they brought us back together again."

"Yes," Owen said, his smile huge.

Cullen asked, "Are we really? A family, that is?"

"I'd never have known how much I missed this place or any of you if I hadn't been sent back," Wyatt admitted. "I lost a lot of years with both of you, but not anymore."

Owen's smile was gone, his dark eyes intent. "And Dad?"

Wyatt had expected this question. "I found out today my anger should've been directed at the Saints all these years. Dad did what he thought was right, having no idea that saving a life would end up costing him Mom's."

What Wyatt was only just coming to realize was that being back at the ranch had torn down the walls around his heart without him even knowing.

He hadn't been able to escape any of the memories— or Callie. She had been there, goading him, provoking him to take off the blinders that only allowed him to see hate.

And when he had, he saw a world he missed. The little boy inside him that had withered away upon finding his mother's body longed to feel free and happy again.

When he'd seen his enemies closing in, he was finally able to grasp that at the ranch, with Callie, he was content.

"I think that's the most I've ever heard you say at once," Cullen said.

Owen started laughing, and Wyatt found himself grinning. He shoved Cullen away and said, "Let's get back to the others."

"Yes. I must get Sergei home," Lev said.

Cullen began the story of how Lev and Sergei had helped him and Mia against the Saints several times.

"It looks like we owe you and Sergei a debt," Wyatt said.

Lev cut him a sideways look. "I say you do, but no doubt Sergei will call it even. He has a soft spot for Mia."

Their conversation halted when they spotted Natalie running toward them. Owen rushed to her where she pointed to the barn and simply said, "Hurry."

Wyatt immediately thought of Callie. His tired, hurting body grudgingly pushed aside the pain as he ran toward the barn. He spotted Callie sitting beside Orrin, who was propped up against the side of the building. Yuri was pressing against a wound in his father's stomach.

Wyatt looked into his father's eyes and saw how close to death Orrin was. Kate had a medical kit out and shoved aside Yuri's hands to look at the wound.

"Wyatt," Orrin said as he struggled to breathe.

Kate looked up. "He needs a hospital. Hell, all of you do."

When Orrin held out his hand, Wyatt went to him as Yuri moved out of the way. The amount of blood pouring from his father's wound was a bad sign, but Kate was moving quickly to staunch it. Lev knelt beside her and offered his assistance.

"It's been a while," Orrin said.

Wyatt looked at him. "Too long."

"There are things I want to say."

"No," Wyatt said with a shake of his head. "There's no need."

Orrin hissed in pain when Kate peered into the wound. "Lay him down," she ordered.

Wyatt put his hand on the back of his father's head

and gently moved him so that he was flat on the ground. "It's going to be fine."

"Your brothers," Orrin said breathlessly, his eyes closing.

Wyatt called Cullen and Owen over. The three of them stared down at Orrin. The thought of losing him was something Wyatt couldn't reconcile. His father had always been a strong force, a man who couldn't die.

"You're going to live," Wyatt stated. "Do you hear me? We have a war to fight, and you need vengeance."

Orrin opened his eyes. "All I ever wanted was my sons back home with me again."

"We're here, Dad," Cullen said.

Owen nodded. "That's right. We're here."

Wyatt frowned when Orrin's gaze returned to him.

Orrin fought against the pain and said, "I'm sorry for my part in your mother's death."

"It wasn't you." With those three words, all the anger Wyatt had felt against his father dissipated. "We brought the fight to the Saints, but we need you."

Orrin looked at Kate. "I'm just so tired."

Wyatt saw the way the woman stared at his father. There were feelings between them. His father was giving up, and Wyatt wasn't going to allow it. "Look at me, dammit. You're a Loughman. We don't give up. Ever."

His father's smile faded as his eyes closed. Kate started barking orders, and Wyatt could only watch as his father was lifted and brought down to the base by his brothers, Lev, Yuri, and Maks.

Mia and Sergei followed them down inside the base as the Delta team fanned out, looking for any survivors.

Was he going to lose his father now after finally forgiving him? Surely fate wouldn't be that cruel.

He dropped his chin to his chest, unable to move from the weight of everything and his wounds.

"He won't die," Callie said from beside him as she watched them take Orrin away.

Wyatt looked at her. "How can you be so sure?"

"Because he's Orrin Loughman, and there is evil to fight." She turned to look at him and smiled. "And because his sons have finally returned."

CHAPTER THIRTY-SIX

Callie looked at Wyatt, the man who had protected her from the Reeds for over fifteen years. The man who was bruised and nearly broken because of his mother's murder. The man who risked his life to save innocents.

The man she loved.

There was no denying it now. Not ever again. What an utter and complete fool she'd been.

"Callie, I—"

"I have something to say, and I don't want you to interrupt me," she said over him.

The words came in a rush because there was so much she needed him to know. And now was as good a time as any. She carefully lowered herself to her knees to see him better.

His eyes grew wide when he noticed the blood. "Your stitches."

"Can wait," she stated. "I have something to say, and besides . . . not only is Kate seeing to Orrin, but you're bleeding from, well . . . everywhere."

He remained silent, his gold eyes watching her

curiously. She had the insane urge to brush back a lock of hair that fell against his temple.

"I can't hide the way I feel about you anymore. I've done it for too long, and I no longer want to," she said, swallowing. "I love you."

If she thought he might respond, she was disappointed. Then again, it was Wyatt. He kept his emotions close to the vest to protect himself.

She licked her lips. "For years, I kept recreating a world in my mind with you. Then I pretended I didn't love you anymore. I knew it for the lie that it was when you returned home. I have no resistance when it comes to you."

Her gaze lowered to the ground for a moment. "I know the life you lead. I know the expectations you place on yourself and the constant danger you're in. But I can't live without you. I don't want to.

"I know what you did for me with my family. Orrin also just told me it was you who found me in the woods that day. All these years, I thought I didn't matter to you, but you always looked out for me." She paused and swallowed. "I never had the courage to tell you that I loved you before you left the first time, but I do now. I don't know if you want me or not, and I understand that you have a life away from here. But I don't want anyone else. I only want you."

He raised a brow when she quieted.

She put her fingers on his lips. "One more thing," she said right before she leaned in and kissed him.

Joy erupted when his arms wrapped around her as he returned her kiss. But it was quickly wiped away when Cullen shouted for them.

With the kiss ended, she and Wyatt made their way

down to the base. She feared that Orrin had died, but when she saw Cullen and Owen standing next to his bed smiling, she knew all was well.

Then Wyatt joined them. Orrin slept through the reunion of his sons, but there would be plenty of time for catching up later.

"It was close," Kate said as she came to stand beside Callie. "We still need to keep an eye on Orrin, but he has something to fight for."

Callie looked at the doctor. "You."

"I'd like to think so," Kate said with a smile. "Really, it's his sons, you, Mia, and Natalie. You're his family."

"Just so you know, we're a crazy bunch."

Kate chuckled. "I've come to realize that, and I quite like it."

"I hope you stick around, Kate."

She looked where Orrin lay in the medical room. "I think I just might. With the way all of you get wounded, you need someone. Now, let's see to your wounds."

Callie looked to Wyatt to find him watching her. Lev was with all three brothers to tend to their injuries. There would be no discussion now about what she had revealed to Wyatt, and with each minute that passed, her heart twisted in fear that she'd lost him.

She had no choice but to go with Kate, who had an iron grip on her arm. Callie was soon lying on a cot while Kate worked on her wound.

Her mind drifted as Kate began talking about the various wounds they all had and how impressed she was with the medical supplies and medicine Orrin had in the base.

Callie opened her eyes when she realized there was

nothing but silence. She looked around and found herself alone. Furious at herself for falling asleep, she slowly sat up and stood. She followed the soft voices to find Kate and Natalie sitting with Orrin, who was still unconscious.

"Did we wake you?" Natalie asked when she spotted her.

Callie shook her head. "How long was I out?"

"Three hours," Kate said.

Her heart fell to her feet. "Where is everyone?"

Natalie rose and walked to her. "Cleaning up everything. Mia is flying around the property in the chopper with Sergei and Lev to try and spot anyone who might be Andrew Smith."

"The Delta team? Where are they?" she asked, praying they were still around.

There was a small frown on Kate's brow. "They left about an hour ago."

"But Wyatt's still here," Natalie hastily said.

Though Callie tried to keep the relief from her face, she knew she'd failed. "How's Orrin?"

"Stabilized," Kate said. "He should be fine."

"Good. That's real good." Callie glanced at the stairs. She had to find Wyatt and get some kind of answer. The waiting was excruciating. "I'm going . . . to look around."

Neither woman said anything as she walked away, and she was thankful for that. Callie reached the top step and looked at the barn that was in need of major repairs. The dead bodies were gone, and much of the debris had been cleaned.

She walked from the barn and saw Cullen and Owen

on horseback, driving cattle back to their pastures. Maks was with them, manning the gates, grinning as he teased the brothers about being cowboys. It didn't take her long to find Yuri, who was sitting on the porch in a rocking chair with a beer in his hand.

Yet no matter how hard she searched, she found no sign of Wyatt.

She wiped the disappointment from her face when Owen rode toward her. He rode as if he hadn't been away for over a dozen years. Callie put a smile in place as he approached.

"It's good to see you up again," Owen said as he brought the horse to a halt. "Wyatt was fit to be tied that you didn't stay inside the base."

She shrugged. "Speaking of Wyatt. Where is he?"

"I'm not sure." Owen's smile dropped, and his gaze darted away.

Which meant that he didn't want to tell Callie anything. And that could only mean that Wyatt was gone. Again. She shoved down her pain and looked around. "We've got quite a mess to clean up. It'll be slow going for some of us."

"We're all injured in some way," he said, his smile letting her know he was grateful for the change of subject.

She nodded, her heart breaking. "We're lucky to have Kate and Lev."

"Kate will stick around, but Lev will stay by Sergei's side. I doubt they'll stay long." Owen glanced over his shoulder. "Take things easy, Callie. I've got to get back to it."

After he had ridden away, she looked toward the house where Yuri was watching her. She gave him a wave before turning in a circle to figure out what she should do. But her mind was in neutral as she fought to keep herself together.

Then her gaze landed on one of the trucks. She had to get away for a while. Just until she could get her emotions under control and not cry every time someone mentioned Wyatt.

She walked to the truck and climbed inside before looking in the center console for the keys. Within seconds, she was driving away to her house.

Callie blinked away the tears. The drive to the old bunkhouse she'd converted into a house didn't take long. Once there, she hurried inside, stripping out of her dirty and bloodied clothes once more.

She cleaned herself up and then curled up on the couch to stare out the window. When the tears came, they came in a flood. She'd honestly thought that Wyatt loved her. Why then had he left without a word?

It was too much for her already bruised heart. She cried rivers until, blessedly, thankfully, they dried up. Her itchy eyes hurt to keep them open, so she closed them and let sleep claim her.

She didn't know what woke her. Her eyes snapped open, and she sat up, looking around. That's when she spotted the pink and white rose lying on the kitchen table.

Callie got to her feet carefully so as not to jar her wound and walked toward the table. Halfway there, she saw the rose petals on the floor. Curious, she followed them to the door. She hesitated only a moment before she opened it and found more petals on the porch and down the steps.

Then her gaze landed on a palomino horse tied to her railing. He softly nickered at seeing her. There was a saddle on him, and another rose tied in with the reins.

The gelding looked familiar, as if she should know it. Then it hit her. He was the horse Wyatt had put her on after they had killed the Saints.

"How did you get here?" she asked as she walked to the gelding and ran her hand up his velvety nose.

"I thought you'd sleep forever."

Her head jerked to the side to find Wyatt leaning a shoulder against the house. He had showered and now wore a pair of jeans, boots, and a button-down. He pushed away and walked down the steps to her.

"I thought you left," she said.

He lifted one shoulder in a shrug. "I did. I went to get him," he said and nodded to the palomino. "He saved our lives."

"So did you," she said, continuing to pet the gelding.

Wyatt walked to the horse and took off the saddle before setting it on the side of the truck. Then he removed the halter and gave the palomino a pat on the rump. The horse took off at a run, tail up.

With nothing to do, Callie had no choice but to face Wyatt. He held out his hand to her, and she took it. He led her into the house to where she had overlooked a bucket of ice and the bottle of champagne it held.

Roses? Champagne? Who was this man?

Not that Callie was complaining. She quite liked it, but she wasn't sure how to act.

"Our conversation was interrupted earlier," Wyatt said as he stopped and faced her.

She noticed how he wouldn't let go of her hand. "Yes, it was."

"I didn't get a chance to speak."

When he remained silent, she swallowed and said, "What's holding you back now?"

"You."

"Me?" she asked in shock.

He nodded slowly. "From the moment you arrived on the ranch all those years ago, you captured my attention. You became like a sister to my brothers, and a daughter to Orrin. But my emotions ran in another direction.

"I found you after your family beat you. I can't describe the rage that came over me when I discovered you. I brought you to the house, and while Dad and Uncle Virgil tended to you, I went to your family. They never deserved you, Callie. You were everything good and whole, and the Reeds tried to destroy you.

"I tried to think of you as a sister, to deny the pull toward you. Then I gave in. Those were the best two months of my life. You made me want to be the man that I saw in your eyes when you looked at me, but I knew I wasn't."

She gripped his hand tightly. "So you left."

"I had to. Everywhere I looked on the ranch was a reminder that my mother had been viciously taken from us and that Dad wasn't doing anything. For my own sanity, I had to leave.

"I thought I was better on my own, far from you and the love I craved. Until I was forced to return. Then I saw you, and I knew, whatever courage allowed me to leave the first time, deserted me now. I paired up with you because I had to be with you in whatever capacity I could."

She shook her head, dismayed. "I never knew. Why didn't you tell me?"

His lips twisted ruefully. "I couldn't. Words have never come easily for me, but after everything you said after the battle, you deserve the truth."

"What are you saying?" Could all her dreams really be coming true? Could she finally have the love of her life? The hope was there, dangling right in front of her.

Wyatt gave her a crooked smile. "Isn't it obvious? I only want you. I love you, baby girl."

Her heart was going to burst she was so happy. She threw her arms around him, both of them then wincing at their wounds. They laughed as they looked into each other's eyes.

"There's some pink champagne waiting for us."

Her eyes widened. "You remembered."

"When it comes to you, I forget nothing."

She took a step back and grabbed his hand before leading him to the bedroom. There was no telling how long of a reprieve they had, and she was going to take advantage of it.

"The champagne," Wyatt said.

She shrugged and dropped his hand to remove her shirt. "Can wait until later."

"And your wound?"

"Oh, I'm sure you'll think of something."

There was a groan that rumbled from his chest before he claimed her mouth in a savage kiss filled with passion and the promise of tomorrow.

EPILOGUE

Airfield outside of Virginia

Andrew Smith strode to the limousine waiting for him. He climbed inside and faced his superior. The elderly man had a kind face that belied the evil inside him.

His eyes had faded to a dull shade of gray, and wrinkles covered his narrow face. His gray hair was thinning and parted on the side impeccably. He was tall, but age had made his frame look frail in a way that even the expensive suit couldn't hide.

"You failed."

Andrew looked into his eyes as the car drove off. "It's merely a battle, and though it might look like I failed, I didn't."

"How so?" he asked curiously.

"I hit Orrin. It was a mortal wound. There's no way they could get him to a hospital in time to save him. It'll be a blow to the sons."

He raised a bushy eyebrow. "It could rally them."

Andrew shook his head. "Then we don't waste any time sending in another strike."

"I want proof Orrin is dead first. And you still need to find Ragnarok, or, barring that, the formula."

"I'll bring it to you personally."

The man snorted and looked away. "Let's hope so because the only thing between you and death is me. The rest of the council wants your head."

Andrew fisted his hand at his side. Damn Orrin Loughman for again ruining things, but it was the last time.

Wyatt ignored the knowing smiles from his brothers and Maks when he and Callie arrived at the base the next day. It was the news that Orrin had woken that brought them all together again.

He walked with Callie into the med room to find Kate and Yuri with Orrin. His father was sitting up but still looked pale. It was a testament to Kate's skill as an ER doctor that she had saved his father's life.

"They are all here," Yuri told Orrin.

Wyatt looked around at Owen and Natalie and Cullen and Mia to find that Sergei and Lev had remained and were standing with Maks.

Orrin cleared his throat and said, "We all learned just how powerful the Saints are, and my family has discovered that we have friends willing to stand with us. Thank you, Sergei, Lev, Maks, Yuri, and Kate. We couldn't have done this without you."

"It is just the beginning," Sergei said.

Lev crossed his arms over his chest. "A war we shouldn't get involved in."

"But we are," Sergei said. "Someone has to make a stand. Everyone will eventually have to choose sides. I've chosen mine."

Wyatt bowed his head to the older Russian. "And we

appreciate it. Lev, thanks for helping the doc out with our injuries."

"Friends," Orrin said. "I think we've all learned we have few of those now that we've stood against the Saints. The only way we're going to win is if we continue to stand together."

Owen frowned. "You mean keep fighting together?"

"Whitehorse is still functional. I just need men."

Cullen draped an arm around Mia and smiled as he said, "I guess now is a good time to let you know that I've resigned my commission."

"Me, too," Owen said. "There was really no other choice."

Natalie kissed Owen. "I'm a quick learner, so just point me in a direction."

"And if I can get my plane here, we'll have wings," Mia said.

Maks ran a hand over his chin. "I was getting tired of the CIA anyway. Count me in."

"You know where I stand," Yuri said.

Kate linked her fingers with Orrin's. "There needs to be a doctor around."

Suddenly, every eye was on him. Wyatt looked down at Callie, who smiled up at him. She gave him a nod. He looked back at his father, staring into eyes that mirrored his own.

"I'm no longer part of Delta Force," Wyatt said. "I couldn't walk away from Callie or this war."

There was a loud cheer. While everyone celebrated, Wyatt made his way to his father. Yuri and Kate walked away so Wyatt and Orrin could be alone.

Wyatt took a deep breath and slowly released it. "I'm sorry, Dad."

"No," Orrin said. "I'm sorry. But let's leave the past in the past and forge ahead in a new direction."

Wyatt considered it and smiled. "I like that idea."

"I never thought I'd see the day I'd be working with my sons. I just hate the reason."

Cullen came toward them. "We have little time to rest."

"They'll attack soon," Maks said.

Owen nodded in agreement. "Unless we strike first."

Yuri crossed his arms over his chest. "We're going to need more men."

"I know someone," Lev said.

Wyatt looked at him, brow raised. "Is he good?"

"He's exactly the type of man you want on your side."

"Call him," Wyatt said.

There was a moment of silence as it all sank in. Every day from here on out was a gift, and Wyatt would make the most of each and every one.

"To Whitehorse," Orrin said.

"To Whitehorse," everyone replied in unison.

Owen then added, "To finding Andrew Smith."

"To taking down the Saints," Cullen said.

Wyatt wrapped an arm around Callie as he looked down at her. "To family."

"To family," rang out around him.

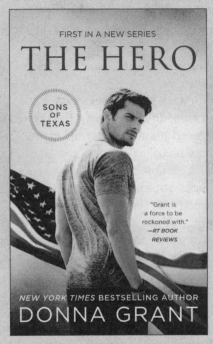